DOMINION KINGS AND QUEENS

CRAIG A. AGUILLARD

Creative Genius Publishing Company
San Bernardino, California 92410
www.cre8tivegenius.com

Library of Congress Control Number: 2020904986

ISBN   978-1-7344385-1-2

A loving shout out to my two daughters for believing in me and without their help this book would not have been finished. I want to thank God for his inspiration and strength in bringing the Dominion series to pass.

TABLE OF CONTENTS

Demon's Realm
Oasis
Rocky mountain
Sky Citadel
Dead Canyons
Sand Province
Dog Town
Grassy Plains
Artic Plains
The Woodlands
the Ecclesians Lair
Lava Pits
Defiled Marshlands
Forest of Doom

CHAPTER 1

THE PROPHECY OF OLD

Ten centuries of rule by the Demon King has left the earth scarred, broken and decayed. Two-thirds of the Earth's population is now dead as a result of war, plagues, diseases and starvation. Earth's once-mighty cities have all been destroyed. Nothing but ruin and devastation are left in them.

Countries that were once world powers and had major influence have been reduced to five surviving clans. North America, China, Russia, South America, and the Middle East are home to the last surviving clans of Earth's decimated population. Nuclear war, earthquakes, tsunamis, and famine have kept these surviving clans isolated from each other for over a century. No word or signs of life exist outside of their own clans, except for the Prophecy of Old.

The Prophecy of Old states, *"and it shall come to pass on that day, that a remnant of mankind, from the five clans of the world, shall no longer remain under the rule of him who conquered them. One child, from each of the five clans scattered throughout the four corners of the earth, will unite and return dominion back to their mothers and fathers."*

Few people know about the prophecy, even fewer know of its existence and only a handful of men and women understand the true meaning of the prophecy. This handful of men and women have never bowed their knee to the will of the Demon King, but by word of mouth have kept alive and passed down from generation to generation the prophecy declared by the Creator.

Caleb, Ruth, Cephas, Kora, and Malachi are the spiritual high priests and priestesses of the five surviving clans. They are dismissed by their clans as harmless, crazy, old men and women, spouting stories of the ancient past. Because of their small numbers and the fact that all the children love their stories, they are tolerated by their clans and are presumed to be insignificant.

That was at least until now, the time and season for the fulfillment of the Prophecy of Old. The chief priests and priestesses from the sole surviving five clans, each told the sons and daughters of their clans about the Prophecy of Old and how the world came to its current state.

"The choices of our forefathers have caused war, death, and destruction to be loosed upon our planet. Men and women, kings and queens have lusted after evil and ill-gotten riches, waged war upon each other and in so doing, lent their strength to the Destroyer of Worlds.

"In the beginning, the world started good and peaceful. People lived in harmony with each other. Children filled the countryside with laughter and happiness. Life and blessing were the reigning choices of mankind and centuries of peace and joy were the result of it. Unfortunately, these good times would not last" they recounted time and time again.

The struggle for the soul of humanity all started with a sibling rivalry between two brothers, Krell and Travius. This rivalry was so fierce, so intense, that even the gods took notice. Their father, King of the Earth, had come of old age and was about to die.

The king had yet to name which son would be his successor to the throne, so he issued a hand-to-hand battle between his two sons — the winner would become Earth's new King. The thought of one losing to the other was a fate worse than death itself. Krell's desire to be king over his brother was so strong that he would do anything to gain an advantage and become the new King.

Two weeks before the impending battle, Krell and Travius trained hard both day and night. During that time, Krell made a three-day trip to find a sorcerer who would give him an advantage over his brother. After two days of travel, Krell finally reached the borders of the Defiled Marshlands. The sight of scorched earth and decaying trees, the rotten stench of death that filled the air signaled his arrival.

Laying in the center of the marshlands stood a decrepit, weather-beaten old cabin. All manner of snakes and serpents slithered about it.

Krell said aloud to himself, "This cabin must be the witch's house."

He was appalled at the site and almost vomited at the ungodly odor coming from the sorceress' lair, but his lustful craving to become King overruled any love or decency he had in his heart for his brother.

Before touching the doorknob to the witch's lair, Krell had a fleeting moment of clarity. He could hear the Spirit of the Creator telling him to turn away from his evil plan before it consumed him. In that moment, Krell made a conscious decision to choose evil over good.

When Krell touched the doorknob a surge of pure evil ran through his veins and seared his conscious mind, turning his heart from all that is good to a heart and mind full of evil, death, and destruction.

The hunchback, wart-faced, decrepit old witch greeted Krell with a wicked grin and said, "I have what you are looking for."

She gave him a vial with a clear, odorless liquid in it.

The witch continued, "This poison drinks life from a beating heart and causes painful instant death."

Krell enthusiastically took the potion, paid the witch 20 pieces of silver and made his journey back to his father's house.

On the day of the battle, Krell instructs the wine bearer to pour the poisonous liquid into both his brother's and father's chalices before the ceremonial toast.

The King stood in the courtyard of the palace addressing all those in attendance. "Raise your drinks, for your future King will be decided today. May the hand of fate decide which of my two sons will reign after me. Long life and peace to the winner."

Everyone cheered and drank merrily. Suddenly, screams could be heard among the people.

"The King is dead. He has been poisoned. Travius is dead also. They both have been poisoned" a sentry shouted.

Chaos erupted in the palace.

Assumptions were made and sides were drawn. Many fled the castle back to their homes. Having killed his brother and father, Krell made his way to the throne room and seized the throne. Rumors of the poisonous death of their beloved King spread throughout the Earth, causing the kingdom to split in two. Those who supported Krell's rule and those who vowed to oppose him. Krell's evil tyrannical rule had begun.

~~~

In the Krellian tradition, many different kings, rulers, and kingdoms would wage war over the next thousand years. The savagery of war made it hard for men and women to choose good over evil. Evil won the hearts of most of the world's population, causing them to unwittingly pledge their allegiance and yield their strength to the Demon King, making him their master. Judgment had finally come.

Humankind, which so freely chose war and death over peace condemned the world and itself. Its love for darkness rather than light and all their wicked deeds forced the Creator, the Maker of all worlds to curse the Earth and allow death to reign.

The Creator, the Righteous One, had no choice but to take dominion over the Earth away from mankind and give it to its new ruler, the Evil One, also known as the Demon King. On that day the Earth shook, the heavens trembled, the sun and moon went dark and stars fell from the sky. The Kings and Queens of the Earth had fallen.
~~~

The Earth's new ruler, the Demon King manipulated mankind into seeking war and destruction on each other, while constantly tempting them with the promise of untold riches and ultimate power. It is the Demon King's rule that the Earth lives under today.

However, the prophecy states that after one thousand years of evil reign, the Creator would raise a remnant from mankind's offspring who would choose good and not evil and he would bless them with special abilities, to unite and destroy the Demon King, thus returning dominion over the Earth back to mankind.

Daily life moves on as normal in the five surviving clans. When suddenly and simultaneously, two mysterious strangers appeared before each clan. The strangers are clothed with long white glistening garments of fine linen reaching down to their feet and girt about the waist with a thick golden belt. The hair on their heads and faces are as white as freshly driven snow; their eyes blaze with flames of fire and their feet are like fine polished brass. Their voices are like the sound of rushing rivers.

They speak saying, "One among your children of this generation has been chosen by the Righteous One to go forth and deliver their people from the dominating rule of the Demon King. They will journey to a far, distant land, where they will grow in strength and power and knowledge of the Creator. And through his power, they will defeat the Wicked One. When the Chosen One touches the altar, a flame will ignite and there will be no doubt that they have been selected as the Chosen One."

As suddenly as the two strangers appeared in the clans, they vanished, leaving behind a stone altar in each of the villages. The multitude of people from the five clans are stunned and bewildered, wondering who these strangers are and what the meaning is behind their incredible statement.

Without any hesitation, Ruth, Kora, Caleb, Cephas, and Malachi, the high priests and priestesses of the clans, shout out, "Finally the time of our deliverance has come! We must find the Chosen One!"

CHAPTER 2

THE CHOSEN ONES

Located in the frozen Siberian Wasteland is the remnant of the Russian clan. The people of the Russian clan are experts in the art of fishing, archery, hunting, and tracking. Every clan member at the age of seven learns how to fish, track and hunt. Their very survival depends on the fish they catch and the prey they can track down and kill in the cold icy tundra.

The bow and arrow are the Russian clan's preferred weapon of choice for hunting. With no trees and very few places to use as cover, camouflage and the ability to shoot from a distance increase the hunter's chances of killing their prey.

When a hunting party goes out to hunt for food they are usually gone for a whole month. It takes weeks to find animal tracks, locate their hideout, kill it and haul it back to the clan.

The Russian clan is abuzz, as excitement about the appearance of the two strangers and the Chosen One spread like wildfire throughout the camp. It was made known that if anyone thought they could be the Chosen One or who the Chosen One was, should go see Cephas, the high priest, immediately.

In the first two weeks after the strangers' visit, hundreds of people came to Cephas to touch the altar and find out if they were the Chosen One. Four weeks pass by and still, the Chosen One has not been identified. The grey stone altar remains unlit and frozen over with ice. Many people start to wonder if the two strangers made a mistake and some start to doubt what they said all together.

Cephas calls a town meeting and asks the villagers, "Has everyone touched the altar?"

The rumbling response from the crowd is a bristling "Yes!"

Several faint voices in the very back can be heard saying, "Twenty members of the hunting party are still out and were not here when the strangers arrived."

"Then one of those twenty must be the Chosen One" declares Cephas.

It is well into the night when the hunting party returns home joyous and tired under the starlit sky. These men and women of varied ages, stature, and personalities successfully killed and brought home two polar bears and a large lion seal. The villagers who normally greet them with a resounding cheer, especially since the last hunting party came back empty-handed, are fast asleep in their ice huts. After storing the carcasses of the dead animals, everyone heads to their homes for the night - all except Obadiah.

Being the youngest of all the hunters, Obadiah was assigned to put away the dogs and hunting supplies before he could go home.

"Youth has its advantages, but it is times like these that I don't know," says Obadiah to himself as he begrudgingly corrals the last dog into the dog pen. "Finally, I'm finished. Now I can go home and sleep in my bed" bellows out Obadiah in a half shout, half whispery shrill.

On his way home Obadiah saw something in the camp that he never saw before. Upon closer inspection, he noticed it was a stone altar, with the inscription "Chosen One" etched on it.

Obadiah put forth his hand to wipe the frost and snow off of it to get a better look. As he touched the altar, the altar burst into flames, knocking him to the ground.

Not knowing what he had done, Obadiah feared that he might have damaged or destroyed the altar. Quickly throwing snow onto the altar he put out the flame before his actions could be discovered. Distraught and overcome with anxiety, Obadiah runs home and goes to bed.

Obadiah is a tall, thin, pale-skinned boy. His blonde hair rests on his broad shoulders and an inner strength can be seen through his light blue eyes. Even though he just turned fourteen, he is wise beyond his years. Obadiah lives alone in the hut his father built when he was a baby. Obadiah's mother was a beautiful, gentle, soft-spoken and religious woman. She caught a disease and died when Obadiah was seven. The day she died, the gentle, soft side of Obadiah died as well.

Tired and exhausted Obadiah falls asleep quickly. He dreams about his father and how he taught him everything he knew - how to hunt, fish, track and most importantly, how to use his natural senses. Not to rely on what you see only, but also on what you hear, smell, touch and your gut instincts.

His dream takes him back to the memories of the story told of how his father, Oshea, was taken from him in a freak hunting accident. The hunting party had spotted a whale shark trapped in a large body of water. The entrance to the waterway was frozen shut, ensnaring the large fish. The hunting party had never experienced this scenario before and was thrilled at the chance to capture this mammoth fish.

Oshea walked over and stood on the frozen entryway of the newly formed pond. Suddenly, the whale shark turned and sped headlong right at him. Crashing into the ice, the whale shark broke through the frozen blockade, simultaneously knocking Oshea fifteen feet into the air. His back slammed onto the concrete-like, icy tundra floor, breaking his spine in four places.

As the hunting party ran to his side, Obadiah's father said one thing before he died, "Tell my son never to forget what his mother and I taught him."

Obadiah's dream also reminds him of the bitterness that sprang up in his heart, and still remains, the day he learned of his father's dying words. On that day, he lost all faith in a good and righteous God.

Obadiah is awakened by a loud ruckus coming from the courtyard. He wipes crusty sleep from his eyes and goes to see what is happening.

The high priest Cephas and all the clan are shouting, "Who lit the altar? Where is the one who caused the altar to ignite?"

Obadiah is glad no one had seen him the night before, especially since he didn't know what the consequences were going to be for the person found guilty. Obadiah asks an older woman in front of him what all the commotion was about. The old lady tells him everything that transpired. Upon hearing her words, Obadiah goes straightaway to speak with Cephas.

~~~
~~~

The remnant of the Asian clan lives together in the hilly, rainy, mountainous regions of China. The Asian clan formed their own values and beliefs. The roles of men and women are clearly defined. Both men and women work on farms and in the rice fields, however, only men are trained to be warriors. Women are trained in the art of cooking and using medicinal herbs.

Kora, the high priestess, tells all the men of the clan to come down and touch the stone altar so the Chosen One can be found. The clan stands shocked and bewildered as the last male of the clan touches the altar and the cold stony mass remains unlit.

One man from the clan shouts, "What kind of trick are the two strangers playing on us? All of the men have touched the altar and it did not light."

Kora ponders under her breath, "Can the Chosen One be a woman?"

She immediately instructs all the women to come down and touch the altar. After half the women in the clan pass by and touch the altar, a young girl shrieks loudly as the altar instantly bursts into flames. She stumbles backwards clumsily, eyes open wide with fear and falls to the ground. The crowd stares at the young girl, in awe and amazement.

"Azra, you are the Chosen One. Come child" says Kora.

Azra's long, straight bluish-black hair swings back and forth as she shakes her head in unbelief. Her black charcoal eyes stare into space for a moment before her legs begin to move on their own.

Azra is a petite, four-foot-tall, soft-spoken little girl with beautiful bright, sun yellow skin. She is the smallest of all the twelve-year-olds in her clan. Azra is viewed by many in her clan as quiet, nonaggressive and insignificant. Her mother is the chief healer and has taught Azra how to pick and mix herbs and prepare healing potions at an early age.

~~~

The remnant of the Middle Eastern clan lives in their man-made oasis in the scorching hot sands of Saudi Arabia. Of the five surviving clans the people of the Middle Eastern clan have twice the muscle mass of the average human. The men and women of the clan are naturally bigger, stronger and slower than the average person in the other clans. Their size, strength, and speed are normal to them since they have no one to compare themselves to but each other.

Life in the desert is very hard. The men carry heavy stones to build their pyramid homes and dig deep wells to secure their life source — water.

Keembo is unusually large, even by his clan's standards. At thirteen years of age, Keembo is already
~~~

the size of the average Middle Eastern man and three times as strong.

Keembo has a bald bronze shaved head and chiseled calves and arms. His abdominal muscles form a noticeable eight pack and his skin is as hard as stone. His deep bearlike voice scares away most girls that hear him.

Because of his abnormal size and strength, Keembo finds himself alone and isolated from the other children his age. No one tries to bully him because of his size, but no one wants to be his friend either. This causes Keembo to be distrustful and distant towards anyone he meets.

Malachi, the high priest, has everyone in the Middle Eastern clan touch the altar. Keembo's turn finally comes to touch the altar. The stone altar ignites causing a perplexed look to come upon Keembo's face. All eyes stare at Keembo, all the while wondering what is going to happen next.

Looking at Keembo, Malachi says, "Chosen One come with me."

~~~

The remnant of the South American clan lives in the lush green tropical rainforest of the Amazon. The Amazon is notorious for its dangerous insects and wildlife roaming the expansive floor.
~~~

To ensure safe passage from place to place the South American clan has mastered a different means of transportation, travel through the web of trees. Using vines and whips that latch onto tree limbs the clan jumps and swings to their destinations. Members of the South American clan are nimble, acrobatic, athletic, agile and excellent swimmers.

Ruth, the high priestess of the South American clan, blows the unicorn trumpet summoning all clan members to the ancient Temple. She instructs each person to pass by and touch the stone altar left behind by the two strangers.

"We must identify the Chosen One" Ruth exclaims.

The beautiful brown-skinned, brown-haired, rambunctious, Sakia, a fearless and very outspoken fourteen-year-old shouts out, "I will go first."

Running to the altar all the while pushing people out of the way, Sakia makes it to the altar first. Taking deep breaths, a little bit winded from her sprint to the altar, Sakia looks up at Ruth and touches the altar.

The altar ignites into flames and the clan is amazed over how quickly the Chosen One is found. Hope, which was thought to be dead and buried, twitched its finger and everyone in the clan felt it.

Suddenly, something happened that hadn't occurred in over a century. Forming on the hardened, stoic faces of the clan was a smile followed by thunderous shouts of joy that could be heard to the heavens — for hope had returned to the South American clan.

The clan watches as Ruth and Sakia walk into the temple.

~~~

The North American clan has made its home in the vast underground sewer ways of the Silicon Valley. Even though the nuclear fallout has long since dissipated, the clan still chooses to live underground. Every day, members of the clan travel back and forth above ground. The people in the clan spend the majority of their time above ground working in the abandoned industrial buildings, tinkering and making use of the technology left behind.

The clan has an endless supply of electricity because of the solar conversion panels and windmills they have reconstructed. Their underground homes and pathways are well lit twenty-four hours a day. All clan members have a natural affinity for technology. However, no one is as gifted and adept at making new inventions and gadgets as Titus.

Titus is a thirteen-year-old genius who, at the age of seven, created an everlasting light bulb out of magnesium which he adapted for the clan's underground lighting system. At age 11, he was instrumental in the development and creation of an
~~~

underground cooling system that pumps cool air through the sewers during the scorching summer months.

This brainy, analytical, over-thinking young black man is a perfectionist in his own right. With light brown eyes and short, jet black hair, he is of average height and build, nonathletic and a little bit of a know-it-all. Nobody in the clan is surprised when Titus touches the altar and it ignites, signifying he is the Chosen One.

Caleb calls and beckons Titus to follow him to his home, "We have much to discuss, my son."

CHAPTER 3

THE CALL

As Obadiah follows Cephas to his home a multitude of thoughts rush through his head. What is going on? Who are these two strangers the old woman was talking about? How can I be the Chosen One?

As if he could read Obadiah's mind Cephas says, "Calm your mind Obadiah, for I will explain everything to you."

As the two enter Cephas' home, the elder motions to Obadiah to have a seat at the eating table and begins to explain. "The altar you touched and caused to ignite was left by two strangers sent by the Creator to identify the person he has chosen to deliver our clan and defeat the Demon King. You are the Chosen One from our clan, Obadiah."

Standing up Obadiah says, "I can't be the Chosen One. For I no longer believe in a so-called 'Righteous

God' who would let my parents die such horrible deaths."

Cephas pauses for a moment and says, "Indeed, Obadiah, you have not chosen him, but he has chosen you and called you to deliver your people."

There is a long, deafening silence in the room. All of Obadiah's emotions of hurt, anger, and pain are etched on his face.

Reluctantly Obadiah replies, "For the sake of my people, I will go."

~~~

Walking quietly behind Kora, Azra's pace starts to slow down as her mind flashes back to the altar and the proclamation that she is the Chosen One. All of a sudden fear and anxiety start to well up in her heart. With every step, these feelings grow in her heart and cause her mind to race uncontrollably. Fear and anxiety quickly consume her whole body. Shaking and breathing heavily, Azra can't take another step. Looking over her shoulder Kora notices that Azra has stopped and is shaking like a leaf.

Reaching out and taking Azra's hand Kora says, "You are trembling. What is the matter, dear?"

In a shaky, high pitched voice Azra says, "I can't do this! There has been a mistake!" All of her insecurities come racing out of her mouth. "I am too small to be the
~~~

Chosen One. There are many others who are bigger, stronger, smarter and more significant than I am. I am not a warrior. I am nobody of importance. There is no way I can deliver our people and defeat the Demon King. I just can't."

Kora looks right at Azra as if seeing her very soul. Leaning over and putting her arm around Azra, Kora calmly says, "The Righteous One has chosen the small and insignificant of this world to defeat the strong and mighty. You must believe that there is something about you and in you that has made you the Chosen One. Now, calm your fears and dismiss all your doubts, for you indeed are truly one of the Chosen Ones. Come now, we are almost at my house."

Kora's soothing words calm Azra's racing thoughts and strength returns to her body. Placing one foot after the other Azra reluctantly continues on to Kora's house.

~~~

Titus triumphantly walks alongside Caleb as the Chosen One of his clan. With a smug grin on his face, he looks at Caleb and says arrogantly, "I knew I had to be the Chosen One, for there is no one in our clan who is smarter than I am or who has created more useful and ingenious inventions than I have. If there is anyone who can deliver our clan and figure out a way to defeat the Demon King, it could only be me."
~~~

Titus' arrogant attitude is nothing new to Caleb who quickly retorts, "Yes, Titus, you are wiser than most people and possess knowledge and wisdom about many things. However, you are ignorant about many more things than you are wise. Remember this always — pride comes before defeat and a haughty spirit before a fall. It is better to have a humble spirit than a prideful heart." Titus remains quiet the rest of the way to Caleb's house, all the while pondering the words Caleb had just spoken to him.

~~~

Ruth and Sakia start walking towards the Temple before Ruth can say anything Sakia blurts out, "I am so excited to be the Chosen One. I hate waiting around for things to happen. I can't wait to fight and deliver our people from this harsh way of life and kick the Demon King's butt. I'll go right now, by myself. I'm not scared. What do you say, Ruth?"

Ruth retorts, "My rambunctious Sakia, you are in need of patience. It is imperative that you learn, understand and walk in what I am about to tell you. It is contrary to your nature, but it will save your life one day."

In a stern but compassionate voice, Ruth says, "You must learn to be quick to listen, slow to speak and even
~~~

slower to get angry. For wrath does not always promote the ways of the Righteous One."

"Oh don't worry yourself, Ruth, my strength and wit haven't failed me yet, but I'll keep that in mind...maybe."

Ruth smiles at Sakia as they walk into the ruined remains of the Aztec temple.

~~~

Keembo unenthusiastically follows Malachi to his pyramid home. Not one word is spoken during the trek to Malachi's house.

Reaching the front door of his home, Malachi turns and asks Keembo, "Why are you here?"

Taken aback by the question Keembo shrugs his shoulders and says, "I don't know, you asked me to follow you."

"Yes, I asked you to follow me because you are the Chosen One and-."

Keembo cuts Malachi off and says, "No one in this clan has chosen me, everyone treats me like an outcast or some kind of freak. They don't like me and I don't need them. Nor will I fight for them, so you can find some other altar boy to deliver this clan and fight that Demon King guy because I'm not interested. Goodbye. I'm out of here."
~~~

Looking at the back of Keembo's shaved head Malachi says, "What about your mother and father, your little brother and sister? Who will protect them?"

Keembo turns around slowly, eyes full of rage, "Don't you even think about threatening my family or I'll..."

"I'm not the one threatening your family; it is the Demon King and his army that threatens our clan and your family" interjects Malachi.

"What? What are you talking about Malachi, explain yourself."

~~~

Suddenly, the two strangers appear in synchronicity before each of the five Chosen Ones saying, "The Demon King knows that the day of the Chosen Ones has arrived. In order to save your clan and all of mankind, you must unite with the other four Chosen Ones, obtain the six pieces to the Armor of God, then face the Demon King and defeat him.

"The Demon King is currently in his realm making plans to defeat you and return here to destroy Earth's five remaining clans. You are mankind's only hope to reclaim dominion over the Earth back from the Demon King. Kings and Queens long ago handed dominion of the Earth over to the Evil One.

"Your journey will be a long and arduous one, full of peril and temptation. You must learn to recognize and
~~~

follow the Spirit of Truth, for it is she who will lead you and guide you through Demon's Realm. Gather your belongings and say your goodbyes for today you will be teleported to Rock Temple, the doorway which leads to Demon's Realm. Now hurry the Spirit of Truth awaits you there."

The two strangers give the Chosen Ones an hour to gather their belongings and say their goodbyes.

Titus, full of confidence, runs home and fills his backpack with his inventor's toolkit and all other strange odds and ends he thinks he will need to defeat the Demon King. He puts on the special goggles he made and takes his expandable steel baton. As he leaves he hugs and kisses his mother, father, and little sister goodbye.

Azra still visibly shaken and stunned by what the two strangers just said, walks with Kora to tell her parents and gathers her belongings for the long journey ahead. Azra tells her parents what the two strangers said and that she has to pack and leave in one hour.

Immediately her father responds, "My daughter isn't going anywhere without my protection, Kora. She is not a warrior nor has she been trained to fight, let alone defeat this Demon King."

Before Kora can respond Azra's mother says, "Azra, I have already packed your satchel full of the medicinal herbs you will need to make healing potions. I also want to give you our clan's Sacred Bracelet of Indestructibility. This bracelet will feel your thoughts and allow you to create an indestructible shield."

Placing the bracelet on Azra's right arm she looks at her husband and says, "Azra is the Chosen One, she must go." With a distraught look on his face, Azra's father slowly nods his head as he reaches out to his little girl, gives her a big hug and his blessing.

Obadiah angrily walks home emotionally torn between his feelings of having to save his clan and his feelings of being abandoned by the Righteous One.

"Obadiah I have something for you" comes a deep voice behind him. Obadiah turns around and sees the chief of his clan, Boldar, holding a large, beautiful, ivory bow. Boldar says, "Obadiah you are the Chosen One from our clan. Take this Bow of Kings. When you pull the string back a powerful fiery arrow will appear and fire upon your release. Take it and represent your people well."

"I will," says Obadiah.

Sakia full of excitement leaves the Temple to gather her things. Her entire clan is standing outside waiting for her. Shouts of, "Sakia! Sakia! Sakia!" shake the Amazonian Rainforest.

Sakia's father steps forward, lifting his arms to quiet the crowd, he says, "Sakia we are all proud of you. Take this 20-foot-long, retractable metal whip on your journey as a gift."

"Thank you, father! Thank you all!" shouts Sakia.

Keembo reluctantly turns to go home and say goodbye to his family when Malachi stops him. "Keembo I have something I would like you to have."

Malachi opens a large silver box, inside are two beautiful, razor-sharp daggers with golden hilts. "These should aid you in your fight, Chosen One."

"Thank you...I think" Keembo responds testily. "I have to say goodbye to my family now. I will be back shortly."

Time is up and everyone has returned to the two strangers in their camps. The strangers give out their final instructions. "Once we teleport you, you must seek out the other four Chosen Ones and find Rock Temple. When you are all together, find the stone altar similar to the one in your village, touch it and the Spirit of Truth will appear to give you direction and guidance. Now be off."

With that, the Chosen Ones disappear from their camps and are teleported near Rock Temple.

CHAPTER 4

ROCK TEMPLE

A weather-beaten old structure, made out of large smooth rocks and pasted together by gray mortar lays abandoned in the center of the woods in Australia. No living soul knows of its location. This small uninspiring rock heap is called Rock Temple. The temple is hidden away amongst trees and overgrown by vines and ivy. No one has been there for centuries. It has been isolated and untouched by human hands for far too long.

Activated by the presence of humans nearby, the stone altar inside the temple starts to quietly pulsate, mimicking the rhythm of a beating heart. Instantly the five Chosen Ones appear dispersed throughout the forest near Rock Temple.

"Well what do you know; all these trees make a girl feel right at home, not to mention I get to try out my new metal whip," says Sakia out loud.

Immediately she sets out to find the others. After a while of unsuccessful searching, Sakia mutters, "What the heck? Where is everybody? I know those two jokers didn't just drop me off in the middle of the woods by myself. Next time I see them, I'm going to give them a piece of my mind."

"Oh, this would be a perfect time to test out my goggles on these so-called Chosen Ones. I'll probably have to save their butts already." Titus switches his special goggles to the infra-red setting which allows him to detect heat signatures from any living thing.

"Ahhh!!" Azra lets out a high-pitched shriek. "Are those Thurmis Blossoms?" Azra squeals excitedly.

"I thought those flowers went extinct centuries ago! I must gather all I can." Ecstatic about her new find, Azra forgets about everything else and doesn't notice the large presence headed towards her until it is too late.

A large hand reaches out and grabs her shoulder. Azra turns around and lets out a scream, "Ahhh, it's a giant! It's a giant!"

Taking his hand off her shoulder Keembo quickly spins around saying, "Where is he? I don't see anything."

Realizing that there is no immediate threat, Keembo turns back to Azra stating, "You must be imagining things, little girl. I heard your scream earlier and came to see who was in trouble." Now, getting a good look at the scared girl, Keembo adds "My word, you are a little person."

"And you are a giant. Are you one of the Chosen Ones?" asks Azra.

"Unfortunately, I am. I am sorry I frightened you. I seem to have that effect on people."

"No, I'm sorry for screaming, you just startled me that's all. Hi, my name is Azra. I am the Chosen One from the Asian clan in China. I'm glad I found you or should I say *you* found *me*. Who are you? What's your name?"

"I am Keembo of the Middle Eastern clan in Saudi Arabia. You seem like a nice person. I hope the others are as nice as you are."

"I'm sure they are" smiles Azra.

Titus is alarmed by a faint clanging sound in the distance. "What's that noise?" Titus says as his goggles detect a figure quickly moving throughout the trees. "Hey, you" shouts Titus. "Are you one of the Chosen Ones?"

Sakia spots Titus shouting and swings to the ground to meet him. "Hi, I am Sakia, the Chosen One of the South American clan. I am glad I found you. And you are?"

"My name is Titus, inventor, and genius of the North American clan and I do believe it was *I* who found *you*."

"I found it. This must be the place the two strangers were talking about" whispers Obadiah to himself.

Obadiah approaches the splintering wooden door of Rock Temple as thoughts of his mother flood into his mind. Struggling to push open the thick temple door, Obadiah remembers his mother praying and worshiping the Righteous One and how she taught him to call upon him and do good. Obadiah peers into the temple but does not go in.

He says to himself, "I will enter the temple when all the Chosen Ones are here."

"Do you see those two forms to the south of us? Of course, you can't, you don't have my special goggles. I invented these goggles myself; they are equipped with infra-red vision, night vision, and binocular vision. They are the only one of its kind" proclaims Titus.

"That's nice," Sakia says dismissively. "Now you stay here while I go check things out."

"No! Wait, Sakia! We should stick together" yells Titus as Sakia snaps her whip and takes to the trees heading south to where Titus said the two figures were.

Sakia quickly reaches her objective and does an acrobatic backflip from a tree to the ground, landing right in front of Azra and Keembo.

With excitement in her voice, Sakia asks them, "Are you the Chosen Ones of your clans?"

Both Keembo and Azra reply, "We are."

"Good that makes four of us," says Sakia. "Four? There are only three of us" says Azra.

"Oh, Titus should be joining us shortly. He's just north of us a little way."

"Then there is only one of us left to find," says Keembo.

Titus finally reaches the others and with a perturbed look on his face addresses Sakia saying, "Why did you leave me and go off on your own? It is safer to travel together."

"I couldn't wait, besides you said there were two people out there and you were right" states Sakia.

"That's not the point," replies Titus.

"We can argue later, but first let me introduce you to Keembo and Azra, the Chosen Ones of their clans."

"It's nice to meet you two, my name is Titus." They shake hands and greet each other, all the while checking each other out wondering what made the other so special that they were selected to be the Chosen One of their clans.

Around three o'clock in the afternoon, Keembo notices smoke rising above the trees. "I see smoke to the west of us," he says.

Looking through his goggles Titus says, "I see a campfire and someone sitting next to it."

"I wonder if that is the last person we're looking for?" inquires Azra.

"It must be. I'll go check it out" announces Sakia.

"Not this time Sakia, we all go together" reprimands Titus.

"I agree," says Keembo.

"Stay with us Sakia" insists Azra.

"Okay, okay. We go together, but you better not drag your big feet Keembo" quips Sakia.

"What did you just say to me?" Keembo asks Sakia in a disgruntled tone.

"You have to keep up" Sakia replies.

"That's what I thought you said" retorts Kembo.

Sakia leads the group through the woods as Titus points out the direction of the campfire.

Obadiah built a campfire right next to the temple hoping the smoke would attract the others. His plan worked perfectly, for bursting through the forest and into the open campfire area are the rest of the Chosen Ones.

The five Chosen Ones have finally come together. They all greet each other politely and sit down around the campfire, talking in detail about their homes, clans, skills, and abilities.

"So let me make sure I have this right" spouts Titus. "I am the resident inventor slash genius. Sakia, you are the whip-slashing, tree-swinging, agile, athletic one. Keembo is super big, super strong and has mastered the use of daggers. Little Azra, makes healing potions from herbs and possesses an indestructible shield she controls with her mind through her enchanted bracelet. Last but not least, Obadiah is a tracker and hunter, as well as an expert bowman, with a sacred bow that shoots fiery arrows."

"Excuse me" interjects Sakia. "I'm sorry, but I just met all of you today and I need to see some kind of demonstration of these alleged abilities before I believe a word any of you have said."

"Are we all agreed that a little demonstration is in order? Who would like to go first?" inquires Titus.

Keembo stands up and says with his bearlike voice, "I'll go first."

Walking over to a massive boulder seven feet tall, weighing well over eight hundred pounds, Keembo attempts to pick it up. He puts his muscular arms around the huge rock, bends his knees and easily lifts the boulder, he takes several steps forward before setting it down again.

"Impressive. So you *are* as strong as you claim" says Sakia. "Now, it's my turn!"

Sakia dashes towards Keembo places one foot on his broad shoulder and leaps upward, flipping midair onto the top of the boulder. Sticking the landing, Sakia flashes the others a smug grin as she snatches the whip from her hip and snaps it onto a nearby tree. Swinging through the air, she gently settles on a tree limb.

"Wow, Sakia! That was great" exclaims Azra as Sakia somersaults back to the ground.

"I have a thought," says Titus. "Let's kill two birds with one stone. Azra why don't you go fifty yards over there and release your indestructible shield and Obadiah you go fifty yards in the opposite direction. Then shoot one of your flaming arrows at Azra's shield."

"Are you crazy?" says Obadiah. "What if her shield breaks and I hit her."

"Oh, my shield won't break. You might miss, but my shield won't break" says a resolute Azra.

"Oh, it's on now! Players, take your positions" shouts Titus with excitement in his voice as if he were making a scientific discovery.

Azra and Obadiah arrive at their spots one hundred yards apart. "Azra when you raise your shield I will shoot my arrow right in the center of it. Keep a close eye on us Titus and be amazed" yells Obadiah confidently.

"Amazed, you'll be lucky to just hit the shield from that distance. Your bow doesn't even have a scope on it. Good luck rookie" says Titus with an inquisitive grin on his face.

"Ready yourself Azra" shouts Obadiah.

With a simple thought, Azra manipulates a round shield from her bracelet that she places in front of her tiny frame, protecting her from head to toe.

"I'm ready!" screams Azra.

With no thought or hesitation, Obadiah pulls the bowstring back on his ivory bow and immediately a flaming arrow appears. The blazing arrow is clearly seen by all as dusk settles on the open area.

CRACK! It takes all of five seconds for the flaming missile to hit Azra's light brown, indestructible shield. Hitting the center of her shield, the arrow disintegrates, leaving Azra a little startled but totally unharmed.

"Incredible! Both of you were incredible! How did you do that?" inquires Titus. "Well done!" states Keembo looking at Obadiah.

"Way to stay alive girl," says Sakia to Azra.

"Now there is only one person left to prove his worth" muses Obadiah. All eyes turn toward Titus. "Demonstrate to us this inventor slash genius ability of yours if you can" Obadiah challenges sarcastically.

"So you all don't believe I am an inventive genius? You doubt my abilities? Good. Let me shock you and I mean that literally."

Titus opens up his backpack and pulls out his inventor's toolkit. "Sakia, may I have your metal whip, please. I am going to give it a little upgrade."

"Okay but you better not damage it, Titus. I'm warning you."

"This will take all of fifteen minutes. I have all that I need here in my toolkit." Titus saws, hammers, welds and drills on Sakia's whip for fifteen minutes.

Everyone else has moved back to the campfire waiting for Titus to complete his masterpiece. Their conversation is abruptly interrupted by a shout from Titus, "It is finished! I am done!"

Evening has arrived and the last glimmer of daylight has disappeared. Titus carries Sakia's newly modified whip over to the campfire.

"Well boy genius what do you have for us?" inquires Obadiah.

"First off don't call me boy genius, plain genius will suffice. Secondly, I have transformed Sakia's ordinary metal whip into an extraordinary electrical whip that dishes out well over one thousand volts of electricity. It can shock and render unconscious a three-hundred-pound grizzly bear with just the touch of a button."

Titus pushes the newly fashioned button on the rubbery hilt of the whip. Several pulsing blue lights quickly travel back and forth from the top of the rubbery handle to the very tail end of Sakia's whip.

"I guess it is true, we have a genuine genius in our ranks," says Obadiah.

"Let me have it! Let me have it! Please let me have my whip back. I can't wait to try it out. Thank you, Titus, I am so excited to play with my new toy I could kiss you."

"Ah, well, okay," says Titus with a blushing look on his face.

"I was just kidding," says Sakia.

Everyone laughs at Titus' bewilderment. "Titus you are definitely science smart, but you are woefully ignorant when it comes to other matters" chuckles Obadiah.

"Hey guys now that we've had our introductions, don't you think it's time we go into the temple?" says Keembo.

The lightness and laughter in the air are quickly replaced by one of tenseness and sobriety, as all eyes turn and gaze upon Rock Temple. The Chosen Ones quietly make their way to the temple door, Keembo leads the way and Obadiah slowly brings up the rear.

Entering the temple they notice an altar similar to the one they touched back in their clans, near the back wall. Everything about this altar was the same except for a large red ruby sitting on top of it.

As the Chosen Ones form a circle around the altar the gem starts to glow. The light emanating from the gem continues to grow brighter and brighter until it explodes into a blinding light. Removing their hands from their eyes, they notice a presence in the blinding light. This presence is the Spirit of Truth.

"Do not be afraid. The Creator has sent me to teach and guide you in all that you must do."

With their hands and arms covering their adjusting eyes the Chosen Ones listen intently to the words spoken by the Spirit of Truth.

"Each of you has been chosen from the five remaining clans on Earth to defeat the Demon King and restore dominion of the Earth back to mankind. In order to defeat the Demon King, you must first find the Armor of God, which is comprised of six items: the Belt of Truth, the Breastplate of Righteousness, the Boots of Peace, the Shield of Faith, the Helmet of Salvation and the Sword of the Spirit. These items are scattered throughout Demon's Realm. The items will be well guarded by beings loyal to the Wicked One.

"Secondly, each of you has been given special talents and abilities. You must learn to become a unit and operate in unity to defeat the Demon King's minions and wield the Armor of God. Lastly, take the jewel on the altar with you. When you build an altar and place the jewel on top of it, I will appear to speak with you. However, when your heart is quiet, still and full of faith, you will hear my voice without the use of the gemstone.

"To find the entrance to Demon's Realm you must head north to Granite Mountain. Somewhere on the mountains smooth surface the gemstone from the altar will fit and unlock a portal enabling you to pass over into Demon's Realm. Do not let your hearts be troubled, neither let it be afraid, for you are the Chosen Ones of the Prophecy of Old. Farewell young ones, until we meet again."

Too stunned to speak or ask questions the five simply reply, "Farewell."

The Spirit then disappears.

"Wow!! That was so cool" says Titus.

"I know, I almost reached out and touched it...her...whatever it was" utters Sakia. "It was a spirit," says Keembo.

"Hey guys can I hold onto the spirit stone please?" asks Azra.

"Sure, why not," says Keembo. Walking over to the altar Keembo removes the red gemstone from its place and gently hands it to Azra saying, "Here you protect the spirit stone and I will protect you."

"Wait a second, I'm not some little girl who needs protecting; well okay I am a little girl, but I can take care of myself," says Azra.

With a sneaky grin on his face, Keembo says, "Sure you can Azra."

"It looks like we'll be sleeping here tonight. Everyone may as well get comfortable and relax, for tomorrow morning we find the entrance gate to Demon's Realm" states Obadiah.

Everyone agrees and starts to unpack their sleeping gear while trying to find a soft spot on the cold hard dirt floor.

Obadiah beckons to Titus and says, "Titus can you help me extinguish the campfire outside?"

"Sure thing" replies Titus. Obadiah and Titus walk outside.

Speaking first Titus says, "What's on your mind, Obadiah? I know you didn't really ask me out here to help you put the campfire out."

"Yeah, you're right. Titus, I want your assessment on what the Spirit said to us and what you think our chances are to successfully complete this task?" inquires Obadiah.

"Hmm. Tracking down the six pieces to the Armor of God in a strange land will take time, but it can be done. Defeating enemies we do not know poses a greater challenge, but with strategic planning and patience, this too can be accomplished. The five of us possess unique skills and abilities that if used in tandem as a cohesive unit we will be a very formidable force."

"Thank you, Titus, for your honesty. I respect your analytical abilities and agree with everything you just said. But my only concern is where you said *'If we work as a cohesive unit.'* We're not a team! We are five individuals who barely know each other, let alone trust each other. I've been part of several hunting parties and it takes time to bond and trust each other with your life. Time we do not have!" exclaims a concerned Obadiah.

"Then we will have to learn and develop as a team on the journey ahead, for there is no other choice" explains Titus.

"That's what I was afraid of," says Obadiah.

The two quickly extinguish the campfire and walk back into the temple. Too excited to sleep everyone stays up longer than they should, sharing stories of life in their home clans. As they share what little food they brought from home, sheer distrust gives way to cautious apprehension. With their bellies full, they finally fall asleep.

CHAPTER 5

THE JOURNEY BEGINS

The morning sunlight shines through the temple windows, birds chirp loudly outside and silent internal alarm clocks go off as the Chosen Ones slowly, one by one, awaken from their sleep.

Obadiah is the first to wake up and without saying a word to anyone, he goes outside. He stretches and yawns loudly, then starts to sniff the cool fresh air. "Ah, there you are. I found you" says Obadiah as he heads southward from Rock Temple.

Everyone else finally wakes up and gives each other an unenthusiastic morning greeting. "Where is Obadiah?" inquires Sakia.

"I saw him go outside," says Keembo.

"We need to pack our stuff and get ready to head out" states, Titus.

Just as everyone finishes packing, Obadiah busts through the front door with eight fish in his hands saying, "I've caught breakfast and we can fill up our water bags at the stream south of here. I see you all have packed already. Can someone start a fire outside and clean the fish while I pack up my stuff?"

"I'll prepare the fish," says Azra.

"I'll start the fire," says Keembo.

After breakfast, everyone follows Obadiah down to the stream to fill their water bags. Returning to the temple they gather their backpacks and satchels for the trek north to Granite Mountain.

Stepping into the woods, all had forgotten the massive thickness of the forest. How its branches blot out the sky like a green carpet, with moth-like holes in it letting small beams of light shine through. The woods force a steady, slow and deliberate pace to be maintained. After two hours of walking, frustration starts to set in.

"Will this forest ever end? Mr. Goggles do you see anything?" cries out Azra.

"I know you didn't just call me Mr. Goggles, little girl. I will step on you" says Titus.

"I don't think that would be a wise move on your part" interjects Keembo.

"Oh, so you want a piece of me too, huh? Well, I've got something in my bag for you; just give me ten minutes big man."

Obadiah steps between Keembo and Titus saying, "What are you doing? Stop fighting amongst yourselves. If we want to defeat the Demon King, we need to work *together*."

"Excuse me, gentlemen, I hate to interrupt this little love fest, but I have one question. Where did the sun go?", questions Sakia.

"The sun?" inquires the others, looking upwards.

"Yeah, it stopped shining through the trees about fifty yards back" Sakia replies.

"Sakia climb to the top of the trees and tell me what you see" instructs Obadiah.

Sakia swings and jumps up through the trees until she reaches a clear vantage point where she can see the blue sky. "Oh my gosh! The sun is being blocked out by a huge mountain" gasps Sakia.

Twenty yards in front of her is a huge stone mountain that stretches for miles in both directions. Sakia quickly rappels down the trees to tell the others. "We are here, we've made it. Granite Mountain is just a few yards ahead of us."

Excitement replaces frustration at the sound of the good news. Everyone walks in the direction Sakia points out. Exiting the forest, they see Granite Mountain looming in front of them.

Granite Mountain stands a thousand feet high and stretches out for miles; the top is flat like a plateau and its face has smoothly uniformed ridges. The dark brown stone is beautiful and ominous at the same time.

The Chosen Ones stand in the shadow of this monstrous mountain, looking at it in awe and amazement. They decide to pause and rest before they resume their search for the gateway to Demon's Realm.

As they talk amongst themselves Sakia says, "I noticed a large, hollowed-out area in the side of the mountain when I was up in the trees. We should probably try looking there first."

"Okay, let's get started" replies the others.

Reaching the hollowed area, investigative eyes look for any signs that would confirm this is indeed the gate entrance.

"This is the gateway," says Azra in a soft, calm voice as she points to a diamond-shaped hole in the mountain wall, the same shape and size as the red gem in her satchel bag. Everyone watches Azra pull the spirit gem out of her bag and gently place it in the slot on the wall. It fits perfectly.

"Everybody takes a step back," says Keembo as the stone wall starts to rumble and shake. A beam of red light shoots out from the gem onto the adjacent wall, the light on the wall grows and expands until the whole wall is engulfed by the red light.

"It's the portal to Demon's Realm, we found it" shouts Obadiah. The excitement of finding the entrance to

Demon's Realm quickly gives way to the stark reality that they will be leaving Earth, their families and their clans, possibly forever.

"Is everyone ready to go?" asks Keembo.

"If this isn't a one-way trip, then, yes" replies Titus.

Walking straight towards the portal Sakia says, "There is only one way to find out, see ya on the other side."

"Sakia wait" yells Obadiah running through the portal after her.

"You have got to be kidding me, nobody in their right mind walks into Demon's Realm by themselves and without a plan to boot. That girl must have a death wish or something" says Titus shaking his head.

"Titus, Keembo, go on after them, I will be right behind you. I need to get the spirit gem" says Azra.

Reluctantly, they say, "Alright, but be quick about it."

Demon's Realm is a world that has been conquered by the Demon King. It is divided into six separate principalities, each ruled by commanders loyal to the Demon King. These six regions are the Sand Province, Underground Caverns, Woodlands, Defiled Marshlands, Sky Citadel, and the Arctic Plains.

Each territory is separated by steep mountain ranges, frigid waters and vast canyon passes. By day a red sun lights up and permeates the atmosphere with an eerie, creepy sensation. By night two bloodshot moons dimly reflect the sun's red light upon this godforsaken land. Dark black clouds drift across the red sky blocking out the already diminished light of day. Vultures roam the skies looking for their daily meal.

Life is harsh and cruel for the inhabitants of this world. They are all pressed into forced slavery or recruited to be guards that protect their master's kingdom. This ominous place is where the Chosen Ones have been teleported.

Passing through the portal, the Chosen Ones enter Demon's Realm on a mountainous cliff overlooking the Sand Province. Each one stands astonished at the sight before them. Their eyes gaze across the vast ocean of sand, looking at the dunes littered with patches of trees and sparse vegetation. Scanning the horizon all eyes stop and fixate on a large, green patch standing like an island in a light brown sea. This large oasis about a mile northeast of them beckons them like a lighthouse to weary sailors.

"What is that?" inquires Azra, pointing to the green patch everyone is looking at.

"That is an oasis, otherwise known as life in the desert. Everything good or bad will eventually make its way there. For the one thing, every living creature needs to survive is there in abundance. Water. This reminds me of home" says Keembo. The stony ledge beneath their feet connects to a winding pathway, leading down the mountainside to the sandy floor below.

Obadiah says, "We need to get off this cliff and establish a base camp below." Everyone nods and follows Obadiah down the twisty rock pass.

"You have been awfully quiet Titus, are you okay? You're not scared are you?" quips Sakia.

"I'm still calming down from that stupid stunt you pulled back at the portal. If anything, I'm scared that your irrational behavior might get us all killed out here" exclaims Titus.

"Irrational! I'll show you irrational" says Sakia glaring just as intensely back at Titus.

"You two really need to calm down. In case you've forgotten, we are on the same team" states Azra.

"Yeah, yeah, yeah" mumbles Titus and Sakia.

Obadiah instinctively goes into survival mode once their feet touch the sand. "Keembo, you know about life in the desert. Can you, Azra and Titus build our shelter for the night? Sakia and I will check out our immediate surroundings while looking for food and water."

"We will take care of the camp, you two can look for coconuts in the trees; they will have water inside them," says Keembo.

"Okay, we will be back before dusk," says Obadiah as he and Sakia walk off.

"I sure hope Obadiah talks some sense into that girl. Sakia could have put the whole team in jeopardy" comments Titus.

Keembo responds, "I think Sakia is a brave girl, she is rash and unpredictable, but brave nonetheless."

Defensively, Azra says, "Why are you guys talking about Sakia when she is not here to defend herself? Besides we are a team, like family, we should all get along."

"A family? This is not my family" retorts Keembo. "The only reason I am here is to protect my family. I like you Azra because you remind me of my little sister and you've been nice to me. So, I'll protect you with my life. And Titus you're an arrogant little man, but the things you say are in everyone's best interest, so you're okay with me for now."

"I guess I'll take that as a backhanded compliment," says Titus.

"Well, I see both of you like my big brothers" smiles Azra.

"Okay, enough of the mushy mushy stuff. Let's get this shelter built. There are three palm trees over there" points out Keembo.

~~~
~~~

"Sakia, I'm not a big fan of Titus, but I too wonder why you abruptly walked through the portal without us all being ready?" inquires Obadiah.

Briefly hesitating Sakia says, "I've always had a love for risk, danger, and excitement. I have a hard time waiting for long drawn out instructions. Sometimes you have to learn as you go and adapt to the situation, you know."

"Oh, I know what you're saying and I agree with having to learn on-the-fly and adapting to the situation. But, when you are part of a team, everyone is counting on you to follow the plan and not deviate from it. Someone could get seriously hurt or killed if you're not where you're supposed to be when you're supposed to be there" shares Obadiah.

"Wow, you sound like Ruth, my clan's high priestess. I know, you're right." Sakia sighs. "And I'll work at being a better team player."

Reaching the palm trees Keembo knowledgeably states, "These three trees and their palm branches should be enough to make our tent for the night. I'll push over the trees and we can carry them back to camp." Keembo quickly and easily pushes over two of the palm trees with a crashing thud.

As Keembo starts to move the third tree, a loud buzzing sound can be heard coming from the branches above. Hundreds of desert hornets fly out of their nest as the third palm tree slams to the ground. These desert hornets have long poisonous stingers that shoot out rapidly. Multiple stings from these hornets have been known to cause paralysis and sometimes death.

The angry hornets immediately attack. Their poisonous stingers are unable to penetrate Keembo's stone-hard skin and fall harmlessly to the ground. Azra instinctively puts up a shield protecting her from the hornets' attacks.

Titus pulls out his steel baton in a feeble attempt to block the stingers. He screams out in agony as numerous stingers penetrate his body, pumping the deadly toxin into his bloodstreams. Running frantically, Titus finally stumbles behind Azra's shield for protection.

Hearing Titus' screams, Keembo snatches the hornets' nest and hurls it as far as he can. The hornets instinctively turn away and follow in pursuit of their nest.

Before making it safely behind Azra's shield, Titus is stung forty-five times. Large welts begin to emerge on his arms, legs, and back where he was stung. Lying motionless on the ground his body starts to go numb.

"Oh no! He's dead! He's dead!" screams out Keembo.

Azra drops her shield abruptly and reaches into her satchel, pulling out one of her healing potions. She calmly lifts Titus' head, pouring the potion down into his mouth.

Swallowing the potion he passes out. Azra removes the stingers from Titus' body and intensely looks at his face for any signs of the poison's remission. After five excruciating minutes, Titus opens his eyes, the swelling on his back, legs and arms are gone. His body has been cured of the poison.

"You are healed now, Titus. How do you feel?" inquires Azra.

"I don't feel that horrible pain anymore, actually I feel normal, better than normal" proclaims Titus.

"I'm glad you made it back from the dead," says Keembo.

"Dead? I wasn't dead...was I?" asks Titus.

"No you weren't dead, but you came close. My healing potions can't revive the dead; they can only cure and heal the living" states Azra.

"You two go back to the campsite. I'll bring the trees" says Keembo.

"Okay, see you back at camp," says Azra and Titus.

~~~

"We've been walking for a while now and I haven't seen any signs of life out here, except for a few trees and some shrubbery," says Sakia.
~~~

"Oh, there's plenty of life out here. I can see their tracks" replies Obadiah.

"Ah, yes the expert hunter and tracker. Wait, those look like coconuts in the trees" shrieks Sakia.

In an all-out sprint Sakia dashes towards the tree. Gauging her steps to leap onto the tree Sakia sees a fiery arrow fly over her shoulder and stick into the tree, causing her to stop dead in her tracks.

Spinning around angrily Sakia shouts, "Are you crazy? You almost hit me with that arrow of yours."

Glaring at Obadiah with her hand on her whip Sakia notices Obadiah pointing at the tree behind her. Upon closer inspection, Sakia sees the arrow sticking in the base of the head of a large red and black diamondback snake, the most lethal snake in the Sand Province.

"A simple thank you will suffice. I suspect one bite would be deadly" quips Obadiah.

"I didn't even see it. How did you see it?" wails out Sakia.

"I noticed its trail through the sand a ways back, but didn't see the creature until you began to run towards the tree," says Obadiah. Causing the fiery arrow to disappear from the snake's head, Obadiah places the snake's carcass into his bag.

"Well thanks for saving my life, but next time can you give a girl some kind of warning?" says Sakia with a sarcastic grin on her face.

"If time permits, I will. Now what were you going to do before I interrupted you?" asks Obadiah.

Sakia leaps upward and grabs a hold of the tree trunk, taking her whip from her side, she snaps it towards the coconuts, four of them fall to the ground. Several whips later ten coconuts lay on the ground.

"That should be enough water for everyone" states Sakia.

"Yeah, I think we have enough food and water. It's about time we headed back to camp" says Obadiah.

Walking back to camp with Azra, Titus says, "Azra that shield of yours is a very powerful weapon, there must be some way I can enhance it to make it bigger and better. I'm going to have to give it some thought."

"That would be great, then I could protect others instead of only myself. Oh, Titus, I found some Thurmis Blossoms earlier. Here take them, in case you need them. My mother told me these flowers were the key ingredient in making the Sacred Bracelet I wear" explains Azra.

"Great! I'm sure I'll need these at some point or another" Titus replies.

Keembo returns to camp dragging two trees under his right arm and one under his left. Keembo drops the trees in front of the mountain and begins to rip off the palm leaves. He takes each tree and snaps them into three long pieces. Taking seven of the long wood poles he secures each one in the sand, then he pushes the top of them snugly against the mountain. Azra and Titus help Keembo drape the palm leaves over the seven pieces of wood, forming a canopy that will keep the desert sand storms out and protect their campfire at night.

"It's finished. What do you think?" asks Keembo.

"It looks like a teepee cut in half by a stone wall. I like it" says Azra.

"Very functional. It's big enough to house the five of us and has an inside campfire with a hole at the top to allow the smoke to rise outside. Well thought out Keembo. I give it two thumbs up" says Titus. Keembo cracks a rare smile from the compliments of his two new companions.

"We're back" yells Sakia as she and Obadiah walk into the camp. "We have enough food and water for everyone. Oh! Nice shelter."

Dusk starts to settle in and the desert temperature drops. Before they know it, the temperature drops forty degrees.

"We need to build a campfire so we can cook dinner and stay warm as the night gets colder," says Obadiah as he pulls out the red and black snake from his bag.

Azra jumps back in surprise and shrieks, "Is that a snake? Don't tell me we're going to eat that for dinner?"

"Snake meat is delicious. We're going to need some dried-out firewood to start a fire to cook it with" says Keembo.

"If I can get some teamwork from Sakia, we can have that firewood in no time" comments Titus sarcastically.

"I'm the girl for the job" retorts Sakia. "What do you need me to do?"

"I need you to electrocute these two leftover sections of the palm tree. The electricity will dry them out enough to burn as firewood. I'll then need you to slice them into small pieces" explains Titus.

"Okay let's give this a try," says Sakia as she pushes the orange button on the hilt of her black metal whip. Blue electricity flashes back and forth along her whip. Sakia snaps her whip, it wraps around one of the trees sending an electric shock through it.

"Good. Now hold it there for a few minutes. Let the electricity dry up the moisture inside the tree. Do the same thing to the other one" instructs Titus. The moisture in the trees dry up and they become lighter and more brittle than before.

Titus directs Sakia to swing her whip in a slicing motion through the trees to cut them into smaller pieces. Sakia excitedly cracks her whip down upon the trees until the large pieces of wood are reduced to a pile of firewood.

"Great teamwork! Now let's get this snake fry started" belts out Obadiah.

Daylight quickly retreats as the darkness of night creeps in over the land. The winds pick up and flying sand can be heard pelting against the palm leaf canopy. Inside the shelter, the Chosen Ones sip on coconut juice and eat snake meat for dinner, safe from the raging elements outside. They talk and laugh about their adventures of the day, all the while strengthening a bond between them, friendship.

"We should be safe tonight; no creature would dare travel out under these conditions. Get a good night's sleep everyone, we rise at dawn" says Obadiah.

They all say good night and retire for the evening.

CHAPTER 6

THE SAND PROVINCE

Night limps away, giving ground to the rapidly approaching red sunlight. Morning has come and finds everyone awake, satchels and bags packed, ready to head out.

"The oasis is northeast of us somewhere over those sand dunes. Take everything with you, we may not be coming back here. We'll head north, then travel east on top of those sand dunes. We have a long trek ahead of us so let's head out" says Obadiah.

After walking several miles north, they start to climb the sand dune and head east. At the bottom of the sand dune, Azra catches sight of two herbal plants used in making healing potions, Milkweed and Willowroots. She stops to collect them and quickly catches up with the others.

Ascending the sand dune is a slow arduous trek. Reaching the top all are surprised at what they see, a valley of lush green vegetation surrounded by three hills to the north, west, and east. Farther to the east is a gigantic body of water.

Titus switches his goggles to binocular vision and is taken aback at what he sees. "Hey guys, I see some kind of castle or stronghold down there amongst the trees. We need to get closer so I can get a better look."

"Everyone quietly climbs down the dune and stay alert, remember we're in enemy territory" directs Obadiah.

Hearing Obadiah's words remind everyone of what the Spirit said about the dangers and battles ahead of them.

Reaching the bottom of the dune, everyone disappears into the thick green brush. Titus starts walking towards a clearing to get a better look at the large structure.

"Dang! That's not a castle it's a fortress and there's tall thin pyramids surrounding it. I can see people, strange-looking people."

~~~

The people of the Sand Province, the Serconians, were a strong, proud, industrialized people before the Demon King conquered their land and destroyed their cities. The Serconians have deep-set eyes with protruding foreheads. They have chocolate brown skin
~~~

and four arms. The top of the men's heads is bald and the black hair on the sides of their head is pulled back into a long ponytail.

The women have similar features except their long straight black hair starts at the center of their heads and flows down past their shoulders. The women wear halter tops and miniskirts during the heat of the day, while the men wear short underpants with no shirt.

The Demon King is a sadistic and unforgiving taskmaster who kills anyone that would try to oppose his rule. Those who serve him and fail or betray him is reserved a fate worse than death. It has been whispered that those poor souls are not killed, but are tortured unmercifully day and night for three years, not allowed to die. Wailing and gnashing of teeth can be heard from their cells. This vision is seared into the minds of all those whom the Evil One places in charge over his kingdoms. Fear and dread are the scepters of his kingdom.

The Demon King had his demon army kill every Serconian man, woman, and child. He only spared two hundred Serconians to serve as slaves in their own land as he moved on to conquer other kingdoms.

Tyk was terror-stricken by the deaths of his fellow Serconians and said in his heart, "It is better to live as a king than to toil as a slave."

To spare his own life he pledged his eternal allegiance to the Demon King and was made Pharaoh over the entire Sand Province. Under the influence of the Demon King, Tyk's heart and soul became darkened and he became a cruel and oppressive taskmaster over his people, killing anyone who would dare resist or disobey his commands.

The mantle of Pharaoh was passed down for generations to Tyk's sons. Each of Tyk's sons possessed the same evil spirit as their father. The new rulers have chosen to be called King instead of Pharaoh.

~~~

"Everybody get down, someone is coming this way," says Obadiah.

Laying quietly on the ground covered by bushes, footsteps can be heard getting louder and closer by the second. The two soldiers stop and pause several feet away from discovering the intruders. The soldiers turn to leave when Azra lets out a scream.

Instinctively, Keembo leaps out of the bushes onto one of the soldiers taking him to the ground. Lefts and rights from Keembo's massive arms quickly knock the soldier out cold.

The other soldier, catching a glimpse of the intruders and seeing Keembo attacking his partner, takes flight
~~~

towards the fortress yelling, "Intruders, the intruders are here."

Sakia vaults from her spot, grabbing her whip she snaps it encircling the soldier's neck, Zzzt! The unconscious soldier hits the ground.

"Are you alright Azra? Why did you scream out like that?" asks Titus.

"Something crawled on my arm."

"Was it a snake?" inquires Keembo.

With an embarrassed look on her face Azra says, "No, it was a caterpillar. I'm sorry, it startled me."

No one says a word, they just stare at the two strange men lying unconscious on the ground. "Look they have four arms and are armed with whips and swords" squeals Azra.

"They must be lookouts patrolling the area. Keembo bind and gag our two prisoners: we can question them when they regain consciousness. Right now we need to assess the situation and come up with a plan. Any ideas Titus?" asks Obadiah.

Rubbing the back of his head Titus says, "Well, the good news is that we took these two patrol guards down in less than a minute. The bad news is, it sounds like they knew we were coming. If that's the case when these two don't report back they will probably send out a search party and strengthen their defenses causing us to lose the element of surprise.

"Before I can devise a plan I need to get a better look at that Sand Fortress and her defenses. Obadiah, Sakia, I need you two to come with me. We need to go now."

Securing the last soldier's arms with tree vines Keembo says, "Hold on Titus I believe one of our prisoners is waking up."

"Good I want to question him," says Titus. Kneeling down and looking the restrained prisoner in the eyes, Titus asks, "How do you know our language? Who taught you English?"

The dazed prisoner responds, "You are speaking our native Serconian tongue."

Titus looks up at the others then asks another question, "How did you know we were coming here?"

Leering at Titus for a few seconds the prisoner retorts, "The Demon King said months ago that invaders from another world would come here seeking to destroy our world. We have been watching for your invasion ever since. I will tell you nothing more."

Putting the leafy gag back in the prisoner's mouth, Titus turns to Keembo and Azra saying, "I need you two to guard the prisoners, while the rest of us scout the area. We'll be back as soon as we can."

Taking the lead Obadiah heads east towards the Sand Fortress, Titus and Sakia follow one step behind on his left and right shoulders.

~~~
~~~

The Sand Fortress is a massive stone structure. Its outer walls are fifty feet high all around. The only way in or out of the fortress is to pass through the front gate. The entrance is a gigantic lion's head with its massive jaws outstretched as if daring anyone to come close. There are seven smooth, sandstone steps leading into the lion's mouth. Along the sides of the staircase are two gigantic lion paws. The fortress' appearance emanates a sense of fear and dread as if one will be eaten alive if they enter the gates.

The King, his army and all the slaves reside inside the Sand Fortress. The small town inside the fortress is constantly patrolled by the King's men. Once inside, only a select few are permitted to leave. A group of slaves are allowed out of the fortress each day to irrigate the crops and tend to the needs of the guards in the four surrounding towers.

Four pyramid-shaped towers encircle the Sand Fortress. The towers are sixty feet tall. The towers facing north and south are lookout towers. The eastern tower is the sorcerer's tower and the western tower is the dungeon, where prisoners are detained, tortured and put to death.

Obadiah stops a hundred yards from the Sand Fortress, safely hiding behind bushes and trees. "This is the closest I can get us without being detected. It's up to you now, Titus." Using his binocular vision, Titus surveys the four towers, the surrounding areas, and the Sand Fortress. After fifteen minutes of deafening silence, Titus turns to face the others.

"Well, tell us what you saw" Sakia barks impatiently.

"Okay, the north and south towers appear to be lookout towers. I don't know what the other two towers are. There are a handful of slaves working the grounds and a few soldiers watching them. The rest of the soldiers and slaves must be inside this Sand Fortress.

"What we're looking for has to be in either the eastern or western towers, but most likely it's inside the Sand Fortress. I'll need some time to figure out a plan of attack."

"Quiet! Get down. There's a group headed our way" says Obadiah. The three of them crouched behind a few bushes.

Ten slaves carrying baskets of freshly picked vegetables and an armed guard pass in front of Obadiah, Sakia, and Titus. Tripping over a rock, one slave falls to the ground. Losing hold of her basket, the vegetables scatter on the sandy ground.

"You idiot" shouts the guard as he repeatedly strikes the slave girl across the back with his whip. The fifteen-year-old girl screams out in pain with each lash of the guard's whip.

Sakia's body tenses and jerks with each blow. Obadiah puts his hand on Sakia's arm and whispers, "We can't get involved Sakia."

"He's going to kill her! I won't let him kill her" shrieks Sakia as she leaps from the bushes.

Running towards the guard Sakia jumps in the air and kicks him in the back of the head, stunning him and knocking him to the ground. "Are you alright? Hurry we must leave before more guards come" says Sakia.

The other slaves seeing Sakia attack the guard shout out, "Guards! Intruder! An intruder is here!"

Bursting around the corner of the Sand Fortress, fifteen armed soldiers surround Sakia. An archer on top of the fortress wall shoots an arrow striking Sakia in the leg. As she falls to the ground in pain, soldiers throw a net over her. Sakia is captured. With her leg bleeding from the arrow, the guards drag Sakia and the Serconian slave to the dungeon tower.

Without a thought, Obadiah instinctively lunges forward in an attempt to help his teammate. Titus frantically tackles Obadiah to the ground before he can enter the guards' line of sight.

"Get off me! Let me go! We have to rescue her!" shouts Obadiah.

On the ground, Titus whispers into Obadiah's ear, "Obadiah, we can't save her if we get captured too."

Knowing Titus is right, Obadiah stops struggling. "If I had to guess, I would say the tower they are taking Sakia to must be the dungeon," says Titus.

"Do you have a plan yet Titus?"

"Yes, I do. But we have to get back to the others quickly before the soldiers come looking for us."

Obadiah and Titus quickly run through the green oasis back to Keembo and Azra. "It's about time you guys got back. Where is Sakia?" asks Azra.

"She was captured" replies Obadiah.

"Well then, we have to go rescue her," says a determined Azra. The bound and gagged prisoners listen intently to the conversation going on near them.

"Azra, I have a plan. We are going to head back to our camp southwest of here by the stone mountain and give the others this location. Once our army comes, we will destroy everything and everyone here. We must go now before they catch us" explains Titus.

"What about the prisoners?" asks Keembo.

"Lay them face down and leave them. When we reach the base camp it will be too late for them to stop us anyway" replies Titus.

The four head south back the way they came from Stone Mountain. Fifty yards out, Titus explains his real plan to the rest of the group. "Okay, everyone listen up, this is the real plan. As we speak, there should be some sort of search party sent out to find us. When the search party finds our two prisoners, they're going to tell them everything they overheard. This should cause the King to send his army towards Stone Mountain to try and capture us before we call reinforcements.

"We'll hide here in the bushes until we see the King's army leave the Sand Fortress. Once they leave, we'll sneak into the dungeon tower and free Sakia. After we get her back, we can inspect the other towers and if necessary we'll head into the Sand Fortress and find what we came here for - a piece of the Armor of God."

The guards drag Sakia into the dungeon tower, she screams as one of the guards pulls the arrow out of her leg. They bandage her leg and throw her into a prison cell next to the slave girl she tried to save.

"Who else came here with you?" inquires the head prison guard.

"I came here alone" Sakia boldly states.

"You are lying. I can see it in your eyes. Lieutenant, inform the King of our prisoner and send out a search party to find our little guest's companions."

The lieutenant commands fifty soldiers to scour the outer grounds for any signs of the other intruders before heading to see the King. The lieutenant kneels before the King in the throne room.

"What news do you have to report?" questions the King.

"My King, we have captured one of the intruders and she is being held captive in the dungeon. Also, I have dispatched fifty of my men to leave no stone unturned in finding any other intruders."

"Good work lieutenant. Let me know what your men find out. After that, we will kill the girl."

The soldiers carry swords and whips in their hands as they walk shoulder to shoulder searching the oasis floor. "I hear something," says one soldier as he walks closer to the sound.

Brandishing two swords and two whips, a weapon in each of his four hands, he holds them high prepared to strike. Pushing back the leaves of a large bush, he sees two soldiers tied and gagged lying face down on the ground.

The entire search party gathers around to hear what the two soldiers have to say. When the freed soldiers finish telling the others of the intruders' plans, the commanding officer instructs everyone to return to the Sand Fortress at once.

Watching his plan unfold Titus laughs, "Ha, ha, ha, they fell for it. Now we need to get closer to the fortress and be ready to move when the King's army leaves."

The King, extremely angry at the lieutenant's report, orders his entire army to pursue and eliminate the intruders. Only one hundred soldiers are left behind to guard the fortress gates.

"What about the prisoner, my lord?" asks the lieutenant.

"We will let her rot until her friends join her. Now go, and don't fail me" commands the King.

The lieutenant leads the King's army to the southern section of the Sand Province to deal with the intruders. Riding eight-legged camels and marching on foot the soldiers leave the Sand Fortress, pass through the oasis, and disappear around the sand dune.

"The King's army has left and most of the remaining soldiers should be inside protecting the Sand Fortress, leaving the towers lightly guarded" explains Titus.

Flipping a switch on his goggles, Titus scopes out the two lookout towers and notices only one guard stationed at the top of each tower. "Obadiah, can you take out the guards in those two towers?" asks Titus.

"Not a problem. Count it as done" answers Obadiah. Pulling back his bow, Obadiah releases a fiery arrow hitting the south tower guard directly in the chest, knocking him to the floor of the tower. Turning one hundred and eighty degrees to his left, Obadiah shoots another arrow striking the north tower guard square in the back. The guard's neck jerks back before collapsing to the floor.

"The coast is clear," says Obadiah.

"Run, now!" shouts Titus.

~~~
~~~

"My name is Tiwa," says the fifteen-year-old slave girl. "Thank you for saving my life. That guard surely would have killed me. Sadly, I fear we'll both die instead. How's your leg?"

"Name's Sakia and I couldn't just stand by and watch you get killed. If what I did was a mistake, it's one that I would probably make again. Oh, you asked about my leg. It hurts like hell. I won't be jumping on it anytime soon, but I'll live" says Sakia holding the bandage over her still bleeding leg. "I'm curious Tiwa, why did the others rat me out?"

Tiwa solemnly replies, "The fear of death is a daily reality for my people. One simple mistake could mean your life. My only guess is that they didn't want to be perceived as helping intruders, for that act is punishable by death."

"I guess it really doesn't matter," says Sakia leaning back against the cold prison wall in her cell.

"You! Halt!" screams the head prison guard before losing consciousness to a forceful, well-placed, straight right hand to the jaw from Keembo.

"Get the keys! I think I hear Sakia behind that door" cries Azra.

Lifting the keys from around the guard's neck, Keembo unlocks the outer door leading to Sakia's cell. "Sakia! We found you!" shouts Azra as she snatches the key out of Keembo's hand and quickly unlocks her cell door. "You're hurt! Take some of this healing potion. It will heal that nasty wound."

"Dang Azra, you are worse than my mother," says Sakia playfully.

"Yeah, well, just drink this and in a few minutes you should be all healed up."

"Sakia, I'm sorry we didn't help you back there," says Obadiah.

"Nonsense! There is nothing to be sorry about. You guys came back to rescue me. If you had tried to help me, we all would be locked up in here" Sakia responds with a smile on her face.

"Sakia, take me with you! I can help you escape from here" cries out Tiwa.

"No way! We can't trust you" explains Titus.

"I owe Sakia my life and if I have to repay it with my own life, then so be it" sincerely declares Tiwa.

"I trust her" insists Sakia.

"I believe her as well" responds Azra.

"Damn! Damn! Damn! Damn!" belts Titus, banging his steel baton on the floor. "If she cries out, we're all going to die. You do realize that, right?"

"I feel she is sincere" states Keembo.

"She could help us navigate this place" shrugs Obadiah.

Looking straight into Titus' eyes, Sakia says again, "I trust her."

Reluctantly, Titus says, "Alright, fine. What's your name?"

"Tiwa."

"Tiwa, what's in that eastern tower?"

"That's the Sorcerers' Tower. All the alchemists and enchanters live there making all sorts of magical things" answers Tiwa.

"Sounds like your kind of place Titus" jokes Sakia.

"They usually sleep during the day and work their magic at night" explains Tiwa.

"Okay, we'll head there next" declares Titus. He then turns to Arza. "Azra, let Tiwa out of her cell. Sakia, is your leg healed yet?"

"This girl's fit and ready for duty" replies Sakia.

Leaving the western tower, the five intruders and Tiwa make their way to the eastern tower, staying as far away from the Sand Fortress and as close to the outer walls as possible.

Reaching the Sorcerers' Tower undetected, Titus gently pulls down on the door latch. To his surprise, the door is unlocked. He slowly pushes the door open revealing a large oval-shaped room consisting of a square eating table, a cooking area with cupboards, a fire pit built into the center of the floor, three tall dressers, and three empty beds. A spiral staircase attached to the tower wall circles its way up to the second floor.

Entering the tower, they all gaze upon the furnished living quarters before abruptly looking up towards the ceiling. Voices can be heard coming from above.

Looking at Tiwa, Titus whispers, "I thought you said these guys would be sleeping during the day."

Tiwa shrugs her shoulders saying, "I guess they woke up."

Keembo says, "I hate enchanters with their hocus-pocus stuff. I will lead the way upstairs and draw their attention. You guys strike when you see an opening."

Keembo walks up the narrow winding staircase followed by Azra, Sakia, Titus, and Obadiah. Tiwa stays downstairs. Preparing for battle, Obadiah cinches his bow, Titus fully extends his steel baton, Sakia uncoils her whip, Azra focuses mentally, and Keembo draws out his daggers.

The three residents of the Tower consist of an alchemist (one who uses science to make powerful weapons), a mighty wizard and a powerful sorceress.

"Be careful with those sulfur bombs, you imbecile! You're liable to blow us all up. Forget it! I will put the bombs away myself" says the alchemist to the sorceress as he places the sulfur bombs into a satchel bag.

"You best watch your tone with me old man, lest I turn you into the pig you are" threatens the sorceress.

"Stop it you two" commands the wizard. "We have more immediate matters to deal with."

Turning away from their work table the enchanters behold five young strangers entering their upper chamber. Looking intently upon them, the sorceress bursts out into laughter and with a raised voice, screeches, "Are these the intruders the Demon King warned us about? They are merely children. I can dispatch of them all by myself."

Angered by the demeaning words of the sorceress, Keembo, with a sudden burst of speed, leaps into the air with both daggers raised above his head, poised to strike the sorceress. Seconds from driving them into the sorceress' neck, the sorceress moves the wand held in her lower right hand suspending Keembo in midair. Keembo hurls one of his daggers at the sorceress, hitting her in the lower right shoulder. Wincing in pain, she drops her wand. As it hits the ground, Keembo is released and falls to the floor.

Screaming in pain, the sorceress pulls out the dagger and tosses it away. She shouts, "How dare you!" Stretching out her upper left hand towards Keembo the sorceress shoots out a firebolt hitting a kneeling Keembo in the chest and hurling him headlong off the second floor, crashing twelve feet below.

Obadiah quickly shoots three fiery arrows at the wizard. Raising his upper right hand the wizard disappears for three seconds, then reappears. The arrows pass through him and strike the wall.

The alchemist shoots fireballs from his staff at Azra, Sakia, and Titus. Azra erects a force shield blocking the fireballs while the others maneuver behind her.

Leaping into the air from behind Azra's shield, Sakia jumps over the sorceress' head, flipping while in the air, her feet pointing to the ceiling she snaps her electric whip, latching it onto one of the sorceress' left arms. Landing on the ground, Sakia pushes the orange button, sending out bolts of electricity. The sorceress' body pulsates as she hits the floor face first.

"One down, two to go," says Sakia.

"Obadiah, keep the wizard occupied with your arrows. Azra, provide protection for Obadiah. Sakia, you and I will take care of the alchemist" instructs Titus.

Obadiah holds the wizard's attention by shooting a barrage of arrows at him. Sakia agilely evades the fireballs shot at her from the alchemist's staff. Titus runs up behind the alchemist knocking the staff out of his hand with his steel baton. Before the alchemist can reach for his fallen staff, Titus delivers several body shots and a crushing head blow to the alchemist with his baton, knocking him out cold.

Seeing his two companions fall, the wizard confidently declares, "I will toy with you younglings no longer."

Raising his four arms up in the air, he clasps his hands together as if squeezing someone's neck. All at once Sakia, Azra, Titus, and Obadiah start reaching for their throats and gasping for air. Dropping their weapons, they struggle to loosen the invisible vice-like grip choking the life out of them.

"You all shall die this day by my hands" roars the mighty wizard. A sinister grin forms on the wizard's face as he sees the four bodies weakening and starting to go limp.

Splashing water on Keembo's face, Tiwa revives him. Looking at the smoking red scar on his chest Tiwa asks, "What happened?"

"Some old hag shot me in the chest with a firebolt. I guess I won't be asking her out on a date anytime soon" says Keembo.

"All the noise and explosions have stopped upstairs" explains Tiwa.

"Oh no. That's not good. I have to get back up there" blurts out Keembo as he struggles to get up and make his way to the stairs. Fighting through the pain Keembo makes his way up the stairs and glimpses the unfolding chaos.

With his back to the stairs, the wizard lets out a loud curdling scream. Releasing his four victims, his arms reach towards his back trying to pull out Keembo's long dagger. Having his heart pierced by the blade, the wizard feels his life force leaving his body. Falling to his knees, the wizard utters his last words, "This can't be."

Coughing violently and rubbing their throats, air refills the near-empty lungs of Titus, Azra, Sakia, and Obadiah. Staggering to the nearby table, Titus grabs some rope and binds the arms of the unconscious sorceress and alchemist behind their backs.

"Is everyone alright?" asks Tiwa as she makes her way upstairs. Still catching their breath, the four nod their heads.

"Azra, Keembo needs your help. He has multiple injuries and a very nasty burn on his chest" says a concerned Tiwa.

Azra rushes over to Keembo, who is laying down on his back at the top of the stairs. Helping him sit up against the wall, Azra gives Keembo a healing potion to drink.

As Keembo drinks the potion, Azra says, "My healing potions will heal any internal problems, but I'll need to apply some healing ointment to your chest wound in order to heal your burnt skin."

"Do what you have to do Azra. I trust you" says Keembo as he rests his head against the wall.

Picking up Keembo's dagger from the floor and pulling the other one out of the wizard's corpse, Sakia says, "The wizard is dead. Good job Keembo; you saved our lives. Should I kill the other two?"

"No. Sakia, we don't kill if we don't have to. Besides, they may have some information about the location of the Armor of God" says Obadiah.

Oblivious to everyone else in the room, Titus becomes fixated on the objects resting on the sorcerer's table. Sulfur bombs, quartz crystals, and enchanted sand are a few of the items that catch Titus' eye.

Titus takes several quartz crystals and puts them in his pouch. He scoops a jar full of enchanted sand and places it in his backpack. Collecting three loose sulfur bombs on the table, he places them in a satchel bag holding several other bombs.

Titus calls Tiwa over and asks, "Tiwa, can you carry this satchel for me? You have to be very careful not to jump around with it because it contains explosive sulfur bombs."

"I will be careful, Titus."

"Thank you, Tiwa."

"Are you done playing with your little toys, Titus? Because we need to get a move on before the King's army returns" states Obadiah.

~~~

Reaching Stone Mountain in the southern section of the Sand Province, a scout from the King's army bellows out, "I have found a camp."
~~~

The lieutenant rides over and dismounts his camel intently inspecting the camp and the surrounding area. Shouting in a loud voice, the lieutenant screams out, "Has anyone found any signs or tracks of an invading army?"

Several scouts reply, "We have only seen the tracks of five people."

Enraged at the thought of being outwitted and played for a fool, the lieutenant commands his soldiers to hastily return back to the Sand Fortress.

~~~

"I'm going to question the alchemist about the location of the Armor of God. Titus, you and Keembo secure the sorceress in that backroom" states Obadiah.

Keembo, totally recovered from his multiple injuries, walks over to the sorceress and picks her up with one arm. He addresses Titus with a smirk on his face, "Move out the way little man. I've got this."

Following Keembo, Titus counters, "You just got off the injury reserve list, Keembo. You keep talking and my steel baton and I will put you right back on it."

"Bah, I'd pick my teeth with your baton" utters Keembo as they both enter the back room.

"Tiwa, dowse some water on him and wake him up," says Obadiah.
~~~

Coughing frantically and realizing he is bound, the alchemist screams, "Release me at once or I'll--"

"Or you'll what," says Obadiah. "What you'll do is answer my questions or die. Do you understand?"

Looking at his dead comrade on the floor, the alchemist starts to tremble and utters, "You wouldn't kill me or you would have done it already."

"Sakia."

"Way ahead of you Obadiah," says Sakia as she snaps her whip, wrapping it around the alchemist's neck.

"With one push of a button, your head will be cooked like a boiled egg. Would you like me to have her demonstrate on you?" inquires Obadiah.

"I'll talk, I'll talk. Don't kill me, please" the alchemist begs frantically.

"Tell me what you know about the Armor of God."

"For years we have studied and analyzed the Breastplate of God, trying to unlock its hidden power, to no avail. Then several months ago, the King ordered the breastplate to be taken from us and brought directly to him. I have no idea where it is now" says the alchemist.

"But you do know your King. Where would such a trusting King place such a valuable item?" inquires Obadiah slowly turning his head towards Sakia.

"Alright! Alright! My best guess would be that he'd hide it somewhere in his royal bedchamber. Good luck getting in there" snickers the alchemist.

After having all his questions answered Obadiah gags the alchemist and locks him in the backroom with the sorceress. "Listen up, everyone. We have a little over an hour left before the King's army returns from their wild goose chase" declares Obadiah. "Anyone have any ideas on how we can get into the royal bedchamber and recover the breastplate?"

Silence fills the room as minds think and eyes look back and forth at each other.

Tiwa's voice breaks the long silence, "I remember hearing my mother say once that there was a hidden passageway to the King's chamber at the back end of the Sand Fortress. I think she said it was used by the previous King to sneak his mistresses in and out of his bedchamber without the Queen noticing. But when the Queen found out she had the entrance sealed. A story I had long since forgotten."

"Our time and options are limited. The only way into the Sand Fortress is through the front gate which is protected and fortified by soldiers. Our only hope is that Tiwa's story is true and we can find the sealed rear entrance to the Sand Fortress" says Titus.

After walking down the tower stairs, out the front door and stealthily to the back of the Sand Fortress, they stop.

"Look for anything out of the ordinary - a boulder out of place, a hole in the ground, fake bushes, whatever," says Titus.

"Fake bushes? Are you serious? Who in their right mind would hide a secret entrance behind some fake bushes? For a smart guy, you sure say some stupid things, Titus" teases Sakia.

"If you move your eyes as fast as you move your lips, we might have found it by now" retorts Titus.

As the two argue back and forth, Azra is drawn to an isolated area under a tree where she spots some herbs. Making her way to the herbs, Azra loses her footing in the sand and falls down. "Ouch" shouts Azra. "That's the hardest sand I've ever felt."

Hearing Azra cry out Keembo quickly walks over and asks, "Are you okay?"

"Yeah, I'm fine. But it feels like something is underneath the sand right here."

Pushing back the sand Keembo and Azra discover metal underneath. Calling the others over, they clear out a large section of sand revealing a large metal door.

"Azra, you did it! You found the secret entrance to the Sand Fortress" shrieks Sakia. "It appears to be welded shut."

"Stand aside, Sakia, let me give it a try," says Keembo reaching down to grab the metal door handle with his right hand. Pulling up as hard as he can, the metal door remains sealed tight.

"Is that it? Is that all you've got big guy, or are you still recovering from that butt whuppin you received at the Sorcerer's Tower" taunts Titus.

Sneering at Titus, Keembo bends his knees and grabs the metal handle with both hands. Letting out a loud grunt, Keembo pulls up on the metal door, straightening out his legs and arms. Straining and pulling with all his might, veins appear on the top of Keembo's bald head. With one deep grunt, Keembo rips the welded door from its place, revealing stone steps leading down into the ground.

"I never doubted you for a second, Keembo. I knew you could do it with just a little bit of motivation" says Titus.

"You might want to stop talking right about now," says Azra as Keembo leers at Titus huffing and puffing.

The stone steps descend fifteen feet underground leading to a small oval-shaped tunnel. At the end of the tunnel, more steps await leading upwards into a small nook hidden behind a large fireplace.

Obadiah leads the way down the dark stairway. Drawing back his bow, a fiery arrow appears, lighting the way through the dank, stuffy passageway. It is apparent to all as they march in a single file through the narrow tunnel, that no one has used this secret passageway in decades. Grabbing several unlit torches from the wall Obadiah lights them with his fiery arrow. Sakia carries a torch as she walks in the middle and Titus carries one as he brings up the rear.

They walk for two minutes in the passageway before reaching the nook. Seeing a long thin strip of vertical light emanating from the wall, everyone searches for a lever or something that will open the secret door. Looking up Sakia notices a strange-looking stone protruding from the ceiling. She reaches up and pushes the stone in.

The stone immediately retracts into the ceiling. Simultaneously unlatching and slightly opening a medium-sized door, four feet high and four feet wide on the right side of a huge fireplace in the King's bedchamber. The massive fireplace consumes half the wall. Shiny glazed bricks with a gold-colored hue surround the square-shaped mouth of the fireplace.

During this time of heightened security, the King commands his two strongest and most skilled soldiers to stand guard by his side at all times. After sending forth his army to deal with the intruders the King decides to rest in his bedchamber.

Ge'ta and Serg the King's personal bodyguards flank the King's bed as he rests on his pillow. Ge'ta possesses unparalleled strength. His broad chest is covered by heavy steel armor and engulfing his massive hands are solid brass knuckles.

Serg has a steel shield and wields a two-handed mace called the Morning Star. The Morning Star has a large steelhead made of six V-shaped spikes mounted on top of a short metal staff.

Pushing the secret stone door open, it slides across the stone floor making a low grinding sound. Entering the room the Chosen Ones and Tiwa notice they are not alone. Ge'ta and Serg slowly turn their heads toward the low grinding sound coming from the fireplace and see six bodies enter the room.

"Ge'ta protect the King! I will deal with these intruders" says Serg as he lifts the Morning Star above his head with his two upper arms. With his lower left arm, he holds his shield at the side of his body.

"Everyone spread out" shouts Obadiah as he shoots a fiery arrow at Serg.

Serg blocks the arrow with his shield and runs headlong at Obadiah with his weapon raised high. Aiming for his opponent's head, Serg swings down with all his might. Instinctively raising his ivory bow to block the oncoming assault, Obadiah knows his bow has no chance of stopping this massive weapon from crushing his skull.

Several inches before impact the Morning Star is blocked. Azra standing directly behind Obadiah raises her force shield projecting it in front of Obadiah.

"What witchcraft is this?" belts out Serg. "A shield appearing out of thin air, deflecting my deathblow, who dares? Ah, I see the source. Little girl, you die first."

Refocusing his attention on Azra, Serg reaches around Azra's shield and backhands Obadiah with a closed lower right-hand, knocking Obadiah to the floor three feet away.

Reaching to grab Azra, Serg shouts out, "Now you die."

In a full out sprint, Keembo charges directly into Serg, knocking him off his feet sending him flying five feet across the room, smashing into a nearby wall.

Popping up from his bed the King commands Ge'ta, "Kill them all."

Ge'ta walks over and picks Keembo up raising him effortlessly above his head with his four arms. With incredible strength and velocity, Ge'ta hurls Keembo headlong into the stone fireplace.

Obadiah sends five arrows exploding into Ge'ta's breastplate with no effect. Sakia latches her whip around Ge'ta's ankle and sends an electric shock through his body. Visibly pained and angered, Ge'ta yanks on Sakia's whip sending her flying across the room, flipping in the air, Sakia lands on her feet unharmed, her whip still around Ge'ta's ankle. Holding his bruised cheek Obadiah makes his way over to Azra, as a groggy Serg stands to his feet.

Standing in a safe corner with Tiwa, Titus observes the skirmish before him ascertaining the strengths and weaknesses of both sides, figuring out a strategy for his team to win.

Abruptly, Titus calls out, "Sakia make your way over to me. Azra, Obadiah, you two keep attacking the guy with the shield and mace. Keembo I need you to re-engage with the big strong guy."

Obadiah continuously shoots his arrows at Serg to slow down his advancement. Crouching down placing his huge shield in front of him Serg advances one step at a time towards Azra and Obadiah.

Sakia makes her way to Titus. "Tiwa give Sakia a sulfur bomb. Sakia be ready to move when I say so" says Titus emphatically. Sakia affirms with a nod of her head.

"Keembo keep an eye on his footwork," says Titus as he points to Sakia's whip still wrapped around Ge'ta's ankle. Standing straight up, Keembo looks Ge'ta straight in the eye before diving to the floor grabbing Sakia's whip.

Pushing the button Ge'ta is stunned momentarily, allowing Keembo to tug on Sakia's whip pulling Ge'ta's foot from under him, knocking him to the floor. Keembo leaps to jump on Ge'ta's chest and is met with two right-hand brass knuckles, one to the head and one to the rib cage.

A thunderous sound like the sound of a cannon being fired is heard as Keembo's body smashes into the ceiling and falls to the ground. Ge'ta stands to his feet and walks over to Keembo to deliver the final blow.

"Keembo" screams Azra turning to run to his aid.

"Azra, focus!" exclaims Obadiah. "I need you here. The others will have to help Keembo."

Turning back around Azra raises her shield just in time to block Serg's attack with the Morning Star.

"Now Sakia, arm the bomb and place it inside the back of the big guy's armor" shouts Titus. Sakia pulls out the detonating pin on the black round sulfur bomb. Tumbling and jumping, Sakia lands directly behind Ge'ta and stuffs the sulfur bomb under his armor in the middle of his back. Spinning around Ge'ta swings at Sakia, who leaps backward out of the way of his attack.

"Everyone take cover! Fire in the hole!" yells Sakia.

The explosion rockets Ge'ta face-first into the stone wall. His limp body crumbles to the floor, smoke rising from his back through the large hole in his armor. Distracted by the blast Serg leaves himself open for one second, Obadiah sees the opening and shoots four rapid arrows hitting Serg in the upper and lower torso. Serg falls to his knees, then flat on his chest. Serg and Ge'ta the King's strongest and most skilled warriors lay dead at the hands of the Chosen Ones.

"Where is the King?" barks out Obadiah.

"I saw him slither under the bed during the battle" quips Titus.

"Azra, Tiwa, Sakia, see to Keembo. We are running out of time. Titus, I believe we have some questions to ask of his Royal Highness" states Obadiah. Bending down and looking at the trembling King underneath his bed, Obadiah says, "King you can come out from under the bed and possibly live or you can die on your belly. Choose quickly."

"I'm coming out. I'm coming out" stammers the King as he crawls from under the bed. "You know my soldiers had to have heard the explosion in my chambers. They will be arriving any moment now."

"Azra, you guys get Keembo into the passageway, drag him if you have to. Move now" shouts Obadiah.

Pulling back his bow and pointing his fiery arrow in the King's face Obadiah says, "Now, I'm going to ask you one time King and if you don't answer me quickly, your soldiers will find your dead body alongside your two bodyguards. Where is the breastplate to the Armor of God?"

Sensing no hesitation in Obadiah's voice or face the King quickly answers, "It is in my chest at the foot of my bed."

Pulling a key from around his neck the King unlocks the chest revealing a shiny, beautiful, gold and silver breastplate with the symbols Alpha and Omega etched on the front of it.

Hearing the sound of footsteps approaching and voices getting louder Titus says, "How do we know this is the real breastplate and not a fake?"

"This is the real one," says Obadiah.

"How do you know?"

"My mother used these symbols sometimes when referring to the Creator. I'll grab the breastplate. You take care of the King."

Expanding his steel baton, Titus strikes the King two times in the back of the head rendering him unconscious.

"Hurry Titus, to the tunnel now, shut the door behind you."

Titus barely pulls the secret door shut when twenty of the King's soldiers burst into the room. Noticing the King and his two bodyguards laying on the floor one soldier inquires, "Is the King dead? And what is the fate of his two bodyguards?"

"The King is alive but unconscious. His two bodyguards are dead" replies several soldiers.

The soldier in charge orders the King to be placed in his bed and five soldiers to stand guard in his chambers. "The rest of you search the palace grounds. The intruders must still be inside."

~~~

Keembo regains consciousness in the escape tunnel. "Keembo's coming around. Good, we can leave now" says Obadiah.

"He has internal injuries and won't be ready to travel for about five minutes," says Azra as Keembo gulps down a healing potion.

"Five minutes? We don't have five minutes! We are in danger of being discovered by the search party and I'm pretty sure the King's army is well on their way back from their fool's errand of looking for us" groans Obadiah.

"All that may be true, but Keembo won't be fit to travel for a couple more minutes" restates Azra. "Besides you could use some healing ointment on that bruised face of yours, Obadiah."

"Calm down everyone, let's take these few minutes to strategize and figure a way out of this place. As a matter of fact, Tiwa, what's this place called and what other provinces or regions exist in Demon's Realm?" inquires Titus.

"Then it's true, you are from another world. Well, Titus, my world, Demon's Realm, is divided up into six provinces; this is the Sand Province. The other five
~~~

provinces are the Underground Caverns, the Woodlands, the Defiled Marshlands, the Sky Citadel, and the Arctic Plains.

"I have never been outside of the Sand Province nor have I seen anyone from the other regions. I only know of these places from bedtime stories my parents told me as a little child. Not far to the north of us is a long wooden footbridge that leads to one of the other provinces. No one who has left the Sand Province has ever returned" explains Tiwa.

Thinking out loud Titus says, "Six provinces, six pieces to the Armor of God. Well, that settles it folks we head north to the footbridge. Have five minutes passed yet?"

"Keembo are you feeling better?" Azra asks.

"As right as sand in the desert" blurts out Keembo.

"Good. I'm tired of waiting, let's go find this footbridge. Wait! Does anybody feel the ground shaking?" inquires Sakia.

"Damn! The King's army is back. We gotta go now!" exclaims Obadiah.

Climbing the steps out of the secret passageway the Chosen Ones and Tiwa head north.

~~~

The King's large army returns and stands rank and file in front of the Sand Fortress. The lieutenant leaps
~~~

off his mount and demands to speak with the King. The soldier in charge greets the lieutenant and informs him of the King's condition and that of his two bodyguards. "I have men searching every square inch inside the Sand Fortress; I should have a status update for you shortly."

"Have the lookout tower guards reported any strange movements outside the Fortress?" asks the lieutenant.

"No word from the lookout towers, sir" replies the soldier.

"I will take over from here," says the lieutenant. "Send a soldier to the North and South tower to find out if they've heard or seen anything."

The soldiers return from searching inside the Sand Fortress, "Sir, there's no sign of the intruders anywhere in the fortress."

Word comes back to the lieutenant that both guards in the lookout towers have been killed, the prisoners have escaped and the sorcerers have been defeated.

"Search everywhere for the intruders I want their heads on a platter" orders the lieutenant.

Moments later, the secret passageway is discovered along with a trail of footprints heading north. The lieutenant mounts his camel and orders his soldiers north towards the footbridge.

~~~
~~~

Switching his goggles to binocular vision, Titus shouts out, "I see the footbridge two hundred yards out. We're almost there. Keep running!" Looking back over his shoulder Titus sees the mounted soldiers racing after them, moving twice as fast as they are. "Ah guys, there are mounted soldiers five hundred yards behind us and closing fast. I estimate that when we're halfway across the bridge and vulnerable the soldiers will reach us."

"Well, brain boy do what you do best and figure a way out of this" barks Keembo. Surprisingly, Titus does not respond to Keembo's remarks. "What? No response? Did I hurt the little brain boy's feelings?" jabs Keembo.

Somberly Titus says, "In order for us to make it all the way across the bridge someone is going to have to stay behind." Titus' words hit the group like a hard punch to the stomach.

"No! Titus, you are wrong. You're not thinking hard enough. We aren't leaving anyone behind" screams Sakia.

The footbridge spans five hundred feet across the Dead Canyons and looms twelve hundred feet above razor-sharp rocks. Wooden planks bound together by ropes make up the slender bridge. The bridge's wobbly walkway is only big enough to allow a single file line of people to cross at a time.

Finally reaching the wooden footbridge Titus says, "Someone will need to stay behind and delay the soldiers while the others cross over the bridge safely."

"I'll stay," says Obadiah.

"No, you can't Obadiah. You're the only one who possesses a long-range attack. You'll be needed to protect the one who stays behind and blows up the bridge."

"Blow up the bridge? Then how's the person who stays behind supposed to get across the canyon?" inquires Sakia.

"There's a seventy-five percent chance that the person who stays behind won't survive. I'm just stating the facts" says Titus.

"I'll stay," says Tiwa. "What do you want me to do Titus?"

"No, you can't stay behind!" screams Sakia.

"Sakia, I owe you my life and now I intend to repay it. I can see the soldiers, you don't have much time" states Tiwa.

With a teary eye, Sakia squeezes Tiwa's hand and reluctantly lets out a faint, "Okay…"

Titus takes three sulfur bombs from the satchel Tiwa is carrying, leaving six left in the bag. "Tiwa use the bombs to delay the King's army, it should take four minutes for us to cross the bridge. When we cross over start running across the bridge and Obadiah will provide some cover with his arrows.

"Obadiah you cross first, Azra you trail last protecting our flank with your shield. Let's move out" shouts Titus as he sticks two sulfur bombs at the base of the footbridge.

The King's men draw closer to the bridge. Tiwa standing hidden behind a palm tree reaches into her satchel and places four bombs in her hands.

As the King's men close to within forty yards, Tiwa throws two sulfur bombs with her two right hands, one landing to the left side of the army and the other to the right side. Two large explosions detonate knocking a group of soldiers off their camels. The sand burns with an orange flame from the sulfur.

The remaining soldiers stop in their tracks to assess the damage inflicted on them and to find the source of the attack. Spotting Tiwa by the palm tree and the five strangers crossing the bridge, the lieutenant orders his men to go around the burning sand. He sends half the soldiers around the left side of the flames and the other half around the right.

Tiwa places two more sulfur bombs in her two right hands. Galloping around the sides of the burning sands, the lieutenant and his men advance closer to Tiwa and the bridge. Noticing the army has divided, Tiwa throws a sulfur bomb at the mounted soldiers approaching on her left, then quickly turns and throws one towards the advancing soldiers on her right.

Two more large explosions send soldiers flying off their mounts to the ground. Both sides of the army stop in their tracks and gaze at the lifeless bodies of their comrades. Tiwa turns and runs to the bridge grabbing the remaining two sulfur bombs out of her satchel.

Just yards away, the lieutenant orders his men to take the bridge. He notices the intruders are more than halfway across the bridge.

"We're almost across" pants Titus.

Tiwa starts to cautiously run across the footbridge, holding the last two sulfur bombs in her upper right and left hands, while holding onto the ropes of the footbridge with her two lower hands. Reaching the bridge first, the lieutenant dismounts and arms his bow with an arrow.

On the bridge, eighty feet away Tiwa turns to throw a sulfur bomb at the dismounting soldiers. Just as her right arm moves forward to throw the bomb an arrow strikes her in the upper left shoulder causing her to throw the sulfur bomb without activating it. The arrows impact also causes Tiwa to drop the last bomb she had in her upper left hand.

All the soldiers dive on the ground expecting an explosion that never comes. Slowly standing up and looking around the soldiers breathe a sigh of relief and let out a euphoric laugh.

The lieutenant walks over to the sulfur bomb and looks at the wounded person still moving quickly across the bridge. Stretching out his right arm and pointing at Tiwa, he commands his soldiers to arm their bows. "Shoot her" shouts the lieutenant.

Boom!

The sulfur bomb explodes, killing the lieutenant and twelve nearby soldiers.

"Great shot Obadiah" cheers Sakia.

Shaken and dismayed at the death of their lieutenant, the remaining soldiers are uncertain of what to do. Then out of anger, one soldier yells, "The lieutenant's last command was to kill the girl on the bridge. Look, there are two bombs at the base of the bridge. If we blow them up she will fall to her death."

Another soldier shouts, "I'll do the honors" as he pulls out both detonating pins. "Run!" shouts the soldier.

"Hurry up, run Tiwa they are going to blow up the bridge!" screams Azra.

Ninety feet away from the end Tiwa runs with all her might. Two loud explosions go off destroying one end of the footbridge.

Tiwa continues to run until the walkway drops from underneath her feet. Her body pauses in mid-air before starting to freefall towards the jagged rocks below.

"Noooo!" screams Sakia as she leaps off the cliff after Tiwa. Keembo holding on to the bridge post with his right-hand snatches Sakia's right leg with his left hand. Extending as far as she can Sakia snaps her whip towards Tiwa's outstretched arm. Tiwa's body jerks as the whip barely secures around her wrist, causing her body to suspend in mid-air.

Obadiah and Titus help pull up a straining Keembo, a crying Sakia and an injured Tiwa. Exhausted and safely out of the reach of the Serconian soldiers, they all lay tired and sprawled out on the cliff, all except Azra who is busy tending to Tiwa's injured shoulder.

CHAPTER 7

THE UNDERGROUND CAVERNS

Twenty minutes quickly pass as the Chosen Ones and Tiwa rest on the mountain ridge. It is four o'clock and the sun is racing down out of the sky. Hunger forces their exhausted bodies to get up while there is still sunlight to look for food and shelter.

"I'm going to hunt for food, anyone want to tag along?" asks Obadiah.

"I'll go with you," says Azra. "I only have two healing potions left. I need to gather some herbs to make more."

"Cool, then Keembo and I will start looking for firewood" states Sakia.

"Oh, we will?" says Keembo with a curious look on his face. "I don't respond well to people who tell me what I'm going to do, Sakia. But because I don't want to be stuck with Titus, I'll go with you."

"Now you went and hurt my feelings Keembo, I think I'm going to cry. Trust me, the feeling is mutual, big guy. Tiwa and I will stay here and set up camp" retorts Titus.

~~~

The Underground Caverns is a region unlike any other in Demon's Realm. At first glance, no one would perceive that there is an underground city. The underground city called DogTown is a labyrinth, an intricate combination of passages in which it is difficult to find one's way through.

DogTown lays hidden beneath the tall prairie grass above it. Golden-brown grass stalks, which grow as high as five feet, engulfs the whole region of the Underground Caverns. Dirt mounds litter the entire grass plain with a few hills scattered about.

DogTown can only be entered through four open dirt mounds which change every day. The inhabitants of DogTown, the Gopher People, keep four entrances open at one given time, providing air ventilation for the city and escape routes in case of emergencies.

The Gopher People are about four feet tall, have brown fur and a stocky build. They have large powerful legs with three razor-sharp claws on each of their paws that easily dig through dirt and rock. Their short tail is used to feel around tunnels when walking backward.
~~~

The Gopher People walk upright most of the time, but when they need to move quickly they drop down on all fours and run very fast. They operate as one big closely-knit family.

~~~

Obadiah and Azra head off to find food and herbs, Sakia and Keembo go looking for firewood, while Titus and Tiwa establish a base camp for the night. Before stepping down off the cliff, Obadiah notices the change in terrain and climate.

"What are you waiting for Obadiah? It'll be dark soon" says Azra.

"Do you notice there isn't one grain of sand here? There's nothing but tall grass as far as the eye can see? Well, I guess we can explore tomorrow. Look over there Azra I think I've spotted dinner" says Obadiah.

Turning her head to look, Azra notices a flock of large birds descending out of the sky and disappearing into the tall brown grass. "Oh, good we're going to have chicken for dinner" cheers Azra.

"Something like that" laughs Obadiah. As the two walks west towards the birds, Azra hesitantly asks Obadiah a question.

"Obadiah do you think I belong here? I mean you're brave and courageous; you provide food for everyone; you're smart and it's obvious you and Titus are the
~~~

leaders of the group. But I don't do anything. I'm small and scary. I can't fight. I just feel like you guys would be better off with someone else here rather than me."

Shocked and taken aback by the words coming from Azra, Obadiah stops in his tracks and responds. "Azra you obviously don't know how important you are to this group. Yes, you're small and get startled rather easily. But no one here has a bigger heart than you and when someone is in danger you respond without fear for your own safety.

"Don't you remember saving my life, Titus' life and Keembo's twice? If you weren't here the three of us would be dead right now. You were chosen to be part of this team. Just do what you do best and you'll supply your part. So to answer your question, yes I think you belong here."

Azra's doubts melt away and she lifts her head ever so slightly saying, "Thanks for the kind words. I'm feeling a lot better now."

"Aw, anytime Azra. Now let's go catch some chickens." They laugh together and continue to walk toward the birds.

~~~

Keembo and Sakia leave the others in search of firewood. They walk several minutes without speaking before Sakia breaks the silence. "Keembo, don't you
~~~

think you were kind of harsh on Titus back there? I know the guy can be sarcastic and get under your skin, but he really does have the best interest of everyone in the group, including you. You two argue back and forth like you're good friends."

"I don't need any friends. I'm more comfortable by myself. Sometimes when Titus says things, I get so mad I just want to punch him in the face. But I don't, because I respect him.

"He is a skinny guy with no muscles, all mouth. But he's come up with several strategic plans that have led us to victory over our enemies. Besides I'm not used to being part of a team or making friends."

"Keembo, all of us here are different and none of us are your enemy. You're just going to have to get used to being around a bunch of crazy people and I'm probably at the top of that crazy list" laughs Sakia.

"Yea, the guys told us how you jumped out of the bushes and got caught trying to save Tiwa. That was stupid."

"Stupid? Keembo you don't want to get started with me, I talk way more than Titus." They banter back and forth as they collect dried-out bushes for firewood.

~~~
~~~

Tiwa and Titus find a clear open area to make camp. Tiwa asks Titus, "Is everything okay between you and Keembo?"

"Yeah, we're fine. I like Keembo. He's as strange as I am but in a different way. The one who I have a problem with is Sakia. She always reacts without thinking, she's too impulsive. I don't know if I can trust her not to deviate from a plan in order to do her own thing, putting us all at risk."

"Titus you speak of Sakia's impulsiveness as being totally bad. Was Sakia being too impulsive when she came out of nowhere and saved my life from the hands of that guard? Was she too impulsive when she jumped off the cliff to save my life a second time? If it were left up to logic, I would be dead *twice* right now. There has to be a balance between logic and emotion. Titus, you may not know if you can trust her, but I trust Sakia with my life."

"Hmm, you put forth a logical argument in defense of Sakia. I'll have to think about that for a while" says Titus.

~~~

Keembo and Sakia returned to camp with their arms full of dried-out brushwood. After greeting Tiwa and Titus they immediately start building the campfire.
~~~

Moments later Azra and Obadiah enter the camp with six pheasants.

"Hi everybody, we're back! Obadiah caught a chicken for everyone" says Azra gleefully.

"We can explore the area and search for water tomorrow. By the way, who wants to play chef tonight?" asks Obadiah.

"I'll prepare dinner tonight" volunteers Tiwa.

"I'll help you Tiwa. I still have some rice left that I brought from home. We can cook that as well" says Azra.

"Great, let's get started."

Tiwa and Azra leave the group to start preparing dinner. Obadiah, Titus, Sakia, and Keembo sit and talk around the campfire.

Looking eagerly at everyone, Titus blurts out, "Describe to me in detail everything you saw out there."

"Well one thing I noticed right away is, there are no trees in this place," says Sakia.

"Yea, the land is covered with dry bushes and grass four to five feet high. The land is pretty flat as far as the eye can see" responds Keembo.

"There are large dirt mounds scattered throughout the tall grass. I also noticed a lot of strange animal footprints around the dirt mounds. I'll look into it more tomorrow. Oh yeah and because the grass is so dry out here I'll have to use my regular bow, so my fiery arrows don't start a fire. I need to make some arrows" says Obadiah.

Thinking out loud Titus says, "Hmm, using deductive reasoning from your descriptions of this place, I know we're not in the Arctic Plains or the Woodlands. I see nothing in the red sky except clouds, so we cannot be in the Sky Citadel. Tall dry grass all over the place with dirt mounds scattered about doesn't sound like a Defiled Marshland. That only leaves the Underground Caverns. So, then what we are looking for must be underground somewhere."

"I knew there was a reason I hadn't beaten you up yet Titus" smiles Keembo.

"You wish you could," says Titus blowing on his fingernails and rubbing them on his chest.

"An underground adventure now that sounds exciting. Obadiah, I want to go exploring with you tomorrow. Don't leave me, okay" insists Sakia.

"Okay, but you better wake up early, I'm not going to wait all day for you to get ready" snaps Obadiah.

"Well a girl must look her best at all times, especially if she runs into strangers," says Sakia with a grin on her face.

"I'm done here. Is the food ready yet? Tiwa! Azra" shouts Obadiah.

Stuffed from a delicious meal, everyone relaxes under the brightness of the two full moons, enjoying a moment of peace.

Azra breaks the tranquil silence saying, "Guys let's build an altar and speak with the Spirit. She...He...It...you know what I mean, may give us some clues to finding the next piece of armor."

Everyone excitedly jumps up collecting stones to build an altar, all except Obadiah. With the altar built Azra sets the red jewel on top of it.

The Spirit appears and says, "Greetings Chosen Ones, you have done a great job in defeating the Evil One's forces and retrieving the Breastplate of Righteousness. Continue to grow together as a team, for in unity you possess great strength.

"Beware of division, for a house divided against itself cannot stand. The enemy will try to divide and separate you any way he can to diminish your strength. Do not allow this to happen.

"Stay in unity with each other no matter the cost and you will be victorious. Be strong and courageous, for many more battles await you."

"Spirit" interrupts Obadiah. "We almost died in the Sand Province and you did nothing to try and help us. You act like you care, but in the end, you don't care if we live or die."

The others look at Obadiah in shock, seeing this anger and rage come out of him.

"Obadiah I know you blame us for the death of your parents, but we did not kill them" replies the Spirit.

"But you could have stopped it, you could have saved them, but you didn't! My mother and father believed in you, prayed to you and you let them die" shouts Obadiah.

"Obadiah your parents chose good over evil and believed in and worshipped the Creator. They knew that mankind had fallen and the Demon King had rulership over the Earth. They knew the Evil One hated them and that their days on the Earth were numbered because they would not bow down to him. But they chose, instead, to worship and obey the Righteous One.

"As a result, the Creator heard and answered their prayers. Their constant prayer, Obadiah, was that you would grow up healthy and strong, live a life free of the Demon King's rule and that you would believe in and worship the Creator. Because of their prayers, we were able to intervene on your behalf and keep you safe. Now you must choose to allow your heart to be healed of the bitterness and anger you possess towards the Righteous One or be consumed by hate."

As his mind replays the words spoken by the Spirit of Truth, tears well up in Obadiah's eyes. Astonishment and guilt are etched on his face as he relives the misplaced anger and bitterness he held in his heart.

"I'm sorry for hating and blaming the Creator all these years. I didn't know my parent's prayers were for my safety and not their own. I have thought and said some terrible things about the Righteous One. My heart has grown numb towards him. I don't want to be like this, but I don't know if my heart can change" exclaims Obadiah.

The Spirit stretches forth her hand towards Obadiah's heart. Gently touching his chest, hardened scales start to break and fall off of his heart, his stony hard heart of bitterness and resentment is changed back to a heart of flesh again.

"You have chosen wisely my son."

Turning to address the rest of the group the Spirit says, "You may use the Armor of God to aid you as you see fit. However, its full power will not be released until all six pieces are together and you are baptized by blood. My Chosen Ones, remember what I have spoken to you and be strong and very courageous."

The Spirit departs leaving the Chosen Ones and Tiwa awestruck, amazed and reflective over the words she spoke.

~~~
~~~

Obadiah slips away to be alone as the others chatter about the Spirit's visitation. Out of the corner of her eye, Azra spots Obadiah and quietly leaves the group to catch up with him.

Slowly jogging, Azra catches Obadiah. "Want some company?"

"Not really" responds Obadiah without looking back at her.

"Well that's not a no, so I'm going to keep you company."

Obadiah's silence signifies it's okay to tag along. They walk for a few quiet moments before Obadiah stops to speak. "Azra you asked me a question earlier today, 'Do you think I belong here?' Well, up until now I didn't think I belonged here. I couldn't believe I was picked to be the Chosen One from my clan. Azra, I hated the Creator for letting my parents die. For seven years I stopped believing in him. I didn't want anything to do with him or his ways."

Starting to cry, Obadiah says, "I was wrong. My parents never prayed for the Righteous One to save their lives, they asked to save mine. How could the Creator care for me, let alone choose me, when I hated him so much?" Drying his eyes, Obadiah continues, "I don't understand how he could love me when I hated him so much. How?"

Azra has no answer to Obadiah's question. After a few quiet minutes, Obadiah turns around and heads back to camp. Azra quietly follows behind him.

~~~

"Wow, what a magnificent creature that was. What was it?" inquires Tiwa.

"It was the Spirit of Truth sent on behalf of the Righteous One," says Sakia.

"Oh! So that was the sworn enemy of the Demon King. And you five have aligned with It to overthrow him. That's an impossible task" states Tiwa emphatically.

"No, we will defeat the Wicked One and free our people and our world, from his dominance" declares Keembo.

"Impossible you say. Was it impossible for us to free you from the Sand Province and defeat the King's army? But we did just that" responds Sakia.

"Good point. Then maybe it is possible for the Demon King to be defeated" says Tiwa with a smile on her face.

Azra and Obadiah rejoin the group. They all continue to talk awhile before calling it a night and falling asleep.

~~~

The red sun rises to meet Obadiah who gingerly wakes up the others. Obadiah's greeting of "Good morning!" is met with groans, grunts, and silence as they painstakingly stand up, yawn and stretch.

"I'm going to scout ahead. All those who are coming with me in search of the Underground Caverns need to be ready when I return in fifteen minutes" states Obadiah.

"It's going to take us, girls, a lot longer than fifteen minutes to get ready Obadiah," says Sakia.

"Then I guess you girls won't be coming" replies Obadiah with a serious look on his face.

"*Somebody* woke up on the wrong side of the bed this morning," says Sakia as Obadiah walks away.

"I won't be going out with you guys today. I need to collect more ingredients for my healing potions" says Azra.

"I'll help you search for herbs Azra. I'm not in an adventurous mood today" says Tiwa.

"I'm going to stay at camp and experiment with some of the knick-knacks I took from the Sorcerers' Tower," remarks Titus.

"Well it looks like it's going to be just the three of us," says Keembo.

"Then we best get to moving before the drill sergeant gets back" teases Sakia.

~~~
~~~

Obadiah returns twenty minutes later. "I came back five minutes later because I knew Sakia wouldn't be ready yet."

"Ha, ha, ha. You're a funny guy Obadiah, besides I was ready a long time ago" declares Sakia as she puts her last item in her backpack.

Standing behind her, Keembo shakes his head and says, "Only Sakia and I will be going out with you today."

"That's fine. We're searching for some kind of entrance that leads underground. We're not looking to engage the enemy in a fight, understand Sakia?" explains Obadiah in a stern tone.

"Why are you singling *me* out? Keembo likes to fight more than I do...well, almost."

"We're not at full strength. With all this dry grass around I can't use my fiery arrows and you can't use the electricity on your whip or we could set this whole place ablaze. We investigate, stay out of sight and defend ourselves if we have to. Got it?" Keembo and Sakia both nod their heads.

"Okay let's go." Obadiah, Keembo and Sakia say goodbye to the others, and leave camp.

~~~

"Tiwa are you ready to go?" asks Azra.

"Yes, I'm ready" responds Tiwa.
~~~

"I'll tell Titus we're leaving," says Azra. Walking over to Titus, Azra notices that Titus has his toolkit out and all the sorcerer's doodads in front of him.

"Titus, Tiwa and I are leaving to gather some herbs for my potions. What are you doing?"

"Hey Azra, I'm glad you stopped by before you left. I'm going to enhance the capabilities of your bracelet with the stuff I took from the sorcerer's lab. Can you give me your bracelet? Promise I'll give it back to you by the end of the day, in better condition than it's in now, of course."

"I, um, well, okay, sure" stammers Azra reluctantly. Slowly taking off her bracelet Azra says, "You're not going to break it, are you? I feel naked without it. Are you sure you don't want to do this tomorrow?"

"Azra it'll be okay. Remember how I enhanced Sakia's whip? You'll love the improvements I make, trust me."

"When I get back will it be ready?" asks Azra.

"Hopefully, now go find some herbs for your healing potions. I'll see you when you get back" says Titus as he excitedly turns back to his work.

Azra slowly walks over to Tiwa and they head out into the grassy prairie.

~~~
~~~

"These are the strange footprints I saw yesterday," says Obadiah bending down and pointing in the dirt. "And this dirt mound looks like it was recently filled."

"Looks like the tracks go right into the mound and just disappear," says Keembo.

"Do you think these dirt mounds are the entranceways to some subterranean city?" inquires Sakia.

"I believe so, everything seems to point that way. Let's dig down a few feet and see what we find. Sakia, you and I can dig. Keembo, you keep a lookout" directs Obadiah.

Shroc. Shroc.

"Did you guys hear that noise, it sounds like a high-pitched bark?" says Keembo.

"I didn't hear anything," says Sakia.

"Me neither," says Obadiah.

"Listen, there it is again, it sounds closer now" points out Keembo.

"I hear it now," says Sakia.

"Hey, something just hit me in the back of the head" blurts out Keembo.

Looking around on the ground Obadiah finds two darts near Keembo's feet. "Get down you two, they know we're here, whoever *they* are. You just got hit with two poisonous darts, but your skins so hard they just bounced off! We have to retreat; we can't afford to fight them here. Stay on your knees and follow me."

~~~

"Azra, over here. I see some strange grassy looking stuff by this dirt mound" says Tiwa.

"Excellent! Those are Wheat Grass and Tamberleek Grass. Good eyes, Tiwa" says Azra.

"There's a large hole leading into the ground on the other side of this mound" exclaims Tiwa.

"This must be the entrance to the Underground Caverns. Want to go and see what's down there Azra?"

"No, we should gather all the grassroots here and get back to camp. We have to tell the others what you found. We also need to make sure we know how to get back here" replies Azra.

~~~

Talking out loud to himself Titus says, "The enchanted sand expands exponentially in size. One handful of sand when activated can expand to the size of a large bus. Crushed quartz makes things harder. Solid quartz is hard and when used as a reflector gives a crystal clear transparent appearance. Now if I fuse it all together --"

Titus utilizes the tools in his toolkit to extract the sulfur from the last sulfur bomb, grind the three quartz crystals to powder, meltdown Azra's bracelet, and fuse elements together. He then recasts Azra's bracelet, using a solid quartz jewel as its new setting.

"Now if my calculations are correct Azra should have an awesome new weapon. Hmm, let me see what I can make with the rest of this leftover stuff" says Titus to himself.

~~~

Passing the last dirt mound on their way back to camp Keembo says, "The barking noise has stopped."

"Yeah, but they're probably still after us," says Sakia.

"No, I don't think so," says Obadiah getting off his knees to stand up.

"Get down you idiot" snaps Sakia.

"It's okay, you guys can stand up now. Nobody's following us. It appears they were defending their home from strangers, the strangers being us. Once we stopped digging and retreated they stopped attacking. We have to figure out a way to communicate, without getting shot by poisonous darts in the process. We mean them no harm" says Obadiah.

~~~

Entering the camp, Sakia, Obadiah, and Keembo see Titus putting his tools away. "Hi, Titus! Did you miss us?" shouts Sakia.

"Well, I did enjoy having the camp all to myself. I managed to get a lot of work done."

"Where are Azra and Tiwa?" asks Keembo, slightly concerned.

"They haven't made it back from gathering herbs yet" responds Titus.

"I'll go find them," says a concerned Keembo. Just as Keembo turns to leave, Azra and Tiwa run into camp breathing heavily.

"You two okay? Is anyone following you?" inquires Keembo.

In between gasps of air Tiwa says, "We're okay. No one is following us. But we did find a hole that leads underground, right underneath one of those dirt mounds."

"Did either of you see anyone, or hear anything?" asks Obadiah.

Azra and Tiwa both respond, "No."

"There is a group or clan of something out there. They shot Keembo with two poisonous darts; luckily they bounced off his hard skin and had no effect."

"Yeah, but the rest of us don't have rock hard skin and those poisonous darts can kill us," says Sakia, interrupting Obadiah.

"Look, they know we're here and didn't try to follow us. I think it'll be okay for us to stay here tonight" finishes Obadiah.

"That doesn't mean they won't try to kill us in our sleep" responds Sakia.

"I can't believe I'm saying this, but I agree with Sakia. We can't stay here tonight Obadiah. Tonight we must find the underground entrance. Whoever they are, they won't think of looking for us underground. Besides we're extremely low on water, there should be an underground reservoir down there" points out Titus.

"Okay that settles it, we head out at dusk. That should give us about three hours to rest up and pack our gear. I have a feeling this is going to be a long night" responds Obadiah.

Keembo and Obadiah stand watch at camp, Tiwa helps Sakia pack her stuff and Azra goes with Titus to get her bracelet back.

"You didn't break my bracelet did you, Titus? Does it still work?" inquires Azra.

"I'm deeply offended Azra, there is nothing I can't fix if given the right materials. And no, your bracelet is not broken. It does look different, better than before I think. Your new bracelet is three times larger than the old one and has a quartz jewel setting on it" brags Titus.

Reaching into his bag Titus says, "Here, look for yourself. What do you think? Put it on."

"It's beautiful, Titus! It looks better than before. I love the violet-purple color of the jewel on my bracelet and it fits comfortably. What improvements did you make to it? Did you test it yet?"

"The enhancements I made to your bracelet are tremendous if I do say so myself. I have transformed your relatively small brown indestructible shield into a transparent impenetrable force field that can extend up to fifty feet."

"You mean I can see through it" interrupts Azra.

"Yes, you should be able to."

"What do you mean should, didn't you test it already?"

"Your bracelet is attuned to your thought patterns, I wasn't able to test it. But according to my calculations, everything I said should happen. Go ahead, give it a try."

Azra concentrates like she normally does. "Titus you broke my bracelet, how could you! I don't see a shield or a force field" cries Azra.

"Wait a minute, keep focusing," says Titus as he pulls out his steel baton. Titus swings his baton as hard as he can at Azra's head.

Bang! The baton is stopped by an invisible shield.

"Ahhh! What are you doing?" screams out Azra.

"Ha, ha, I knew it would work!" shouts Titus. "Look, here. Do you see the distortion of space? That's the edge of your shield. You should practice making different shapes and sizes with it."

"Thank you! Thank you so much, Titus, you're the best" says Azra as she gives him a big hug.

"That is true, I am the best" smiles Titus arrogantly.

Azra runs over to Sakia and Tiwa to show off her new and improved bracelet.

Titus grabs his bag and walks over to Obadiah and Keembo. "Obadiah, Keembo, I was thinking since you two generally attack first, Obadiah should wear the Breastplate of Righteousness for protection."

"Yeah, Obadiah you should be the one to where the breastplate armor. My skin affords me some protection, but you have nothing" says Keembo.

"Okay, I'll wear it. Thanks, guys" says Obadiah.

Reaching into his bag Titus pulls out two quartz-tipped, sand arrows and hands them to Obadiah. "These sand arrows will explode on contact and crystallize anything it hits, transforming it into crystallized sand. I only had enough materials left to make two arrows" says Titus.

"Thank you, Titus, I'll put these to good use, don't worry." Obadiah turns to Sakia and Tiwa and asks, "Are you two finished packing yet?"

Sakia and Tiwa respond, "Yes."

"Good. Can you two take our place at lookout till we finish packing and, Azra, can you make some rice for dinner? It looks like that's all we have time for."

Everyone executes their respective tasks as the sun inches its way down the sky.

Chewing their last mouthful of rice, the Chosen Ones grab their bags and prepare to depart, waiting for the last shred of red sunlight to disappear.

Obadiah puts on the breastplate armor and finds it to be light and very durable. He places his ivory bow over his left shoulder and his regular bow over his right. As the sun finally sets, Titus switches his goggles to night mode.

"Everyone ready to go?" asks Obadiah as he looks at each person nodding their head. "Tiwa, Azra point the way to the dirt mound you found earlier."

Titus and Obadiah take the lead, Keembo takes the rear and Azra, Sakia and Tiwa follow in the middle. Retracing the steps Azra and Tiwa took earlier, the group comes to a dirt mound.

Recognizing the stone she placed by the dirt mound Tiwa says in a whispery voice, "This is the dirt mound with the entrance. That's the stone I used to mark it."

They look all around the mound and find no entrance.

"Are you sure this is the place?" asks Obadiah.

"I'm positive. Somebody must've filled it up with dirt" says Tiwa in astonishment. "We'll just have to check every mound until we find an entrance. If someone or something is living underground they must have air ventilation somewhere above ground" declares Titus.

An hour later, frustration and boredom start to set in.

"I can't take this anymore. This is our twelfth dirt mound and no sign of any entrance. I'm about to make camp right here" whines Sakia.

"Let's try one more then we can stop and figure something out," says Obadiah. As they approach the mound everyone feels the air surrounding them become a bit warmer.

"Jackpot! I see a big hole in the ground. Persistence pays off" says Titus.

"Are you trying to say something to me, Titus? Because I'm right over here if you are" says a perturbed Sakia.

"If the shoe fits, buy you a pair" quips Titus.

"Titus, I'll wrap this whip around your neck so fast-"

"Stop it you two, we're about to go down into, God knows where and you two are fighting each other. Come on" barks Azra.

"Alright. You're right Azra. I'm sorry little man" says Sakia to Titus.

"That's, little big man to you" retorts Titus.

"Quiet, you two! We are entering the Underground Caverns now" snaps Obadiah. Obadiah pulls his ivory bow off his shoulder and pulls back the string to summon a fiery arrow to light the way. Everyone tenses up slightly as they descend into the Underground Labyrinth.

The dirt opening turns into a very narrow, lengthy tunnel. Everyone has to bend down to walk through the tunnel, while Keembo has to crawl to make it through. A light at the end of the tunnel forces Obadiah to stop and extinguish his arrow. Signaling the others to be quiet and stay put, Obadiah creeps closer to see what lies ahead.

Inching his way to the light Obadiah spies out about fifty furry, brown, creatures moving around in a large, expansive oval-shaped room. Most of the creatures appear to be talking to each other or laying down. A handful of them have weapons in their hands, walking back and forth like patrol guards.

Turning to go back and tell the others, out of the corner of his eye Obadiah notices a patrol guard heading towards the tunnel. Scurrying back Obadiah informs the others of the approaching guard and makes plans to capture him quietly.

As the patrol guard reaches the tunnel he stops and takes three whiffs of the air. Smelling several strange odors the patrol guard turns and yells, "Intruders in tunnel four! Intruders in tunnel four!"

Shocked at what they hear and surprised they can understand the furry creatures' language, Obadiah shouts, "Quickly, we need to get out of this tunnel so we can be in a better position to fight."

Simultaneously, the gopher soldiers grab their weapons and prepare to meet the intruders head-on. The sound of a loud piercing whistle travels through the tunnels of the Underground Labyrinth, sending an intruder alert to all its occupants.

Upon exiting the tunnel Azra puts up a large invisible shield to protect her and her five teammates.

"Fire!" yells, Puma leader of the four gopher clans. Dozens of spears and poisonous darts are hurled and shot at the intruders. The projectiles seem to hit a wall and fall straight to the ground.

Tiwa emphatically shouts out, "We are not your enemy, we mean you no harm!"

Upon seeing Tiwa with her four arms up in the air Puma says, "Hold your fire. We have a Serconian in our midst. I would like to hear what she has to say." Stepping forward the chief says, "I am Puma, chief of the Gopher People. Who are you and why have you invaded my land?"

Clearing her throat Tiwa states, "My name is Tiwa. I am a Serconian of the Sand Province. I was freed from captivity by these five outworlders. We mean you and your people no harm nor do we wish to fight you."

"And yet you break into my city uninvited. Serconian, your people serve the Demon King. Did he send you here?" asks the chief.

Sakia interjects, "We're here to retrieve a piece of the Armor of God from this region and then we'll be on our way. The Demon King didn't send us here. We came here to destroy the Demon King."

Puma laughs hysterically out loud, "Anyone crazy enough to say those words out loud must be from another world. Strangers, you are welcome here. We too, wish the destruction of the Demon King. Soldiers lower your weapons. We have guests."

Shocked at what just transpired, introductions are made. Shaking everyone's hand the chief says, "As our guests, we offer you food, drink, and lodging for the night. I will give you a tour of our city, DogTown. We can talk as we go, for we have much to discuss. Please excuse me if I stare, you outworlders are some strange looking creatures" says Puma.

"Forgive us as well, for we've never seen talking gophers before. How is it that you speak our language?" inquires Titus.

"All the kingdoms under the Demon King's rule speak the same language. Your world must be under the Demon King's rule as well. You all appear to be from different regions of your world, yet you all speak the same language, as do the citizens of this world.

"The Demon King keeps us isolated and divided so we will not rise up together against him. But the Gopher People no longer serve the Wicked One, so we live underground away from his prying eyes" says Chief Puma, with an angry look on his face.

"Now, let me show you our city. The area we just left is our army command post and barracks for our on-duty soldiers. We mobilize to attack and defend our city from there. Follow me as we go down to the next level."

Moving downwards through another tunnel the Chosen Ones emerge into DogTown. DogTown consists of twenty-eight buildings, fourteen on each side of the street. A single long dirt road called Main Street divides the town.

DogTown has merchant stores where vendors trade and sell food and merchandise. It also has a blacksmith, nursery and doctor's office. On the opposite end of town is the living quarters of the Gopher People.

"Wow, chief, I never would've guessed all of this would be underground," says Azra in amazement.

"Chief, do you have a place where we can fill our canteens with water" inquires Keembo.

"Oh yes, you must be starving as well. Behind the buildings to your right is our water basin that catches fresh rainwater. Fill your containers and rejoin me at my house over here, where a meal will be waiting for you" says a smiling Puma, pointing to his home.

"Thank you, Chief Puma, we'll be over there shortly for dinner, I'm starving," says Sakia.

Filling their containers with water, Obadiah asks Titus, "Do you trust the chief?"

Pausing a moment to think Titus responds, "Well, if the chief wanted to hurt us he wouldn't have shown us his city, offer us food and water and let us keep our weapons. So, yes, I trust him."

"Okay, just needed a second opinion," says Obadiah with a reassured look on his face.

"Hurry up you guys, I'm hungry!" shouts Sakia. With their water supplies full, again, they walk over to Puma's house for dinner.

Puma's wife greets them at the door and welcomes them into their home. She escorts them to the dining area where a feast is laid out for them. All sorts of fruits, vegetables, and unknown meats are spread out on the table.

"Eat my friends; eat to your heart's content. Then I will show you the lower level of the city" says the chief.

Bellies full and smiles on their faces, Obadiah takes this moment to have a discussion with the chief. "Chief Puma, do you know where a piece to the Armor of God is located in your kingdom? We retrieved the Breastplate of Righteousness, which I'm wearing from the Sand Province. There's another piece somewhere in the region of the Underground Caverns. Once we recover it, we must get the remaining pieces from the other provinces here in Demon's Realm."

"I see. Then what you seek must be below our city in the Lava Pits. My father and grandfather told stories about a corridor that leads to a neighboring province hidden in the Lava Pits. They said it is protected by a two-headed dragon. Once, out of curiosity, I went down as close as I could to the Lava Pits and there I saw a treasure chest. It was sitting on a large rock in the middle of the lava. I took a few steps closer when something started to rise out of the lava. I turned and ran as fast as I could, without stopping to see what it was. Was it the two-headed dragon? I don't know. But something is guarding that chest and blocking the path to the neighboring region" explains Chief Puma.

"That sounds like the place we're looking for chief," says Titus.

"Very well then. You all can sleep here tonight and tomorrow I will take you down to the Lava Pits" offers Puma.

"Thank you" replies everyone as they follow Puma to their room for the night.

CHAPTER 8

THE LAVA PITS

Morning comes quickly and Puma enters the room waking his guests from their slumber. "Rise and shine folks, today we visit the Lava Pits."

"Puma do you have a spare weapon I could borrow? I left the Sand Province with only the clothes on my back. When I make it back this way I'll return it to you?" asks Tiwa.

"Let me see what I can find Tiwa. Come out to the eating area when you are ready. My wife has prepared breakfast for us" says Puma as he leaves the room.

Excited about the prospect of getting a second piece to the Armor of God everyone quickly packs their gear.

"Alright everyone let's go see Chief Puma. Azra you still haven't packed? Why are you moving so slowly? Just hurry up and meet us in the eating area" says Sakia a little irritated.

Everyone leaves Azra and heads to the eating room except Keembo who stays behind. "What's bothering you Azra? It normally doesn't take you this long to pack. Why are you stalling?"

"Keembo, you always read me so well," says Azra pausing a few moments before continuing. "I'm afraid to go down to the Lava Pits. I don't want to face that two-headed dragon. It probably breathes fire! Keembo, I'm scared."

"Azra we'll be with you all the time. I won't let anything happen to you. Hey, we made it this far. We'll make it through this as well" reassures Keembo.

Hesitantly Azra says, "Okay, let's go."

Meanwhile, in the eating room, Puma gives Tiwa four ebony colored metal boomerangs. These two sets of boomerangs glisten brightly through the brown leather holsters securing them.

"Tiwa, these boomerangs are my fathers and grandfathers. They were forged from the lava in the Lava Pits themselves. They are made of shuminite, the strongest, densest material known to my people. Use them on your quest and may they serve you well."

"Thank you Chief Puma; I'm honored to wield your father's and grandfather's weapons in battle" replies Tiwa.

Keembo and Azra enter the room and quickly eat some food.

"Good, we are all here now. Gather your belongings my friends and let's be on our way" says Puma.

"Yee-ha!" shouts Sakia as they head out.

They walk for about twenty minutes down a long twisty tunnel that leads to a large cave high above the Lava Pits. The chief points to the lava below and says, "I had the rest of the path destroyed so no one would accidentally walk all the way down. This is as far as I go, my friends. Good luck and be careful."

Sakia attaches one end of her whip to a nearby rock and tosses it over the ledge. She quickly descends, sliding down her whip, as the others follow suit. Everyone turns to see the lake of lava in front of them. Lava flows through the cave from one end to the other.

There is no way to walk around the massive lava flow. Surrounded by lava is a large rocky patch of land. On the other side of the lava in the left corner of the cave is a small landmass.

"It would seem the story Puma told us is true," says Sakia as she retrieves her whip.

"We have to assume that there's a two-headed dragon in the lava lake and that a piece of the Armor of God is in a chest on that rocky mound in the center of the lava," says Tiwa.

"So what's our plan of action?" inquires Obadiah.

"Yeah, how do we get across the lava?" asks Keembo.

Looking intently at the lava Titus begins to speak, "We'll need to break up into two groups. Obadiah and Tiwa you two will stay on this side of the lava and use your long-ranged weapons to draw the dragon's attention.

"Azra, Keembo, Sakia and I will cross the lava and find the chest on that slab of rock. Azra, you'll have to expand your shield as large as you can over the lava so the four of us can safely stand on it. Then Sakia, you'll need to latch onto one of the rocks in the middle of the lake of fire with your whip. Keembo, you'll pull us across the lava in Azra's invisible shield boat."

"Titus that sounds like a good plan in theory, but I'm still not sold on it. Azra are you sure your indestructible shield can withstand hot lava?" Sakia inquires.

"Positive," says Azra rather curtly.

"Well if anyone has a better idea I'm open to hear it" states Titus. Everyone looks at each other, but no one offers any suggestions.

"I guess we'll go with Titus' plan then," says Obadiah.

Walking close to the bubbling lava, Tiwa and Obadiah find an advantageous spot from which to attack. Azra stretches out her invisible shield over the lava, just as a large head slowly starts to rise out of the lava.

Orange hot lava drips off the dragon's long black snout and head as it continues to rise out of the lava.

The dragon's neck is ten feet long. Its yellow snake-like eyes scan the area looking for intruders. It sets its eyes on Azra's group and turns its head, coiling back to attack.

Obadiah quickly shoots off four fiery arrows that hit the dragon in the head, having no effect. Tiwa immediately throws two boomerangs at the dragon smacking him on his long snout.

Irritated but unharmed, the dragon turns his attention towards Tiwa and Obadiah.

Taking advantage of the distraction Titus, Keembo, Azra and Sakia climb aboard Azra's shield. Sakia flings her whip, which securely wraps around a boulder on the rock mound in the center of the lava lake. Keembo grabs hold of Sakia's whip and pulls them across the orange hot lava they clearly see beneath their feet.

The dragon lunges at Obadiah and Tiwa, snapping its jaws.

"Aim for its eyes!" screams Tiwa as she hurls two more boomerangs at the dragon.

Obadiah shoots two fiery arrows into both the dragon's eyes.

"I got him!" he yells.

The dragon blinks and lunges at Obadiah knocking him off his rocky perch.

"My fiery arrows have no effect," says Obadiah out loud.

Keembo pulls the others to the mound and they jump onto its rocky surface.

Looking around Sakia points to a carved out hole in the rock and shouts, "It's the chest!" Sakia runs over and touches the chest. As soon as she touches the chest a second head slowly rises out of the lava.

"Uh, guys, I think we have company," says Titus.

"Obadiah, something is glowing in the dragon's mouth," says Tiwa.

Obadiah looks up at the dragon and yells at Tiwa, "Get behind a rock now!"

Without hesitation, Tiwa dives behind a large rock, at the same moment, the dragon spews a stream of fire at them. The fire smashes against the rock spattering off to the sides.

Azra lets out a high-pitched scream. "I knew they were fire breathing dragons, I knew it!"

"Okay guys, it's time to move on to plan B" explains Titus.

"Plan B? You didn't tell us about a plan B" says a startled Keembo.

"Yeah, I know. I'm making it up as we go along. Everyone move back towards the chest. Azra throw up a protective shield over us" commands Titus.

Backing up towards the chest, Azra sees a glowing light in the second dragon's mouth. She puts up her invisible shield just in time to block a stream of fire pouring down on them out of the second dragon's mouth.

The two-headed, fire breathing dragon holds the intruders at bay.

"I can't hold this shield up forever. I'm starting to get tired" says Azra.

No one responds to Azra's sobering comment.

"We have to think of something. The others won't last much longer" cries out Tiwa.

Obadiah suddenly sits up straight and says, "I'll use the arrows Titus made me. Tiwa distract the dragon with your boomerangs and I'll shoot him with my sand arrow."

Tiwa jumps from behind the rock and throws all four boomerangs at the dragon, hitting it in the head and neck. Angered by the blows the dragon focuses his attention on Tiwa. Obadiah takes aim and fires a sand arrow, striking the dragon on the side of his face. An explosion occurs on impact and sand crystals quickly spread over the dragon's head and halfway down its neck.

"Now Tiwa! Hit him with your boomerangs" screams Obadiah. Tiwa hurls her four boomerangs again at the dragon's crystallized head, shattering it into pieces.

"Yes! Did you see that?" yells Sakia.

"Shoot this one over here. Hurry up, guys! I can't hold the shield up much longer" says an exhausted Azra.

Obadiah shoots his last sand arrow at the dragon's second head. The arrow explodes on impact and the dragon's head starts to crystallize.

"I got this one" shouts Keembo.

"You can lower your shield now Azra" instructs Keembo. Picking up a large boulder, Keembo launches it at the dragon's crystallized head shattering it to pieces.

"We did it! We did it!" yells Sakia.

"Indeed we did. We need to give Azra some time to regain her strength before we move on" says Titus. Everyone agrees and lets out a big breath of air, relieved that the battle is over, for now at least.

As Azra rests, Titus, Sakia, and Keembo turn their attention to a rusty old chest nestled in the rocks. Keembo rips off the rusty lock with his bare hands. Gingerly opening the chest they see a beautiful helmet made out of gold and silver. Carved on the front are the symbols Alpha and Omega.

"This is a piece to the Armor of God. Two down, four to go!" exclaims Titus.

After a few minutes pass, Azra is ready to wield her shield again. Traveling on top of Azra's shield, they pick up Tiwa and Obadiah and let the lava's current carry them to the small landmass in the left corner of the cave. As they approach, an opening in the cave wall becomes more visible. Reaching land, they sprawl out and reflect on their victory over the two-headed Lava Dragon.

Azra quietly gets up and walks over to the lava. Staring intently into the lava, images of the entire ordeal playback in her mind. She recalls all the fear and anxiety she felt during the fight and remembers how close to death they came.

Thoughts start flooding into her mind, some her own and others not her own. These thoughts question her, *What are you doing here? You almost died. You are too young and too small to fight in these battles. Aren't you the weakest of the whole group? They will probably do better without you. How will you live with yourself if one of them dies because you're so weak?* Listening to these thoughts Azra's confidence melts away and is replaced with fear, doubt and a feeling of being insignificant.

The others ready to move on call out to Azra, "Let's go Azra, it's time to move out!"

Azra still staring at the lava pit responds, "I'm not going."

"Stop joking around Azra and let's go," says Sakia.

"I told you, I'm not going. I'm not cut out for this. I never should have come here" says Azra in a teary melancholy tone.

"What are you talking about Azra; you've done great all this time, especially this last battle. We couldn't have won without you" explains Obadiah.

"You don't understand! I'm scared! I can't do this anymore!" sobs Azra.

"You guys leave her alone. If she doesn't want to go then she doesn't have to go. I'll stay here with her" says Keembo.

"Keembo, what are you thinking? You of all people should know we have to defeat the Wicked One before he destroys our clans and kills our families, your family" explains Titus.

"Yes, I know that, but down here Azra is the closest thing to family I have and I won't leave her alone" declares Keembo.

"Let's leave them then. We don't need them anyway!" shouts Sakia as she starts walking up the cave pathway with Tiwa right behind her.

"Keembo, talk to Azra, we'll scout ahead and come back for you two" states Obadiah as he and Titus follow Tiwa and Sakia.

"This team is falling apart, Obadiah. It's going to take all of us to accomplish our tasks and defeat the Demon King. We don't stand a chance if we separate or worse disband as a team. We could all wind up stuck out here" says Titus.

"The Spirit said to beware of division. That the enemy would try to divide and separate us any way he can to diminish our strength. She said don't allow it no matter the cost. I won't let this team be divided, you hear me, Titus, I won't let it" declares Obadiah.

Titus and Obadiah catch up with Tiwa and Sakia. Looking back at Obadiah and Titus, Sakia sarcastically says, "So it's just the four of us now?"

"No, the others will be joining us later. For now, we can scout ahead and see what province lies ahead of us" states Obadiah.

It is quiet as the group ascends the large oval arched tunnel. Finally, they reach the mouth of the cave, their eyes adjusting from the darkness of the tunnel to the light of day.

The landscape opens up to a small patch overlooking a beautiful waterfall. Water plunges from one level to the next, cascading down rocks till it reaches the bottom and flows into a river. The thundering roar of the water hitting the cliffs and rocks can be heard from far away. The area at the base of the last waterfall is open and surrounded by hills with green trees and vegetation.

"Don't tell me, let me figure this out," says Obadiah. "This definitely isn't the Arctic Plains, nor the Sky Citadel. It appears to be more of a woodland than a marshland, so we must be in the Woodlands Province."

"That was some great detective work there, I don't think any of us would have figured that out" sneers Sakia.

"Sakia, why are you being so mean and rude? You're acting like you're mad and upset with everyone. What's eating at you?" says Titus sincerely.

"Titus I'm tired of people whining and crying. I'm tired of people saying hold up let's plan and strategize. I'm tired of waiting. I want to move forward, I want to go; I don't want to wait or plan anymore. I just want to do it, fight and react, fight and react, that's all!" bellows Sakia.

"I understand what you're saying and how you're feeling Sakia. But that bold and reckless attitude can be dangerous to both you and your teammates" interjects Obadiah.

"Teammates? Two of our teammates just quit on us! For all, we know we could be trapped on this planet and have to forge out a new life for ourselves here" blurts out Sakia.

"Azra and Keembo haven't quit the team; they just need some time to regroup. Now that we've found the exit, I'm going back to get them. Anybody want to go back with me?" inquires Obadiah.

"No, I'll stay here," says Sakia.

"Me too," says Tiwa.

"I'll go back with you" answers Titus.

"Tiwa, Sakia don't wander too far from the cave, the rest of us will be back soon" instructs Obadiah. Obadiah's instructions receive no response as he and Titus walk back down the cave pathway.

After a long period of silence, Keembo speaks, "So what do you plan to do now Azra?"

Azra hesitates, then mutters, "I don't know. Maybe live here with Chief Puma and the Gopher People."

"What about your family back home? Are you just going to forget about them, let them die? I understand you're scared, but you can't let fear paralyze you and cause you to give up and quit. You can't let fear stop you from doing what you know in your heart must be done. The Demon King must die for our clans and families to survive" says Keembo.

"Keembo, I agree with everything you just said. But how do I defeat these thoughts and images that bind me? *Immobilize* me? They keep me from doing what I know I should do. Tell me, Keembo?" asks Azra, tears welling up in her eyes.

"I don't know Azra; fear has never really been a problem for me. My problem is I don't trust people; I don't let them in my life. Therefore, they can't hurt me."

"Then we both have problems neither of us knows how to fix" replies Azra.

Walking up unnoticed, Obadiah interjects, "I know someone who can help. The Spirit should have an answer to your question."

Azra, with a surprised look on her face, smiles at Obadiah and Titus who just arrive and says, "I was so caught up in my own thoughts, I forgot about the Spirit. Let's build an altar and call her. I'd love to hear what she has to say." They quickly gather rocks and build an altar, Azra places the red jewel on top of it.

The Spirit appears and says, "Greetings, Chosen Ones. Congratulations on retrieving the Helmet of Salvation, it will help the wearer remember who they are and what their purpose is during times of trial and uncertainty.

"I see the Wicked One has unleashed his spiritual attacks against you, as well as his physical ones. You have been victorious against his physical attacks, you defeated the Demon King's two-headed dragon. But you have not yet overcome the spiritual attacks of fear and division that are trying to sever your bond of unity.

"Azra, the Creator has not given you a spirit of fear, timidity, or cowardice, but he has given you a spirit of power, love and a calm and well-balanced mind. Paralyzing fear and doubt are lies that come from the Wicked One.

"Your life will reflect what you choose to believe Azra. Will you believe what the Creator has said about you, that you are the Chosen One from amongst your clan, that you will deliver your clan and that you will aid in defeating the Demon King? Or will you believe what the Wicked One says about you, that you are too small and weak to be the Chosen One, that you are insignificant and that the others would be better off without you? Choose now Azra, whose words you will believe and whose you will follow, those of the Righteous One or those of the Wicked One."

Azra pauses for a moment, her understanding being opened, she realizes for the first time that certain thoughts in her mind are from the Wicked One. "I choose to believe the words of the Creator."

"Excellent choice my dear," says the Spirit as she places her hand on Azra's head. "Azra you must practice tearing down and eradicating every thought and imagination that sets itself against the truth of what the Righteous One has said about you. If you do this, fear will no longer be able to control or paralyze you."

Looking at the others, the Spirit says, "Overcome fear, division, and selfishness for they stand in your way and seek to defeat you. Go now and find Sakia and Tiwa. Remember, believe what you know in your hearts to be true, no matter what contrary thing you hear, see, or think. Farewell, my children, be strong and very courageous."

The Spirit departs.

Azra retrieves the spirit jewel and puts it away in her backpack and says, "Guys, I'm sorry for quitting on you. I let fear and my insecurities get the best of me."

"Don't worry about it Azra, you chose to come back and that's all that matters. Besides, we all have our own issues to deal with, no one's perfect" says Obadiah.

Departing the Underground Caverns, they walk up the cave tunnel together to meet up with Tiwa and Sakia.

CHAPTER 9

THE WOODLANDS

The Woodlands is an ancient forest that has large green trees commingled with still-standing, dead trees. Its branches form a multi-layered canopy allowing patches of sunlight to shine through. Thick coarse plant life carpets the forest floor. The Tiger River is also part of the Woodlands. The waterfalls flow into the Tiger River which borders the Woodlands and flows for several miles.

The inhabitants of the Woodlands are the Viragosians, an all-female Amazonian-like clan. The Viragosians have light gray skin and long brown hair. They have long, pointy, elvish ears and wear skirts and robes made out of deerskin.

The Viragosians are skilled woodsmen and excellent hunters and trappers. They live a communal life; everything is used and shared by everyone in the clan.

Myra is the ruler of the Woodlands Province and Queen of the Viragosians.

From the cave opening Tiwa and Sakia look down into the Woodlands. They take in the magnificent sight of three waterfalls cascading down rocky cliffs, splashing into pools of water and finally reaching the mighty Tiger River below. Following a dirt path that leads from the cave and runs along the top of the waterfall, the two girls stop and look over the first waterfall.

"Wanna take a swim? It'll ease your mind while we wait for the others" suggests Tiwa.

"That's a great idea, a nice cold swim should take my mind off of things. Tiwa, I don't see a path leading down the waterfall. Do you see one?" asks Sakia looking around the top of the waterfall.

"No, I don't. I guess we'll just have to jump down" says Tiwa as she leaps feet first off the cliff, splashing into the pool of water below.

Surprised by Tiwa's fearlessness Sakia dives off the cliff head first, arms extended and explodes into the water. Rising out of the water, she looks at Tiwa and says, "I didn't know you were so reckless. You remind me of myself. Tiwa, you can hang out with me any time."

"Well you're not the only one who likes a little thrill and adventure in their lives" replies Tiwa.

"Hey, who's that down there?" inquires Sakia pointing at several figures moving around at the bottom of the third waterfall.

"I can't make them out from here, but they must be the inhabitants of the Woodlands. We should wait and tell the others" suggests Tiwa.

"Wait for the others? Now, where's the fun in that? We should follow them to their home, then come back and tell the others" says Sakia with a wild look of adventure in her eyes.

Seeing Sakia's eagerness to go, Tiwa offers several words of caution, "What if we get lost on the way back?"

"Don't worry, Obadiah and Titus will track us down. They'll find us if we get lost" replies Sakia, disregarding Tiwa's warning.

"You presume a lot Sakia. I wonder, would you do the same for them?"

Sakia ignores the question and dives to the bottom of the second waterfall. Tiwa stands at the edge of the waterfall, thinking about the others for a moment. She reluctantly decides to jump down after Sakia finally catching up with her at the base of the third waterfall.

~~~

Exiting the cave, Azra, Keembo, Obadiah and Titus marvel at The Woodland's beauty.
~~~

Hearing the crashing sound of the waterfalls Azra inquires, "Can we get closer to the waterfalls? I'd love to see them up close."

"Sure, why not. It looks like this trail will take us right to it" says Obadiah.

"Where are Tiwa and Sakia?" asks Keembo a little concerned.

"They should be somewhere close by waiting for us" states Titus, reaching the end of the dirt path, standing at the top of the waterfall.

"Sakia and Tiwa's footprints indicate they jumped down the waterfall. They're probably waiting for us at the bottom" explains Obadiah.

"You're not suggesting that we jump down these waterfalls are you? There could be jagged rocks down there. We could be jumping to our deaths" comments Keembo.

"Are you afraid Keembo?" asks Azra.

Keembo turns and looks at Azra, "I told you before, fear is not my problem, but I do have a problem with stupidity. Jumping down a waterfall, not knowing if deadly rocks lay below, is just plain stupid. Unless there's no other way."

"Keembo, there's no other way down. The only way down is to jump, I'll go first" says Obadiah.

Reaching the bottom of the waterfalls safely, they see no sign of Tiwa and Sakia.

"The sun is starting to go down. We should set up camp here. We have freshwater, plenty of fish and Sakia and Tiwa should be able to find us when they return. Let's get a fire going and catch some fish" suggests Obadiah. While pitching camp embers of concern burn in their minds, as they wonder about the safety of their teammates.

~~~

Sakia and Tiwa follow a safe distance behind five Viragosian warriors as they enter the ancient forest. Traveling deeper into the forest, Tiwa notices the sunlight waning.

"Sakia, don't you think we should turn back now and find the others? It'll be dark soon."

"Just a little bit longer, I want to find out where they live. This forest is much different from the Amazon where I grew up, but I could get used to living here-- hey. Where did they go?" asks Sakia looking around.

"They must've spotted us following them. Let's head back now. Be prepared for anything" Tiwa says, as she reaches back and grabs her four boomerangs.

"Darn it, which way is back. I don't recognize anything!" blurts out Sakia as she uncoils her whip.

"Get down!" shouts Tiwa, as she tackles Sakia to the ground saving her from two arrows whizzing by.
~~~

Tiwa quickly stands up and hurls two boomerangs at a couple warriors sitting on tree branches several feet above the ground. As they reload their crossbows, Tiwa's boomerangs sever the tree limbs beneath them, plunging them into the ground. Both crash hard to the ground and are rendered unconscious.

Sneaking up from behind with knives drawn, two Viragosian warriors attack Tiwa and Sakia. One leaps on Tiwa and stabs her in the lower right arm causing her to drop one of her boomerangs. Tiwa grabs the female warrior with her three good hands and throws her to the ground.

The other Viragosian warrior lunges at Sakia, slashing her across the stomach before she can jump clear of the attack. Sakia swings her whip at her attacker who catches it with her left hand. *Zzzt.* The warrior crumbles to the ground out cold.

Seeing her three comrades fall in battle, the warrior fighting with Tiwa turns and flees through the forest. Tiwa flings a boomerang, hitting the retreating warrior square in the back; the non-lethal blow knocks her off of her feet. Unconscious, she hits the ground.

Holding their wounds, Tiwa and Sakia look around. They are shocked to find that their four assailants are all women.

Simultaneously they both say, "I thought there were five of them."

While looking at each other, they realize that one of the five Viragosians has gone missing.

Hearing several loud clicking sounds, Sakia and Tiwa look up to see twenty-five Viragosian crossbows aimed at them. A female voice utters, "There *were* five of us. Now drop your weapons."

As the Viragosians retrieve their wounded, they take Sakia's whip and Tiwa's three boomerangs back to their camp. With their prisoners in tow, the Viragosians arrive at their massive wooden lodge just before sundown. Sakia and Tiwa are taken into a large room where Myra, Queen of the Viragosians, sits on her throne.

Queen Myra wears a jewel-encrusted, circular crown that covers her forehead. Her stoic face and piercing stare accentuate the ghastly scar on the right side of her face, which stretches from her crown all the way down to her neck.

"My Queen, these are the two intruders I told you about," says the fifth warrior in the woods.

"Bring them before me" commands the Queen.

Pushed and nudged forward, Tiwa and Sakia are forced to walk between two long rows of female warriors before being made to kneel before Queen Myra.

"I will ask you a few questions and you will answer me truthfully or I will have your heads removed from your bodies. Do you understand?" demands the Queen.

Sakia and Tiwa both respond, "Yes."

"Who are you and how did you come into my land?" inquires the Queen.

Tiwa answers first, "My name is Tiwa and I'm a Serconian."

"My name's Sakia and I'm of the Amazonian clan. The two of us and one other female were captured and set to be sold as slaves to the Gopher People. As our three male captors negotiated our sell price with the Gopher clan, the two of us escaped and retrieved our weapons" answers Sakia.

"Why did you leave the other female behind?" asks Myra. "She was too small and weak to make an escape" replies Sakia.

"Why did you attack my warriors?" asks the Queen in a stern voice.

"We didn't attack them. We spotted them when we came out of the cave, not knowing if they were friend or foe we simply trailed behind them. Then we lost track of them and they attacked us. We had to defend ourselves" explains Sakia.

"I will have your story checked out. If you have lied to me, I will have you both beheaded" says Myra as she summons over one of her warriors.

~~~
~~~

Night falls on the Woodlands and looming dark storm clouds inch their way ever closer. Eating fish and leftover bread packed away in their backpacks, Keembo, Azra, Titus, and Obadiah sit around the campfire.

"I guess they won't be joining us tonight," says Azra in a somber voice.

"I told them to wait for us" snaps Obadiah.

"We have to assume they've been captured. We must find out who and what we're up against and figure out a way to rescue them" states Keembo.

"Is this déjà vu or what?" blurts out Titus. "I'm sick and tired of Sakia's recklessness and impatience putting everybody's lives in danger. Maybe we should call it quits and everybody just goes their separate ways."

"You can't be serious, are you Titus? We've come too far to stop now!" says a passionate Keembo.

"No, I'm not serious Keembo! I'm just pissed off at the moment. What about you Obadiah, no comment?" says Titus looking intently at Obadiah.

"Yes, I have a comment. Everyone be still, we're being watched."

Leering through the trees a Viragosian spy scouts out the Chosen Ones' camp. She observes three males and one small female who appears to be guarded by the largest male. She lingers a while longer to see if reinforcements arrive. Content with her findings the spy leaves to report back to her Queen.

"The coast is clear" breathes Obadiah with a sigh of relief.

"How many of them were out there?" inquires Titus.

"I'd say just one. A scout sizing us up and reporting their findings."

"Then we should leave here and find another place to hold up for the night" suggests Keembo.

"We should be okay for the night. Our new adversaries should be fortifying their defenses for an anticipated attack. We'll head out first thing in the morning. Get some sleep everyone" states Obadiah.

The campfire is extinguished as the four call it a night, uncertain of what the morning will bring.

The scout finally returns to report her findings to Myra who is sitting on her throne. "My Queen, I found the intruders and it is as the female stranger said. There are three males and one tiny female who appears to be their captive. They are camped out in the open by the river as if they are waiting for others to arrive. I tarried as long as I could without being spotted and saw no one join them."

"Were you discovered?" inquires the Queen.

"They seem to have sensed my presence for they all looked my way. However, I am positive that I was not followed, my Queen" states the spy emphatically.

"Very well," says Myra turning in her throne to speak to her warriors in the hall. "I want our defenses reinforced and strengthened. I also want guards posted all night for a possible attack. If any army dares to attack our land, we Viragosians will send them speedily to the afterlife. Now go my warriors prepare for battle."

The hall quickly empties, except for Tiwa, Sakia and three armed guards. The Queen orders one of the guards to bring in the four warriors who were injured by Tiwa and Sakia.

Sitting on the floor, Sakia and Tiwa continue to put pressure on their bleeding and untreated wounds. Several minutes later the guard returns with the four warriors, who kneel before their Queen.

"Rise, my warriors. I have a few questions to ask of you. Did these two strangers come from the cave and follow you into the woods?" inquires the Queen.

One of the four female warriors respond, "Yes my Queen. We saw these two females exit the cave and follow us into the woods. We sent Neeka ahead to inform you of the strangers and the four of us traveled at a slower pace, with them following at a distance behind us."

"Did the two of them attack you?" asks the Queen.

Hesitating for a moment a different warrior responds, "No, my Queen. They did not attack us. We decided to capture them and bring them to you."

"I see. You four attacked these two and were defeated. Yet, they let you live when you did not have the same intentions towards them" states the Queen.

Several warriors quickly respond, "Your highness we were merely--"

"Silence!" commands the Queen. "You four go to your posts and send a medic in here immediately."

The four warriors leave and the Queen commands Sakia and Tiwa to be brought before her.

Peering at Sakia's and Tiwa's injuries Myra says, "I am impressed that the two of you survived an attack from four of my warriors. Not only did you survive, you utterly defeated them. You are no longer our prisoners. I invite you to live here and become one of us. Your fighting spirit will fit in well here. Give me your answer in the morning, after your injuries have been treated" states the Queen.

The medic arrives and escorts Sakia and Tiwa to the infirmary to treat their wounds.

~~~

Morning arrives to find Keembo, Obadiah, Titus, and Azra packed and heading into the ancient forest. "We need to track down Sakia and Tiwa before the approaching rain washes away any signs of them" instructs Obadiah.

"How long before it starts raining?" asks Azra.
~~~

"It should start raining within the hour. That's my best guess" says Titus.

"Have your weapons ready everyone, we don't know what to expect. So be ready for anything" utters Keembo in a tense voice, pulling out his two daggers.

Titus pulls out and extends his steel baton. Obadiah pulls his ivory bow off his shoulder as he leads the group through dead trees and lush green vegetation. He follows the trail of tracks made yesterday and suddenly stops. Everyone stops and clinches their weapons tightly.

"What is it, Obadiah? What do you see?" inquires Keembo.

Walking slowly, bending and touching the ground Obadiah says, "There was a fight here. I see drops of blood from more than one person."

"Do you think Sakia and Tiwa have been injured?" mutters Azra.

"I don't know, there's no way to tell," says Obadiah.

"The chances of that being their blood has just gone up," says Titus, as he holds up Tiwa's lost boomerang.

"Oh no, they could be captured, injured, or worse. They could be dead!" exclaims Azra.

"Calm down Azra, control your thoughts. Remember what the Spirit said, *'Cast down, ignore and rid yourself of every thought that would cause you to be paralyzed with fear,'*" recalls Keembo.

Obadiah interjects, "They aren't dead. There isn't enough blood on the ground for someone to die from. Plus, I see over twenty-five pairs of footprints encircling this area. Which indicates someone was surrounded and probably captured."

"They're not dead. They're not dead" Azra repeats over and over several times, to drown out the lying thoughts entering her head.

Just as Obadiah says, "We'll follow these tracks wherever they lead us" a drop of rain hits everyone on top of their heads.

"It's here," says Titus, looking up at the darkened sky. "The storm has arrived. Obadiah, we need to find some shelter before the skies open up on us" exclaims Titus.

Rain starts to pour down as the thick black clouds roll overhead.

Still looking for shelter Titus says, "Hold up everyone I think I see something." Using his binocular vision Titus spots the Viragosian's stronghold. "I see some kind of base a quarter of a mile ahead of us. We're too far away to be spotted. Obadiah, do you think Tiwa and Sakia could be in there?"

"The tracks head in that direction. Scan the surrounding area. Do you see anything else nearby?" asks Obadiah.

Scanning the area Titus replies, "There are no other nearby structures, but to the left of us is a dense collection of trees that should provide shelter for us from the storm."

"Since we know where Sakia and Tiwa are being held captive, let's head for the shelter and get out of this rain" suggests Keembo.

"Yes, let's get out this rain! Somebody lead the way before my hair frizzes up" retorts Azra.

The guys stop and stare at Azra.

"What? I'm still a girl you know. Now stop gawking and let's get out of this rain" says an irritated Azra.

The guys look at each other and snicker at Azra as they head towards the Forest of Doom.

CHAPTER 10

THE FOREST OF DOOM

Sakia and Tiwa wake up in the infirmary, a small room with three tables and two beds, all bandaged and stitched up.

"Good morning," says Sakia, rubbing her right hand on her bandaged stomach and looking at Tiwa's bandaged lower right arm.

"Good morning, Sakia" responds Tiwa. Sitting up and looking around the room she continues, "That was one mighty big lie you told the Queen."

"Yea, but if I hadn't we would be dead right now. We also need to accept the Queen's offer to stay and live with her people. This should buy us some time to find the location of the Armor of God. Tiwa, I need you to follow my lead on this, okay."

"Okay. You have gotten us this far, but what about the others? You know they're probably searching for us as we speak" states Tiwa.

"I know they are Tiwa. We'll have to cross that bridge once we get there" responds Sakia.

"I was afraid you were going to say something like that. I can't help feeling like we're abandoning them" Tiwa says feeling conflicted.

"Tiwa, we have to make the best of a bad situation. If we make one wrong move, they'll kill us. So, follow my lead no matter what! Now let's find Queen Myra."

Opening the infirmary door, the two walks into a long hallway passing several closed doors. The enormous wooden lodge is home to the Viragosians. All of the women sleep and eat here. There are several kitchens and lots of shared bedrooms. The Queen's throne room and living quarters are in the center of the lodge. Several other meeting halls surround the Queen's quarters. The massive lodge has an octagonal shape with towering guard posts at each endpoint.

One of the Queen's guards greet Sakia and Tiwa and escort them in to see the Queen. Queen Myra sits on her throne between two spear-wielding guards. Warriors file in and out of the hall keeping the Queen updated on the morning events. Sakia, Tiwa, and the guard approach the throne and kneel before the Queen.

Myra greets them and asks, "How are your wounds?"

Rising they respond, "Much better, thank you."

"Good. I am glad you are feeling better. Have you made a decision regarding my offer last night?" inquires the Queen.

Sakia responds, "Yes, we have Your Highness. We'd love to live here and become part of your Viragosian army."

A smile forms on the Queen's face as she says in a loud voice, "We have gained two strong warriors today. Tonight, I will announce to all my warriors that they have two new sisters. A guard will show you to your new living quarters. There you will find your weapons and a change of clothing waiting for you. After you have settled in, come back and see me" commands Queen Myra.

~~~

The Forest of Doom is a long dense patch of trees inside of the ancient forest. The trees are tightly packed together, leaving the ground beneath them completely dry. Their branches and limbs intertwine at the top like braided hair and form a closed canopy with no gaps or openings. The lowest hanging branches are nine feet above the ground. No sunlight or rain ever touches its dry brown floor.

"We made it out of the rain! Finally!" blurts out a relieved Azra.
~~~

"Wow, this forest is totally different from the rest of the Woodlands. It has an ominous feel to it. I don't hear any sounds of life in here, no birds, nothing but dead silence" says Obadiah.

"It's dark in there, maybe we should stay close to the edges until the storm passes" suggests Keembo.

"I'm with you Keembo, I'm not going any deeper into that dark forest! I have no plans on fighting the boogeyman today, tomorrow, or ever" exclaims Titus.

"Then let's rest here, we'll probably be here for a while," says Obadiah.

The four sits under the dry trees on the fringes of the Forest of Doom, quietly thinking and looking at the wind-driven rain.

~~~

Sakia and Tiwa change into their new deer-skinned garments and collect their weapons. Walking around the entire compound, their exploration ends in the throne room. The Queen's harsh gaze softens as she sees two Viragosian warriors kneeling before her.

"Lovely! Absolutely lovely! My two new warriors, you look like one of us now. Sakia! Tiwa! Arise. I want you to meet Captain Penar, you will be serving under her. Reports say that there are no signs of an invading force and that the three males and small female have moved
~~~

from the waterfalls. Did you overhear any of their plans while you were held captive?" inquires the Queen.

Pausing for a moment Sakia speaks up, "I overheard them talking about finding a piece to the Armor of God somewhere in the Woodlands and how they would defeat the Demon King with it. That's all I can remember."

"Are they so arrogant as to think they alone can march into the Forest of Doom and seize the treasure from the Giant Ogre's hand? We send all our unwanted males into the Forest of Doom and they never come back. Even I, Queen of the Viragosians, dare not provoke the sleeping giant. And yet, I am intrigued.

"Penar, take Sakia, Tiwa, and twenty-five, other warriors, to search the outer rim of Doom Forest for any sign of the male intruders. We will keep one male and sacrifice the other two" schemes, Myra.

"At once my Queen," says Penar. The rain finally breaks allowing Captain Penar's troops to advance towards the Forest of Doom.

<p style="text-align:center">~~~</p>

"Oh! Look, the rain is letting up now" says a jubilant Azra.

Rising up off the cold dry ground, Titus peers out of the Forest of Doom into the Woodlands and says, "You're right Azra. It looks like there is a break in the rain. Wait a second. What's that?" Adjusting his binocular vision Titus says, "There's a regiment of at least twenty-five warriors headed straight towards us."

Keembo and Obadiah move forward to take a better look. "Is that Sakia and Tiwa marching with them? They have on the same garments as the rest of them. What's going on?" inquires Titus.

"I don't know, but there's only one way to find out and that's to ask them. You guys wait here and back me up if necessary" says Keembo boldly.

"Be careful Keembo" utters Azra. Keembo walks several feet in front of the Forest of Doom to meet the oncoming troops.

"Sakia is that one of the male dogs who tried to sell you and Tiwa into slavery?" Penar inquires, her voice filled with disgust.

"Yes, yes it is" replies Sakia, looking at Tiwa.

"Good. You and Tiwa will have the first opportunity to take him down."

Looking at Keembo, Penar shouts, "Slaveowner, where are your female captive and your two scumbag friends? You can tell me willingly or we can torture it out of you."

Confounded by Penar's words, Keembo replies, "Slaveowner? You're mistaken. I'm no slaveowner. Tiwa, Sakia tell this woman who I am."

"Sakia, Tiwa take him down now" commands Penar. Tiwa grabs two of her boomerangs and hurls them at Keembo. Keembo catches one in his left hand and the other in his right.

"Are they attacking Keembo?" questions Azra angrily, as she starts to move forward to aid Keembo.

"Hold on Azra, we need to see how this plays out. We stay hidden, but be prepared to attack at any moment" says Titus. Obadiah and Azra nod, intently watching and preparing to attack if necessary.

Putting both boomerangs in his left hand Keembo says, "Tiwa why are you attacking me? Are you--"

"You know why we're attacking you," says Sakia, interrupting Keembo. Sakia walks closer towards Keembo, with Tiwa following close behind. Pulling her whip from off her hip Sakia continues, "You tried to sell us as slaves to the Gopher People. We'll never forgive you for that."

Sakia swings her whip at Keembo who catches it with his right hand.

Zzzt!

Electricity flows through Keembo's body dropping him to his knees. Dazed, Keembo tightens his grip on Sakia's whip and pulls Sakia towards him.

"Help me Tiwa! Hold onto me! Pull!" Tiwa wraps her four arms around Sakia's waist.

"Let go of the whip, Sakia!" screams Penar.

Suddenly, Keembo stands up and with all his might yanks upward on Sakia's whip sending Tiwa and Sakia flying over his head and landing right in front of Obadiah, Titus, and Azra.

Obadiah and Titus emerge from the Forest of Doom and pull Tiwa and Sakia unharmed, into Doom Forest.

"Attack them!" shouts Penar. Immediately twenty-five crossbows raise up and fire.

Keembo stumbles and staggers his way back toward Doom Forest. Glancing over his shoulder he sees the arrows rapidly approaching. He stops accepting his fate, knowing that death will one day catch us all, only to see the arrows hit something and fall to the ground.

"Azra! You saved my life again!" exclaims Keembo.

"Yes, I did. Now hurry up and get in here." Keembo staggers into the Forest of Doom as the Viragosian troops look on in bewilderment.

"How could all of our arrows miss him? What kind of sorcery does he possess? They have recaptured Sakia and Tiwa, we do not have orders to enter Doom Forest" declares Penar.

Without warning, a thunderous explosion is heard and lightning flashes across the sky. "Captain a severe storm will be upon us shortly, what are your orders?" asks one of her warriors.

Angry and upset at how things have transpired, Penar reluctantly commands her troops to withdraw and head back to camp. Another thunderous explosion echoes across the Woodlands, just before raindrops start to pelt the forest floor again.

Hitting the dry ground inside the Forest of Doom, Keembo rests a moment to clear the cobwebs from his head. Feeling better Keembo stands up and demands, "Where's Sakia and Tiwa? What the hell just happened out there?"

"Calm down Keembo, they're over there sitting against a tree. They're still a little groggy" says Obadiah.

Marching over to Sakia and Tiwa, Keembo shouts, "Why did you two attack me? Were you hypnotized? Under some sort of spell? What?"

"Oh no, we weren't under any spell. This was my plan all along. Get close to the Viragosians, collect information regarding the Armor of God, then find a way to escape and get back to you guys. We were ordered to attack you Keembo. We had to play along" explains Sakia.

"I understand you had orders" retorts Keembo. Balling up his fists Keembo punches a hole in the tree Sakia is leaning on, inches above her head.

Sakia quickly jumps to her feet pulling out her whip. "You zapped me with your whip, not because you were given orders, but because you wanted to. So fight me now Sakia. Defend yourself" blurts out Keembo.

Keembo lunges at Sakia throwing a cocked right hand and Sakia swings her electric whip. Sakia's whip and Keembo's fist collide into an invisible shield.

"Stop it you two, you're on the same side!" screams Azra.

"Anyone who gleefully attacks me isn't my friend, but an enemy who cannot be trusted. Sakia I don't see you as a friend anymore, but an enemy. I won't help you in battle and I don't want your help either. It's in your best interest to stay out my way" declares a pissed off Keembo.

"Okay, Keembo. I'm sorry. I got caught up and wanted to see how much of an effect my electric whip would have on you. I admit that was wrong and stupid. I apologize. I'll never do something that stupid again" pleads Sakia.

"Apology not accepted! Stay away from me, for your own good" exclaims Keembo, as he turns his back to Sakia and walks away.

Titus and Azra walk over to Keembo as Tiwa and Obadiah walk over to Sakia.

The rain continues to pound the forest, pushed left and right by gusting winds. Yet not a drop falls inside Doom Forest.

"Keembo can you find it in yourself to forgive Sakia?" asks Azra.

Keembo pauses, ignoring her question he asks, "Titus would you forgive Sakia if she did the same thing to you?"

"Since she came clean and gave a sincere apology I'd forgive her. Because I too make mistakes and would want to be forgiven. But it would be hard for me to trust her again. She'd have to work hard to repair that trust" responds Titus.

"See Keembo, Titus would give her a second chance and so should you" interjects Azra.

"I don't give people a second chance to hurt me. That's why I'm a loner. You can't trust people" states Keembo.

"You can trust me Keembo," says Azra.

"You can trust me too. I know you think I'm smart and perfect, but I make mistakes to Keembo" expresses Titus sincerely.

"I know you're not perfect Titus, but you try to do the right thing. I do trust you two. But I am the way I am and I'm not changing for anybody" declares Keembo.

~~~

Returning to the Viragosian Lodge, Penar reports to Queen Myra. Kneeling before the Queen, Penar makes her report. "My Queen we have found the intruders hiding in the Forest of Doom. Unfortunately, they recaptured Sakia and Tiwa and retreated back into
~~~

Doom Forest. Without orders from you to enter the forest, we dared not pursue them."

"You made the right decision Penar. Were any other warriors killed or injured?" inquires the Queen.

"No, my Queen" insists Penar.

"Good. The loss of Sakia and Tiwa is unfortunate. However, they and the other four intruders will serve as our weekly sacrifice to the Ogre. This will allow us to keep our peace agreement that we provide living flesh, animal or human once a week in exchange for him leaving our people alone and staying inside the Forest of Doom.

"Penar, tomorrow morning send out a pair of scouts to see if there are any survivors. Send two to scout the perimeter of Doom Forest and another two by boat to check along the river" orders Queen Myra.

"It shall be done your Majesty" grins Penar.

~~~

Sakia and Tiwa tell Obadiah all they have learned from the Viragosians regarding the Ogre and the Armor of God. Obadiah followed by Tiwa and Sakia walks over to the others.

"We need to go further into the Forest of Doom and defeat the Ogre protecting the next piece to the Armor of God" announces Obadiah.
~~~

"Are you talking about a giant, man-eating Ogre" interjects Titus.

"That's the kind," says Tiwa.

"That's worse than the boogeyman. Hey Tiwa. Here, I believe these are yours" says Titus, as he hands Tiwa her three boomerangs.

"Thank you Titus" Tiwa replies.

"You're welcome. I just better not see one of those things flying at me" says Titus disdainfully.

"Hey! That was uncalled for Titus" remarks a flustered Azra.

"Hey, I'm just saying" mutters Titus.

"Let's move out everyone and please no talking. It would be to our advantage to approach the Ogre unnoticed" interjects Obadiah.

With tension in the air, the six head deeper into Doom Forest.

~~~

Deep in the heart of the Forest of Doom lies an enormous mound. From a distance, a flickering light can be seen through a large open door. Inside, is one gigantic room with very little furnishings. A broken-down bed rests up against one wall, a fire pit surrounded by bones is located in the center of the room and several water jars are placed in the corners of the room. However, in the corner of the room next to the
~~~

foot of the bed sleeps a large wolf the size of a small horse. This is home to the Ogre, who is resting comfortably in his bed.

"Shhh" whispers Obadiah, turning his head towards everyone with his finger pressed against his lips.

"There's a flickering light up ahead. It must be the Ogre's hideout. Titus do you have any ideas on how to fight this thing?" asks Obadiah.

"I need to see it first, so I know exactly what we're dealing with" utters Titus.

"The rest of you stay here, Titus and I will get a closer look at this Ogre," says Obadiah. Walking as quickly and quietly as he can, Obadiah reaches the hideout first and stands with his back against the wall just to the right of the open door. Still walking up the hill, Titus steps on an old, dry stick, snapping it in two. The stick makes a slight sound.

Immediately, the wolf's head and ears pop up. He growls and starts walking towards the door. The Ogre sits up in his bed and says, "Fido, go fetch dinner."

The wolf reaches the front door of the den and locks eyes with Titus. Titus' eyes grow wide with astonishment at the sight before him.

The thick black, four-foot-tall wolf has amber-colored eyes. Its eyes are fixated on Titus as it snarls bearing its razor-sharp teeth. Instinctively, Titus turns and runs down the hill where the others are waiting, the wolf takes off after him.

Obadiah quickly pulls his bow off his shoulder and shoots three fiery arrows at the wolf, which misses and explode into the trees. The wolf quickly gains on Titus, leaping into the air to pounce on its prey; he is tackled from the side by Keembo. Rolling on the dry ground, they both slam into a tree.

The wolf quickly gets to its feet and sinks his razor-sharp teeth into Keembo's left arm. Keembo lets out a scream just as two boomerangs hit the wolf in the head, causing it to lose hold of Keembo's arm and turn its attention towards Tiwa.

Running towards Tiwa with drool and blood dripping from its mouth, the wolf slashes at Tiwa with his paw. Tiwa blocks the wolf's paw with her boomerang but is knocked to the ground by the force of the blow. The wolf opens its mouth to tear open Tiwa's neck when Sakia's whip wraps around its neck and zaps him. The wolf yelps and is dazed for several seconds. Tiwa scampers away behind a nearby tree.

"Fido! You okay" calls out the Ogre as he leaps off his bed and heads outside to see what caused his pet to cry out.

"Azra I need you to come with me up the hill to check on Obadiah. He's up there alone with the Ogre" explains Titus.

"What about the wolf and the others?" asks Azra.

"We have two enemies to deal with. The others will have to handle the wolf by themselves. We'll have our hands full with the wolf's master" explains Titus.

Azra and Titus make their way up the hill leaving the others to fight the wolf.

The Ogre steps outside his den and catches sight of Fido attacking three victims.

"Good boy Fido. We going to eat good tonight. I come give you a hand."

The Ogre takes one step then stops to sniff the air with his crooked, bumpy nose. Standing nine feet tall and very strong, the Ogre's large head is covered with stringy, unkempt grey hair. Cross-eyed, his vision is fair, but his keen sense of smell compensates for any loss of vision.

"Come out! I know you here somewhere, I can smell ya" blurts out the Ogre, looking around.

Obadiah, standing behind and to the right of the Ogre, fires four arrows that hit the Ogre in the back, exploding on impact. Obadiah's arrows have the effect equivalent to that of a wasp's sting, against the ogre's thick skin.

"Ouch! Now I kill you" screams the Ogre, raising a wooden club over his head. Obadiah falls to one knee, raising his bow to block the Ogre's attack. Swinging the club down at Obadiah's head, Azra winces in pain as her invisible shield blocks the giant Ogre's clubbing blow.

"Are you okay Azra? What happened?" asks Titus.

"Strong impacts against my shield send psionic shock waves to my mind. A strong enough impact can render me unconscious" explains Azra.

"How come you not dead? Something blocking my stick. I break through it" shouts the Ogre, as he puts two hands on his club and swings down at Obadiah again.

The Ogre's club hits Azra's shield with a thunderous bang, sending a large psionic wave crashing into Azra's mind. Azra screams and falls to her knees. "Titus, I can't take another blow like that," says Azra in a low voice.

"Obadiah get out of there!" screams Titus, running towards the giant Ogre with his extended steel baton in his hand.

"I get you now" bellows out the Ogre staring at Obadiah. Raising his club over his head again the Ogre swings with all his might at Obadiah's head.

Boom!

Azra lets out a loud shrill and falls to the ground, her indestructible shield disappears as she loses consciousness.

"Barriers gone. Now I kill and eat you" declares the Ogre, still bent over with his head close to the ground from delivering his crushing blow.

"This is for Azra!" yells Titus, as he jumps up and rams his steel baton into the right ear of the Ogre.

"Argh" screams the Ogre, dropping his wooden club. Blood oozes out of the Ogre's ear as he pulls out Titus' steel baton, throwing it to the ground.

"I no hear! I no hear! I crush you bug man and feed you to my dog" says the Ogre, turning all his attention upon Titus.

"Tiwa! Keembo! While the wolf is dazed we all need to attack it at the same time" says Sakia.

"I told you Sakia I wouldn't help you in battle. So, I won't be going along with your plan" states Keembo stubbornly.

"Keembo, I'm not asking you to help me, but to help the team. Obadiah, Azra, and Titus are facing the Ogre while we fight his mutt down here. Titus isn't a fighter, but a strategic genius. Azra is a defensive juggernaut but has no offensive capabilities. Obadiah is the only offensive person up there. They cannot defeat the Ogre by themselves. We need to finish the wolf off and help the others" pleads Sakia.

"Sakia!" shouts Tiwa, as the wolf turns his head grabbing hold of Sakia's whip with its teeth, snatching it out of her hand.

"There goes our chance to take him out quickly," says Tiwa.

Picking up a dead piece of lumber Keembo says, "I'll draw the wolf's attention, when its back is to you, Sakia, regain your whip and we'll attack together."

Keembo slams the dead log against the right side of the wolf's body. Whirling around the wolf lunges towards Keembo, who pulls out his two daggers. Sakia runs and flips over the wolf picking up the handle of her whip, which is still around the wolf's neck.

"Now, Tiwa!" shouts Sakia as she zaps the wolf, stopping him dead in his tracks.

Tiwa hurls all four boomerangs, two hitting the wolf on both sides of his head. Keembo leaps into the air with his daggers above his head, thrusting them into the wolf's neck. The wolf lets out a shrieking howl and then falls to the ground breathing heavily. Not wasting any time, Tiwa, Sakia, and Keembo make their way up the hill to find the others.

The Ogre picks up Titus with both hands and slams him to the ground rendering him unconscious. Obadiah continues to shoot his arrows at him even though they have no real effect. The Ogre picks up his club to smash Titus' head. Lifting the massive club high above his shoulders, the Ogre is suddenly shaken to his core by the spine-tingling, death howl of his pet. Turning in the direction of the howl the giant Ogre runs to find Fido, leaving Titus laying on the ground.

Focusing only on finding his pet the Ogre doesn't notice Keembo, Tiwa and Sakia pass by him on his way down the hill. The three reach Obadiah and see Titus' broken body lying motionless on the ground.

"Is he dead? What happened? Where is Azra?" inquires a frantic Keembo.

"I'll tell you everything later. Right now, we need to get out of here before the Ogre comes back. Keembo, Azra's laying over by those trees. Can you carry her and Titus away from here?" asks Obadiah.

"I'll get them both to safety," says Keembo, heading over to Azra. "Sakia, Tiwa I need you two to help me search the Ogre's den for the Armor of God" instructs Obadiah.

"We're right behind you" responds Tiwa. Entering the Ogre's den they look around. "There's hardly anything in here. Where would he hide something like that? I know he's not stupid enough to hide it under his bed" says Sakia, as she kneels down and pulls back the covers.

"I can't believe it. Here it is" utters Sakia, pulling an old unlocked chest from under the bed. Tiwa and Obadiah hasten over to the chest.

"Open it" insists Tiwa. Sakia opens the chest and finds a silver and gold belt with the symbols Alpha and Omega etched on it.

"We have three pieces to the Armor of God. Let's go before the Ogre comes back. Sakia hold onto the belt" says Obadiah.

Tiwa, Obadiah, and Sakia run outside to meet Keembo who has Titus draped over his right shoulder and Azra tucked under his left bleeding arm.

"Keembo your arm is bleeding," says Tiwa.

"I'll tend to it once we get these two to safety" responds Keembo.

"It's time to put some distance between us and the Ogre. Keembo follow me. Sakia, Tiwa, protect our rear" directs Obadiah.

Obadiah quickly and quietly leads the group away from the Ogre's den. Tiwa picks up Titus' steel baton off the ground as they move on through Doom Forest.

The Ogre, searching for his pet, shouts out, "Fido! Here boy! Where you at? Fido!" to no avail.

He stops looking around and closes his eyes. Tilting his head upwards the Ogre takes three strong sniffs, smelling blood, he follows the scent to find his pet wolf barely alive bleeding on the ground. Gently picking him up the Ogre carries Fido to their home, just missing the Chosen Ones.

The Ogre sets Fido on the floor and bandages his wounds, oblivious to everything else. "You no die on me Fido!" yells the Ogre as he lies beside his beloved pet and only friend.

~~~

The back end of the Forest of Doom runs into the Tiger River. Rain is still pouring down from the storm.

Upon reaching the back end of Doom Forest, Obadiah notices it is still raining and says, "We'll camp here for the night, tend to our wounded and watch out for the Ogre."

Keembo lays Azra and Titus on the ground.

"Sakia I need you to take first watch and keep an eye out for any signs of the Ogre. Tiwa can you tend to Keembo's wounded left arm? I'll try and catch some fish for dinner from the river. Let me know when Azra and Titus regain consciousness" says Obadiah.

Keembo, Sakia and Tiwa each nod, yes, in response to Obadiah as they look at their unconscious comrades. At that moment Azra starts to stir. Opening her eyes she gingerly pushes herself up.

"Azra!" shouts everyone with genuine excitement.

"Are you okay?" asks Sakia.

"I'm okay. I just have a splitting headache. How long have I been out? I remember now. Where is Obadiah and Titus?" asks a concerned Azra.

"I'm right behind you and Titus is still out, we have no clue if he has internal injuries or not. You got knocked out and the Ogre was about to smash me. Then Titus charged at the Ogre like a madman and stabbed him in the ear to save my life. But the Ogre grabbed him
~~~

and slammed him incredibly hard into the ground. He's been out ever since" explains a somber Obadiah.

Looking through her pouch Azra finds three healing potions. "Get some water and splash it on Titus' face. I need him conscious so he can drink a potion" instructs Azra.

Obadiah runs to the river to get some water, while Sakia, Tiwa, and Keembo look on hopefully. Obadiah pours a handful of water over Titus' face; he coughs and opens his eyes, trying to sit up.

"I can't move. I think my back is broken" utters Titus.

"Don't talk! Drink this quickly!" asserts Azra. Titus drinks the healing potion.

"He'll be okay now. Keembo what happened to your arm?" questions Azra. "That wolf bit me, but I'm alright" states Keembo.

"Here drink this in case the wolf has rabies," says Azra.

"Yes, mother," says a smiling Keembo.

Caught up in the joy of everyone being together again and on the mend, no one notices that they are being watched.

Titus sits up and then stands up. "Wow, my back is healed!" exclaims Titus.

Azra runs and hugs Titus saying, "I heard how you fought and saved Obadiah from the Ogre when I went down."

"You know, I'm not just a great thinker. I *can* get physical if I have to" says Titus in a serious voice.

"Well next time leave something for the rest of us little big man" jokes Keembo taking the bandage off his left arm.

"Is your arm totally healed Keembo?" asks Tiwa.

Stepping from behind a tree the Ogre points at Azra and says, "You come with me. Heal Fido, like you heal bug man."

Startled by the Ogres appearance everyone jumps into a defensive position. "Come now or he die," says the worried Ogre.

"She's not going anywhere with you" shouts Keembo, standing in front of Azra.

"Hold on Keembo, there has been too much fighting and pain. I will go with you and heal Fido if I can" says Azra.

"Not without the rest of us," says Titus reaching for his missing baton. Tiwa reaches over and hands Titus his bloodstained baton.

"Hurry, we go now" quips the Ogre, turning and heading towards his den.

Anxious about Fido's poor health the Ogre runs and kneels at his pet's side.

As soon as Azra steps into the room the Ogre says, "Help him. He barely breathe."

Giving the Ogre her last healing potion Azra tells him, "Hold Fido's mouth open and pour the potion to the back of his throat. Make sure he swallows it."

The Ogre opens the wolf's mouth being careful of its razor-sharp teeth and pours the potion into its mouth. Fido swallows the healing potion.

"Good, now we wait," says Azra.

"By the way, what is your name?" Azra's question takes the Ogre by surprise. "My name. My name Kroc. I live in Woodlands seventy-five year. I raise Fido from puppy. You first person ask my name in long time."

"Kroc, my name is Azra. My friends and I want to leave the Woodlands. Where can we go?"

"Kroc overhear Queen lady say river take you to cold place. Kroc never go cause Kroc have no boat."

As Kroc talks a cold wet nose touches his arm. Looking down Kroc sees his pet wolf standing totally healed from his massive injuries.

He screams, "Fido, you live! Come here, boy!" Fido licks Kroc on his face as Kroc squeezes him tightly. Rolling on the floor Kroc notices his open chest. Kroc stops and stands up looking at his empty chest.

"Who take Kroc's belt? You keep as gift for healing Fido. Belt no fit anyway."

Everyone in the room sighs a breath of relief.

"Let me put some ointment on your ear Kroc and then we'll be leaving," says Azra.

"Okay, Azra. Fido sit" says Kroc. The wolf sits down as Azra treats Kroc's injured ear. The ointment is applied and goodbyes are exchanged between enemies who have now become friends.

Walking back to camp stomachs grumble and all heads turn towards Obadiah inquiring, "What's for dinner?"

Obadiah catches eight large fish that are shared between them all. Night arrives and the storm is still raging outside. Everyone sits quietly around the campfire cleaning and checking their weapons. Azra diligently works on creating more healing potions. Confident they are safe in Doom Forest, everyone exhausted from the days battle, turns in for the night. All except Azra, who works well into the night creating ten more healing potions.

~~~

With the storm now gone, it leaves the skies spotted with dark clouds. The Viragosian scouts rise up early to search for any survivors near the edge of the Forest of Doom and along the Tiger River. As Tiwa and Sakia bathe in the river, they spot a rowboat heading their way. Scampering to shore they get dressed. They hear voices from the boat calling their names.
~~~

"Tiwa, Sakia, you are alive" shouts two Viragosian warriors as they jump out of the boat and drag it onto dry land.

"We had feared the worst. Everyone will be glad to know their new sisters are alive" says one of the warriors.

Hearing unfamiliar voices the others come out of the forest to see who it is.

Catching sight of Keembo, Titus, Obadiah, and Azra coming out of Doom Forest a Viragosian warrior shouts, "Sakia, Tiwa, the four of us can take them down, prepare to attack!"

Sakia takes out her whip and swings it around both the unsuspecting Viragosian warriors. Giving them an electric shock, they fall to the ground.

"Well done Sakia. I was wondering how we were going to get to our next destination without a boat, but that question has been answered" says Titus gleefully.

Packing their gear into the boat, they shove off catching the river current heading southeast. They leave the two unconscious warriors laying safely on the riverbank.

The wooden rowboat sits all six comfortably. It has three rows of seating. Keembo sits in the middle by himself rowing the oars with his back to the front of the boat. Sakia, Obadiah, and Tiwa sit in the front row of the boat looking out on the water. Azra and Titus sit in the back of the boat facing Keembo. The river's current takes the boat down the river at a brisk pace.

The Woodlands start to get smaller and smaller as the boat moves further and further away. The river twists and turns down a long canyon pass with steep mountains on both sides.

They travel four straight hours through the tight canyon pass before finding a small dirt riverbank adequate enough for them to stop and stretch their legs. Keembo navigates the boat to the riverbank and pulls it onshore. Everyone exits the boat and walks around stretching their arms and legs.

The sun at high noon peeks out occasionally through the heavily clouded sky. "I'm starving. Are we staying here awhile?" inquires Azra.

"Yes, we can rest here for an hour or two. Sakia can you help me catch lunch?" asks Obadiah.

"Sure, okay" responds Sakia.

"I'll try and find something to start a fire with," says Keembo.

"I'll help you Keembo," says Tiwa.

"No thanks, I can do this by myself" retorts Keembo rather quickly.

Ignoring Keembo's response Tiwa says, "Here I come."

"Girls" mutters Keembo under his breath, as Tiwa catches up and walks alongside him.

"Well, Titus looks like it's you and me," says Azra with a smile on her face.

"What are we going to do?" asks Titus.

"We can sit and talk" replies Azra.

"Now, that sounds like fun," says Titus rolling his eyes.

Sakia and Obadiah walk to the edge of the river. Pulling his regular bow off his shoulder Obadiah ties a long string to an arrow and attaches the other end of the string to his bow. Spotting a nearby fish he fires the arrow, skewering the fish he pulls it in.

"Nice shot. I see you clearly don't need my help catching fish. So, why did you ask me to join you? Do you want to lecture me or what?" blurts out Sakia.

"No, I didn't ask you to come with me to lecture you. I want you to explain to me why you did what you did to Keembo" states Obadiah in a stern serious voice, looking directly at Sakia.

Caught off guard by the question Sakia pauses, then tells Obadiah the truth. "Obadiah what happened yesterday was not planned. Keembo is a fierce warrior and I wondered how I would fare against him in battle. That curiosity lingered in my mind, so when the opportunity presented itself, I reacted without thinking. I've done a lot of bonehead things and regret not a one. But this one, I truly regret."

Tears start to form in Sakia's eyes as she continues, "I've lost a good friend and a trusted ally. Keembo saved my life on the bridge in the Sand Province and this is how I repay him. I know the others have thoughts in the back of their minds regarding me. Wondering if they can trust me or will I turn on them as well."

"You haven't destroyed everyone's trust, but you have damaged it. There *is* a difference. Damaged trust can be repaired. Just as your honest answer has restored my trust in you. I understand you made a mistake and your actions weren't full of malice and evil intent. Over time the others will see that you *are* still trustworthy. Now as far as Keembo is concerned, I have no answer for you" says Obadiah as he gives Sakia a big hug.

Wiping away her tears Sakia says, "Thank you, Obadiah, you're a true friend." They both laugh and joke around as Obadiah continues to fish.

~~~

"How are you doing Keembo?" asks Tiwa.

"How am I doing? Well, let's see. Hm, your best friend stabbed me in the back, making her a backstabbing rat. And if you keep hanging out with her you'll probably turn out to be just like her" answers Keembo irritably.

"That's not fair Keembo. I haven't wronged you, nor am I your enemy" replies Tiwa.
~~~

"I never said *you* were" retorts Keembo.

"Sakia isn't your enemy either," says Tiwa emphatically.

"Now that is where we disagree" Keembo declares.

"Keembo, Sakia made a terrible mistake in shocking you with her whip. She was totally wrong in doing that and I know she's truly sorry" Tiwa explains.

"Tiwa I'm glad to hear you say, your best friend was wrong, that says a lot about you. I have no beef with you. My problem is with your friend. So be smart and stay out of it" stresses Keembo in a stern voice.

Speaking in a compassionate voice Tiwa says, "I side with the truth and the truth is, what Sakia did was wrong. So is not forgiving her Keembo."

"Okay, you spoke your piece, now can you kindly be quiet and help me find something that burns around here" concludes Keembo.

~~~

"Titus do you think we are going to be able to collect all the pieces to the Armor of God and defeat the Demon King? I mean, we have three pieces of the Armor already, but we seem to be breaking down as a team. It appears that everyone's personal flaws and weaknesses are being exposed. Surely the Righteous One was aware of our faults before he chose us. I don't understand this Titus" expresses Azra, confused.
~~~

"Azra I don't understand everything yet, but I do know the five of us, I mean the six of us, form a powerful team. One that's very difficult to defeat. But when one or more of us are separated from the group we *are* drastically weaker. The Spirit is right, division is our greatest enemy and if we become divided as a team we can and *will* be defeated" answers Titus.

~~~

Keembo and Tiwa build a fire from the dry bushes, leaves and splintered wood they gather on the shore of the river. Obadiah and Sakia bring back several medium-size fish to eat. An awkward silence permeates the camp, while the Chosen Ones eat and prepare to make sail again.

Breaking the deafening silence, Azra stands up and says, "Hold on everyone. I think this would be a good time to check in with the Spirit before we move on."

Everyone agrees and gathers stones to build an altar. Completing the altar Azra places the red jewel and summons the Spirit of Truth.

"Greetings Chosen Ones. I congratulate you all for overcoming hardships and adversity from outside forces and from within. You have retrieved the Belt of Truth despite the disunity in your group. The Belt of Truth will help the wearer discern between what is the truth and what is a lie. However, the rift that is forming in your
~~~

midst must be fixed and healed before it destroys you all. Sakia and Keembo, step forward."

Surprised they are called out by name, Sakia, and Keembo cautiously steps closer to the Spirit.

"Sakia you are impulsive and act before thinking. That is why there is strife between you and Keembo right now. Sakia anyone who does not learn self-control or how to rule over their own spirit is like a city with no defenses and broken-down walls. They are easily defeated and captured. You need to practice patience and start thinking more about the effects your actions have on others."

"Spirit I've always been this way and I haven't wanted to change, until now. I'll think about how my actions affect others, instead of just doing what I want to do" says Sakia sincerely.

"As you overcome this area in your life Sakia, you will become a wise and fearless warrior" declares the Spirit, turning her attention to Keembo.

"Keembo, my lone wolf warrior, it is not good for you to be alone. Most people are afraid of you because of your size and appearance, but you are fearfully and wonderfully made. It is because of your uniqueness that you fit perfectly in this group of Chosen Ones. Keembo, you have been hurt by people, so you protect yourself by pushing them away and choosing to be a loner. It is not good for people to be isolated and alone. For two are better than one, for if one falls the other is there to lift him up, but woe unto him that is alone when he falls, for there is no one to help him up. Also, none of you will be able to defeat the Demon King alone.

"Keembo, Sakia made a mistake when she zapped you with her whip. She has since given you a genuine apology. For your sake, to break your loner ways, you need to forgive her."

"Forgive her! If I forgive her then I will be weak" blurts out Keembo.

"If you forgive her, you will start to free yourself from the fear of being hurt by others. If you choose not to forgive her you will fall deeper into the pit of loneliness and isolation. The choice is yours to make Keembo. I know you will make the right choice" replies the Spirit.

Keembo says nothing as the Spirit turns to address the others. "Wear the Armor of God you have collected to strengthen yourselves against the spiritual and physical attacks of your enemies. Continue to keep the bond of unity between you six and farewell my Chosen Ones."

The Spirit disappears leaving the six to ponder the words spoken to them.

Azra collects the spirit gem from the altar as Titus breaks the noticeable silence. "Is it just me or did the Spirit include Tiwa as one of the Chosen Ones? As she was departing she said, *'Keep the bond of unity between you six and farewell my Chosen Ones.'* That sounds to me like Tiwa is the sixth Chosen One. I don't know. What do you guys think?"

"Wow, Tiwa you might be one of us, that's great," says an excited Azra.

"But how can that be, I'm a slave. I've been a slave all my life. I've never seen this Spirit before until I met you outworlders" explains a puzzled Tiwa.

"I guess we can ask the Spirit next time we see her. But right now we need to get sailing again" says Obadiah.

No one addresses the obvious conflict between Keembo and Sakia as they enter the rowboat and begin sailing again.

CHAPTER 11

THE ARCTIC PLAINS

Traveling down the river the temperature abruptly drops, sending a cold chill through everyone's body. Touching the water they notice that the warm Tiger River has turned very cold. The Chosen Ones have reached the end of the Tiger River as it empties into a larger body of water called the Icy Sea.

"We must be nearing the Arctic Plains," says Keembo steadily rowing the boat.

Using his binocular vision Titus notices a long sheet of white ice in the distance. "Keep rowing Keembo, I see icy land straight ahead."

After twenty minutes of rowing, everyone can see the large sheets of white ice in the distance. Still using his binocular vision Titus spots eight people attacking a large white bear and says, "Hey everybody! I see a group of people attacking a large bear and it just fell to the ground. It appears they've killed it…. Oh my gosh! Three bears just came out of nowhere and started attacking the people. I see four running away. The bears just killed four of them and are pursuing the ones that ran away. What kind of place is this?"

"These Arctic Plains remind me of home. What you've described sounds like a hunting party that got outsmarted by its prey. The hunters have become the hunted. The animals here appear to be very intelligent. Keembo bring us to shore closest to the attack" instructs Obadiah.

"Are you sure? I don't want to get off the boat fighting bears if you know what I mean" Keembo says.

"I know what you mean Keembo, but we need to know who and what we're dealing with here. The dead bodies should provide some information" informs Obadiah.

"Be on guard, we're about to reach land," says Keembo.

Reaching the icy shore everyone draws out their weapons. Keembo lifts the rowboat up out of the water and places it safely onshore. Cautiously heading towards the white bear's dead corpse, everyone looks around anticipating a sneak attack that never comes.

"Dang! That's one big bear!" exclaims Sakia.

"Standing on its hind legs it's about ten feet tall" states Obadiah, as he walks towards one of the dead bodies and turns it over.

"What kind of being is that?" asks Azra.

"I don't know, but they must be the inhabitants of this realm" answers Obadiah.

Tiwa pulls a long, clear blue crystal tipped spear out of the bear's chest. Titus collects the crystal tipped knives off the dead corpses and Sakia collects the other three spears. Obadiah takes the thick hooded bear coats and boots off the bodies and gives them to Tiwa, Sakia, Azra, and Titus. Immediately their shaking bodies begin to warm up.

"The sun will be setting in about two hours. We need to build a shelter to shield us from the cold at night. Let's make camp at the base of this glacier. Keembo, can you bring the bear over here? It'll be our food for a few days" says Obadiah, gathering the backpacks off of the fallen hunting party.

The four humanoid corpses laying on the frozen icy shore are long lanky creatures with red eyes, long white hair, and pale gray skin. They have long necks, arms, and legs. Their square jawbones and facial features give the appearance of highly intelligent beings. These humanoids are called Ecclesians, the ruling inhabitants of the Arctic Plains.

The Arctic Plains is a frozen tundra. Its permanently frozen soil covers eighty percent of the region. Ice glaciers of various sizes are surrounded by snow-packed mountains. Because of the thick permafrost, no trees grow in the Arctic Plains. Winds often blow upwards of thirty to sixty miles per hour.

During the summer months, only a handful of plants are able to grow. Moss, Crowberry and Lichen are three rare plants that can exist in this cold environment. Temperatures rise to about fifty-four degrees Fahrenheit during the day and drop well below zero at night.

Working on the shelter, Keembo and Titus cut out five ice slabs to make the walls and roof. Sakia and Tiwa prepare the floor of the shelter, by removing the soft snow covering the solid ice beneath. Obadiah and Azra skin the bear. Azra fashions coats and boots out of the bearskin for Keembo and Obadiah. Obadiah cuts off a section of the bear meat for dinner and prepares the rest to be put on ice for later.

With less than an hour of daylight left, the temperature starts to drop quickly and the wind starts to blow. Completing the shelter Sakia, Tiwa, Titus, and Keembo walk over to Azra and Obadiah.

"I'm finished! Here you go" says Azra, as she hands Keembo and Obadiah their hooded bearskin coats and matching boots.

"Thank you. The cold was starting to get unbearable even with my thick skin" responds Keembo.

"Even though my body is used to this type of weather, I have my limits" explains Obadiah as he and Keembo quickly put on their coats and boots.

"Keembo, I need your help securing the bear meat and burying these corpses. Can you four look through these bags and pull out anything useful?" asks Obadiah.

"No problem, we'll also build a fire and get dinner going," says Tiwa, as each of them picks up a bag and head towards the shelter.

"Girls, do you really need my help with dinner and starting a fire? Because I really would like to inspect the weapons left behind by the recently departed" inquires Titus.

"Go play with your toys Titus, we girls can handle this" replies Sakia.

"Yes!" says Titus, dropping his bag and running into the shelter.

The girls enter the shelter and begin emptying out the backpacks.

"All these packs have the same stuff in them, a cooking pot, some thick pasty liquid, beef jerky or bear jerky and a big yellow crystal rock" states Sakia.

"Oh, let me see the yellow crystal, please" quips Azra.

"Careful Azra before you drop it," says Sakia, as the crystal falls out of their hands. Upon hitting the hard-icy floor, the crystal starts to emit a bright yellow light that illuminates the entire shelter.

Titus turns around from his corner and says, "Can I have one of those?"

Tiwa picks up one of the yellow crystals and hands it to Titus.

"Thank you," says Titus with a smile on his face, as he returns back to his corner.

"Each of us gets a light crystal. Hit it and it turns on. Hit it again and it turns off. Now we can see what we're cooking. Let's get started" says Azra.

As the sun retires for the night, dinner is cooked, the corpses are buried and the bear meat is put on ice. The winds start to blow picking up speed as it howls across the frozen tundra. Securely closing the shelter for the night, the Chosen Ones eat supper by yellow crystal light and converse about the new region and the inhabitants in it.

"I've examined the light blue crystal blades on the spears and knives. They're as hard as diamonds and can cut through almost anything. Keembo be careful, these blades will slice through even your hardened skin like butter. We have four spears and knives, take what you want" says Titus.

Azra, Titus, and Obadiah each take a knife as their weapon of choice. Sakia, Keembo, and Tiwa take spears. No one objects to Tiwa taking two spears.

"I have two sets of hands" laughs Tiwa.

"I'll hold onto the extra knife. Now we need to decide who will wear the Helmet of Salvation and the Belt of Truth" states Titus.

"I think Azra should have the Belt of Truth," says Keembo.

"Sakia should have the Helmet of Salvation," says Tiwa.

All agree to the wearers of the Armor of God. Azra and Sakia excitedly put on their piece of Armor. More talking ensues before the yellow crystals are turned off and everyone gradually falls asleep.

Waking up early, Obadiah catches and prepares fish for breakfast. The smell of freshly cooked fish causes the others to rise up and start the new day.

"Today we break up into two scouting parties to locate the inhabitants' lair. Keembo, Azra and Tiwa you'll be together searching the northeast area. Keep your distance though, we're not trying to fight, we just want to discover their location.

"Titus, Sakia and I will search the southeastern area. Be alert for animal attacks. Any questions?" asks Obadiah, pausing a moment. "Good, let's head out and meet back here before dark."

Both groups head in opposite directions as they leave camp.

"Have you guys noticed there's very little plant life in this frozen desert? This is the first plant we have come across in an hour" says Azra, scooping up the plant.

"No, I haven't noticed. Plants aren't my thing Azra. What I *have* noticed though is that bear has been tracking us for the last five minutes" states Tiwa.

Keembo and Azra turn around to see a large white bear staring at them. "Should we kill it?" asks Azra.

"Not if we don't have to. Let's hide in that cave at the base of the mountain and see if it goes away" suggests Keembo.

Following Keembo's lead, they walk into a small cave on the side of the mountain. They wait fifteen minutes before exiting the cave.

GRRAAWLL!

The large white bear leaps into the air with both paws raised high, pouncing and landing on top of Azra's shield, inches away from them. The bear stops clawing at the invisible shield as it tries to figure out what is blocking its attack.

"Drop your shield Azra" instructs Keembo as he widens his stance.

"What?" screeches Azra.

"Azra drop your shield," says Keembo again in a stern voice.

Azra drops her shield and Keembo punches the bear in the chest, sending it sliding ten feet across the snow.

Getting up slowly the bear leers at its three would-be victims, then turns and walks away.

"Did you see that? Did you just see that? That bear just sized us up. He waited for us to come out of the cave and then sprung a sneak attack on us. Maybe we should've killed it!" shouts Tiwa.

"No, you did the right thing by sparing the bear's life," says a voice coming from inside the cave.

Whirling around Tiwa pulls out her four boomerangs and demands, "Come out where we can see you. Who are you?"

The visage of someone begins to appear as they walk closer saying, "I am Tricar chief of the Pulka clan."

A medium height, pasty white-skinned male with oval-shaped eyes wearing a hooded white bear coat and boots steps out of the small cave. Cinched in his waist are two curved, sharp-bladed weapons that resemble sickles.

In a strong commanding voice, Tricar says, "You are not of this world. What do you strangers seek here in the Arctic Plains?"

"We seek a piece to the Armor of God. You look different from the four dead bodies we found near the shore. Do you know anything about them?" inquires Keembo.

Chief Tricar begins to explain, "There are two races dwelling here in the frozen tundra, my people and the

Ecclesians. My clan used to live on the icy floor in harmony with the animals of this realm. That was until the Ecclesians waged war on us and drove us up into the mountains. We taught the bears and snow leopards how to fight against the Ecclesians who are ruled by three Ice Lords. They are brothers Hyrue, Egill and Halfdan. Halfdan is the strongest and the leader. He wields a powerful scepter which shoots out a blast of ice, freezing whatever it touches. They have pledged their allegiance to the Demon King, who in return has given them power and rulership over this land. The Ice Lords do and take whatever they want. They fear nothing and no one. Yet they cower before the might of the Demon King and follow his every command. Halfdan and his people have killed many of my people and have no desire for peace. If what you seek is valuable and possesses power, it is probably in the hands of Halfdan and his brothers."

"Will you help us find and retrieve what we seek?" inquires Azra.

"My young child if you help us overthrow the Ice Lords, I promise to help you find what you seek" replies Tricar.

"We need to discuss this over with our friends before we can give you an answer" responds Keembo.

"Very well. If you desire to speak with me again come to this cave and I will find you. Until we meet again" says Chief Tricar, as he heads back into the cave and disappears.

"That was interesting. Let's look around a little longer, then head back to camp" says Tiwa.

"Good idea, we can look for more plants before we head back," says Azra.

"I wonder if this Tricar was telling the truth. I can't wait to tell the others and see what they've found" comments Keembo, as they continue to trek through the frozen tundra.

~~~

"We've been walking for two hours straight Obadiah and haven't seen a thing. Do you have any idea where you're leading us?" questions Sakia with an attitude.

"Well since you asked so nicely Sakia I'll tell you. I recently noticed some fresh footprints and have been following them" retorts Obadiah.

Sniffing the air Obadiah asks, "Do you guys smell that?"

"I don't smell anything," says Titus.

"Me neither" answers Sakia.

"Titus look to the east of us at that massive glacier, tell me if you see anything" instructs Obadiah.

Using his binocular vision Titus says, "I don't see anything. Wait, let me switch to infra-red vision. Hold on, I see multiple heat signatures inside the glacier. I
~~~

count twenty-five, thirty-five, more than fifty bodies moving around inside. I think we've found the inhabitant's lair."

"So, what do we do now?" asks Sakia.

"We get a closer look and let Titus observe their comings and goings, to find a way inside" explains Obadiah.

Moving closer but staying hidden, Sakia and Obadiah wait patiently for another hour while Titus gathers intel on the movements of the Ecclesians.

"Okay, folks I've seen all that I can from the outside. The home base of the inhabitants is inside that massive glacier. I can clearly make out two levels inside, but there may be more. People are entering and leaving through a large iron gate at ground level. There's also a small iron door or hatch on the very top of the glacier. I've only seen a handful of people use that entrance. They have an army well over three hundred strong. We should head back and see what the others have found," states Titus.

Obadiah, Sakia, and Titus make the long trek back to camp.

~~~

Tiwa, Azra, and Keembo make it back to camp first. They start a fire and begin to prepare dinner. "I hope the
~~~

others get back soon it'll be dark in a few hours," says Tiwa.

"Do you think they're all right? You don't think they're hurt or lost or anything" frets Azra.

"I'm sure they're okay Azra. Obadiah and Titus are definitely not lost. Now Sakia, on the other hand, may have been captured" says Keembo.

"That's not fair Keembo, talking about Sakia behind her back. She's made her share of mistakes, but she's also done some incredibly brave and courageous things that have gotten the team further along than if she wasn't here. Have you forgotten she's also a Chosen One despite her faults? It's obvious that unforgiveness is one of your faults" states Tiwa.

"Stop arguing you two" interjects Azra.

"I haven't decided if I'm going to forgive her or not. I don't know if I even want to" retorts Keembo, as he walks away.

Sakia, Titus, and Obadiah finally make it back to camp. Obadiah beckons Keembo to come into the shelter to share scouting reports.

"Glad you guys made it back in one piece. We were worried about you" states Azra.

"She was worried about you guys, Keembo and I knew you'd be alright. We have a lot to tell you. Keembo would you like to do the honors of reporting our findings?" asks Tiwa.

Keembo tells the others everything that happened to them on their scouting expedition.

"So Tricar will help us find the Armor of God if we help him defeat the three Ice Lords. We don't know if he's the good guy or bad guy in this situation" exclaims Titus.

"It doesn't matter, as long as he's willing to help us find the Armor of God" states Sakia.

"Yea, but we don't know if we can trust him" responds Obadiah.

"Look, everyone, why don't we go see him tomorrow. Then you can talk to him yourselves and get a better feel of who he is and what his motives are" suggests Azra.

They all agree to go see Chief Tricar of the Pulka people in the morning. Over dinner, Titus details their findings regarding the Ecclesians and their icy lair. Eager to meet Tricar, they all turn in early for the night. Keembo has another bad night's sleep, dreaming of what Sakia had done to him. The visual images replay over and over again in his mind.

Keembo wakes up upset, with fresh images and thoughts of what Sakia had done to him. Even more short-tempered than normal, Keembo snaps at everyone. "Titus, why is your toolkit always out in the open? It's an eyesore. Why don't you clean it up?" barks Keembo.

"You talking to me? Keembo, I know you're not coming at me like this. First off my toolkit is on my side of the room and I'm using it. Secondly, I don't appreciate the attitude. And if you ever lay a hand on my tools without my permission you and I will be mixing more than just words, big man" states Titus emphatically.

"Is that right little man?" says Keembo, standing up and moving towards Titus. Titus reaches for his steel baton.

Azra shouts, "Stop it! What are you doing?"

"Apparently Keembo thinks he can intimidate me, but I will *not* be punked by anyone" declares Titus.

"Titus, without time to plan you are nothing," says Keembo.

"Who says I haven't already planned out this scenario" states Titus in a serious tone.

Keembo contemplates Titus' words and says, as he sits back down, "Bah, you aren't worth the effort."

Staring at Keembo, Tiwa asks, "Why are you acting like this Keembo? What is your problem?"

"My problem is that girl standing right next to you. She stabbed me in the back and I can't stop thinking about it. Maybe you and I should settle what you started outside, Sakia" utters Keembo.

"I already apologized to you Keembo and I meant it, but I won't apologize to you again. If you've decided you want to battle me, then let's take it outside and have at it big boy" retorts Sakia.

"I accept," says Keembo, standing up with an angry look on his face.

"We won't let you fight each other" declares Obadiah as he, Azra, Titus, and Tiwa stand between them. "Listen! We have a mission to accomplish before we can go back home and we won't accomplish it if we fight amongst ourselves. Keembo, you need to calm down. We need to find Chief Tricar. We'll stay in our same groups as yesterday until tempers settle down. Alright, let's pack it up and get out of here."

The two reluctantly turn away from each other, rolling their eyes simultaneously.

Azra, Tiwa, and Keembo walk fifty yards ahead of the other group, leading the way to the small cave where they met Tricar. Keembo walks a few paces ahead of Azra and Tiwa.

"What's crawled up his butt? Did you see how he picked a fight with Titus for no reason? And here I thought they were friends. Next, he'll probably pick a fight with you" says Tiwa.

"You need to cut him some slack Tiwa, it's not every day you get betrayed by a trusted ally. Some wounds cut deeper and take longer to heal than others. Besides, how would you respond if the same thing happened to you?" Azra asks.

"I don't know, probably the same way" Tiwa answers.

"Okay, my point exactly" states Azra.

"There it is," says Keembo, pointing to the small cave opening.

As they walk towards the cave, seven large white bears appear out of nowhere walking in a straight line. "Hey, where'd they come from?" shouts Titus.

"Everyone keep walking towards the cave, but be ready in case they attack" states Obadiah.

The bears stand perfectly still, only their heads move as their eyes follow the Chosen Ones into the cave. Inside the cave, a deep strong voice says, "I see you have come back to see me and you brought your friends. I will tell *my* friends they can go home now."

Tricar steps out of the cave and beckons the bears to go home. Seeing Tricar, the bears turn and leave the cave.

"How did you command those bears to leave?" asks an astounded Obadiah.

"We have an agreement and an alliance with the animals of the Arctic Plains. Oh, I'm sorry we haven't met. I am Tricar, Chief of the Pulka clan."

"Hi, I'm Obadiah, this is Titus and Sakia. You've already met the other three."

Looking at Keembo, Azra and Tiwa, Tricar says, "I trust you have discussed my proposition over with your friends. What is your answer?"

"Trust is the issue, Tricar. We don't know if we can trust you. For that matter, we don't even know you. Are you the good guy or the bad guy" comments Titus.

"Does it really matter if I am the good guy or not, as long as you obtain what you seek?" replies Tricar.

"It might" states Titus.

"I see you have a conscience. Very well then. Follow me back to my clan and there you will get to know me and hopefully trust me" says Tricar.

Everyone agrees and follows Chief Tricar. He leads them to the back of the small cave and through a secret passageway, up into the snowy mountains.

They are led through a narrow mountain pass which opens up to a large valley surrounded by mountains. There they see children playing outside in the snow while their mothers sit nearby talking.

"My people dwell in the surrounding mountain caves. I will call them out and tell them of our impending battle with the Ecclesians" states Tricar pulling a horn from his belt.

"Wait, we haven't agreed yet" protests Titus.

"You will," says Tricar, blowing the horn three short times. Hundreds of people from the Pulka clan emerge from the mountain caves and assemble in the snow-filled valley.

Tricar walks up a hill to address his people. He beckons the Chosen Ones to join him. They reluctantly walk up the hill to stand alongside Chief Tricar.

"My people the time has come for us to reclaim our rightful homeland back from the Ecclesians. These outworlders will aid us in defeating the three dreaded Ice Lords. They may not look like much." Turning to the Chosen Ones, Tricar says, "No offense."

"None taken," says Obadiah.

"I take offense. Ouch" says Titus, as Azra jabs him in the ribs with her elbow.

Tricar continues to address his people, "However, they are very powerful beings who will help turn the tide in our favor. Prepare for war, my people. Ready your weapons for tomorrow we march on the Ecclesians."

The Pulka clan erupts with a loud roar shouting, "Tricar! Tricar!, Tricar!" as they raise their arms. Slowly they disperse, the women to prepare a warrior's feast and the men to secure their weapons and armor.

"My wife Neeka will show you to your lodgings. Feel free to look around and ask questions. I will meet up with you later to talk over battle strategy" instructs Tricar. The Chosen Ones follow Neeka, who is standing at the bottom of the hill, into a mountain cave.

"Keembo, may I have a word with you" calls out Tricar.

"Sure. I'll catch up with you guys later" says Keembo. Tricar and Keembo walk together outside.

"Keembo my friend, what weighs so heavily on your heart and mind? What is this rage I see on you?" inquires Chief Tricar.

"First off pal, we are not friends. Secondly, what ails me is none of your business" replies Keembo rather curtly.

"Are the dreams becoming more frequent? Do you find yourself getting angry with everybody?" states Tricar.

"How do you know this? Are you some kind of warlock?" Keembo replies.

"I am not a warlock, but I have had my battles with unforgiveness on numerous occasions and know its effects on others. Who betrayed you my son?" asks Tricar sincerely.

"What are you talking about?" says Keembo, trying to avoid Tricar's probing question.

"Who betrayed you?" asks Tricar in a loud stern voice.

"Sakia!" shouts Keembo. "I thought she was my friend. I trusted her. I risked my life for her and she attacks me because she wants to know how she would fare in battle against me. If she wanted to test her skills against mine in a friendly duel, I would have gladly welcomed that. But to attack me the way she did is unforgivable" declares Keembo, in an angry voice.

"You have every right to be angry, my friend. But in order to free yourself from the debilitating toxins of bitterness that unforgiveness forms in you, you must forgive her. Unforgiveness will turn you into a person unrecognizable by your close friends and family. If left unchecked it will ultimately destroy those relationships. Keembo, granting forgiveness is for your freedom and peace of mind, not just the offending party. Understand this, forgiveness is not weakness. Forgiveness will help you sleep at night and bring peace to your raging heart. I believe I am speaking to a wise man, hear my words Keembo."

Tricar walks away without saying another word, leaving Keembo alone.

After several minutes of standing alone, Keembo utters, "I forgive you Sakia. I forgive you for attacking me. I forgive you for betraying my trust. I forgive you for hurting me and destroying our friendship. Forgive you I do; trust you I do not."

Immediately a heaviness lifts off of Keembo's heart because of the decision he makes to forgive Sakia. Taking in a deep breath of fresh air, he exhales with a big sigh.

He turns and starts walking in the direction Neeka took the others. He finds the others in a cave relaxing and eating some bread Neeka prepared for them.

"Hey, can I have some?" asks Keembo, as he sits down with them.

Several minutes later, Tricar summons the Chosen Ones to join him and his first commander Belix in the war room to discuss battle plans. "We have a big day ahead of us tomorrow. So how do *you* plan on defeating the Ecclesians?" asks Belix.

"What! You're joking, right? You must have some plan of attack already drafted for such an occasion as this" quips Titus.

"No, we do not have a plan. That is why we are teaming up with you guys. You must be pretty smart to get this far into Demon's Realm and just for the record kid, Pulka people do not joke" states Tricar.

"That being the case, I need more information before I can formulate any kind of plan. How many warriors do you have? What kind of weapons do you use and do they have these sharp blue crystal blades on them?" inquires Titus, showing them his blue crystal knife.

Answering all of Titus' questions Belix says, "We have two hundred warriors. We use spears, shields, and sickles as our primary weapons. Those blue crystal blades are formed by the Ecclesians who control the only crystal mine in the Arctic Plains. Their blades slice through our shields and armor giving them a major advantage over us."

"Hmm, let me see if I have this right. We are outnumbered two to one. The Ecclesians have roughly four hundred warriors compared to your two, they have superior weapons and live inside an iron gated glacier. Is there anything else I need to know?" inquires Titus.

"You have not factored in our allies the snow bears and snow leopards. They number about one hundred and will fight with us against the Ecclesians" states Tricar.

"That'll help us. We won't be able to defeat the Ecclesian army with our numbers in a frontal attack. So, we'll need to draw them out. I propose a two-pronged attack. Belix, your allies, and warriors will attack the crystal mine forcing the Ecclesian army to leave their stronghold and come out to fight you. The second attack will be from the top of the glacier and aimed at defeating the Ice Lords. Tricar, two snow leopards and the six of us will battle with the Ice Lords. Belix, you must keep the Ecclesian army engaged until we defeat them or all will be lost" declares Titus.

"A sound plan my friend, we will follow it and be victorious. Now let us feast, for tomorrow the Pulka people regain their homeland" shouts Tricar.

The Pulka women have been diligently preparing a humongous feast that will feed the entire clan. They cooked stored up whale, seal and fish meat from last summer. They also made a rare vegetable delicacy. The food prepared feeds six hundred men, women, and children.

As evening settles in, the sound of a loud horn is heard throughout the entire camp, signifying the food is ready and that the feast has officially begun. There is eating, dancing, singing, and drinking. Merriment goes well into the night as the Pulka people celebrate the possibility of recapturing their homeland. Nine o'clock the feast comes to an end and everyone slowly makes their way home.

Once home, merriment gives way to somber reality, as wives and children think this could be the last time they see their husbands and fathers alive. Fathers and husbands reassure their families that they will return safe and victorious, but deep down they are not certain if they will return at all. Kissing their sons and daughter's good night, the men retire to bed with their wives, for tomorrow the battle against the Ecclesians begins.

Darkness fades and the crimson night sky starts to brighten to a light red hue. People begin to stir, morning has come. All the Pulka men assemble in the open valley area with their shields, armor, and weapons.

Tricar greets his warriors with sharp sickles in his hands. Standing on the hill he shouts, "My brave warriors, I am proud to be your chief. Today we will wage war against the Ecclesians who have killed our brothers and sisters and have stolen our land. Today we right the wrongs and injustices that have been perpetrated against our people and the animals of this realm. We fight for a brighter future for our daughters and our sons. We fight to live free!"

All the warriors raise their weapons and shout, "Tricar! Victory! Tricar! Victory! Tricar! Victory!"

Belix leads the army through the secret passageway down to the icy tundra floor. Tricar and the Chosen Ones are the last ones to exit the small cave. Tricar emerges from the cave and blows his horn two times. Several minutes later, a hundred large white bears and two dozen long white leopards arrive.

Tricar and Belix communicate Titus' plan to the leopards and bears. "Tricar we need two leopards to come with us to the top of the glacier" instructs Titus.

Belix leads the soldiers and animals to the crystal mine controlled by the Ecclesians. The Chosen Ones, Tricar, and two snow leopards head to the top of the glacier where the Ecclesian stronghold resides.

The crystal mine lies five hundred yards from the Ecclesian stronghold. Belix gets his men and the animals in position, awaiting Tricar's signal.

Scanning the Ecclesian escape hatch with his infra-red vision Titus says, "The coast is clear, give the signal."

Tricar gives one long blow on his horn, signaling Belix to attack. The loud trumpet sound causes the Ecclesians to freeze for a moment, before realizing their crystal mine is under attack. Ice Lord Egill, commands the Ecclesian army to attack the intruders and secure the crystal mine.

Four hundred Ecclesian soldiers march out of the large iron door at ground level. The Pulka army manages to kill fifty unarmed miners and ten Ecclesian guards before their army arrives. Belix commands his two hundred soldiers to fall back.

The Ecclesian army full of rage, charge after the retreating Pulka army. Abruptly, the Pulka army stop running and Belix signals the hiding bears and leopards to attack the advancing Ecclesian army from behind.

The unsuspecting Ecclesians yell and scream as they are clawed and bitten to death. Belix commands his army to attack, sandwiching the Ecclesian army in a bloody fight to the death.

~~~

While the chaos of battle ensues, Tricar and the others sneak inside the escape hatch atop the Ecclesian's lair. They find themselves in a small empty
~~~

room with a closed door. Beyond the door is a hallway that leads directly to the Ice Lords' throne room.

Opening the door, they can hear an Ecclesian soldier shouting orders, "Protect the throne room and the Ice Lords with your life."

"How many soldiers are guarding the throne room Titus?" asks Obadiah.

"I can make out a little over twenty guards" answers Titus.

"Are the three Ice Lords in the throne room?" inquires Sakia.

"I see three figures in the back part of the room," says Titus, adjusting his goggles.

"Those are the Ice Lords" states Tricar.

"We need to quickly take out the soldiers before engaging them" directs Titus.

"Attack!" shouts Tricar.

The two leopards run and leap, taking down two soldiers by surprise, biting and clawing them to death. Obadiah fires four arrows each hitting a soldier in the neck. Sakia swings her whip and latches it around a soldier's arm sending electricity through his body.

Seven soldiers fall by the surprise attack. The remaining eighteen soldiers stand close together, raising their shields to form a strong defense that blocks Obadiah's, Sakia's and the leopard's attacks. Keembo with a quick burst of speed runs headlong into the soldiers' shields bowling them over.

Everyone pounces on the fallen soldiers killing all but two. Angered at how quickly his soldiers are defeated, Halfdan points his scepter at the two remaining soldiers, freezing them instantly in a block of ice.

Hyrue, Egill, and Halfdan fight together as one. Hyrue holds a large shield in his left hand and a long broadsword with a blue crystal blade in his right hand. He stands at the left of Halfdan. Egill holds a large shield in his right hand and wields a long spear with a blue crystal tip blade in his left hand. He stands to the right of Halfdan. Halfdan stands arrogantly in the middle wielding his golden scepter, which holds a large white crystal at the end.

"Did you see that? He killed his own men" utters Tiwa.

"You see this is the kind of tyranny the Ice Lords and the Demon King have brought to our ice lands," says a repugnant Tricar.

Everyone stands behind the large pillars in the Ice Lords' throne room. Obadiah and Azra pop out from behind a pillar. Obadiah fires three fiery arrows at the Ice Lords which are blocked by Hyrue's and Egill's shields. Halfdan fires an ice beam at Azra and Obadiah. Azra raises her invisible shield to block the attack. The blast hits Azra's shield covering it with ice, making it impossible for her to move the shield forward.

"I can't move us closer to them from behind my shield. I can't move or break through the frozen ice" explains Azra.

"My arrows are ineffective against their shields" states Obadiah.

"It seems like quickness and agility are in order here. I'll test Halfdan's skills with his scepter" says an excited Sakia.

Leaping into the air, Sakia emerges from behind a pillar. Halfdan shoots three ice beams at her, missing horribly as she hides behind a pillar on the other side of the room.

"It seems Sakia and the snow leopards are the only ones quick enough to avoid Halfdan's ice beams. Tricar, tell the leopards to get as close to them as possible" orders Titus.

The lean, fierce snow leopards have razor-sharp teeth and long sharp claws. Their long white tails wag back and forth as they receive instructions from Tricar.

Having received their instructions, the leopards walk up to Titus and each of them takes a blue crystal knife from Titus' waist with their tail. The leopards swing the knives with their tails like well-trained assassins.

With a loud growl, the leopards jump out and head towards the Ice Lords, bounding left and right. Crisscrossing each other they evade Halfdan's ice beams. Launching into the air, the leopard's attack the Ice Lords with their claws, knives, and teeth. Hyrue and Egill protect Halfdan and themselves with their large shields, deflecting and knocking back the leopards.

Egill thrusts his spear at one of the leopards, rising off the floor. *Clang.* Egill's spear is redirected by one of Obadiah's arrows, saving the leopard from certain death. The leopards quickly run back to the others behind the pillar.

"By now you cowards should know you cannot penetrate our defenses. Soon reinforcements will come and you will be pinned in. I assure you, you will meet a cold, quick death by my hand. But before you die, tell me why you foolishly attacked us and tried to take that which belongs to me?" declares Halfdan.

"You stole our land, killed my people and indiscriminately kill every animal you see. For these crimes, you will die by my hand" replies Tricar Chief of the Pulka clan.

Holding Tricar back Obadiah says, "You also have a piece of gold and silver armor with specific markings on it. We want it."

"Ha! Ha! Ha! You dare enter my castle and try to steal from me! I tell you what, defeat us and you can have the gold and silver shield you seek. It is hidden underneath my throne. However, before I kill you, you will tell me how to unlock its power. As for you Tricar, Chief of the Pulka clan, we defeated you once and let your people live. This time we shall kill every man, woman, and child in your clan" laughs Halfdan with a sinister grin.

"He's right we don't have much time before reinforcements arrive" states Titus.

"Then come up with a plan young man" stresses Tricar in a stern voice.

"The only plan I can come up with is very risky, not all of us will make it out alive."

"My boy, war *is* risky; you risk your life to protect your family and the ones you love. If I must die to save my people, then I will die. Tell us your plan Titus, I know it will work" says Tricar in a reassuring voice.

Apprehensively, Titus explains his plan, "Okay, first we need Sakia and the snow leopards to draw Halfdan's fire. When he attacks them Azra you place a large shield as close to the Ice Lords as you can. The rest of us will run behind it, drawing Halfdan's attention away from Sakia and the snow leopards. At that time Sakia or one of the leopards *must* get the scepter out of Halfdan's possession. Once the scepter's out of his possession we all attack, overwhelm and defeat them."

"Young lad you are right, that is a risky plan. Alright, ladies and gentlemen, you heard the boy, let's take down these three devils. Attack!" yells Tricar.

The snow leopards and Sakia run towards the Ice Lords. Halfdan fires upon them, missing poorly. Azra projects her shield ten yards in front of the three brothers.

"Everyone run now!" screams Azra.

Halfdan seeing the others running towards him turns and shoots his ice beams hitting Azra's shield. Closing in, Sakia swings her whip around Halfdan's scepter sending electricity through it. Halfdan drops the scepter yanking back his burnt hand.

One of the leopards grabs the scepter in its mouth. Egill thrusts his spear into the leopard's rib cage and through its heart. Hyrue smashes Sakia in the face with his shield sending her flying, unconscious across the room. Tiwa runs over to check on Sakia.

Seeing his leopard friend go down, Tricar screams out, "NO!" and runs with both sickles drawn straight towards Egill. Simultaneously, Obadiah shoots arrows at Halfdan's hand as he tries to retrieve his scepter.

Keembo pulls out his daggers and runs to engage Hyrue who hands his shield over to Halfdan. Hyrue swings his long broadsword down at Keembo who blocks it with both daggers. Halfdan uses Hyrue's shield to block Obadiah's arrows and tries to regain his scepter.

Inches away from securing his scepter Halfdan says, "My scepter will change the course of this battle back in my favor. What is this? Something blocks my hand from recovering my scepter. It is the little girl, it must be her doing!"

Halfdan looks up at Azra who projects an invisible barrier around Halfdan's scepter. Titus extends his steel baton as he and Obadiah stand in front of Azra, to fight a fast approaching Halfdan. Tricar and the other snow leopard are engaged in battle with Egill. Keembo is in combat with Hyrue. Sakia is out cold being attended to by Tiwa, who is oblivious to the battles raging on behind her.

Halfdan continues to block Obadiah's arrows and Titus' steel baton with his shield. Halfdan rushes hard into Obadiah with his shield knocking him to the ground, the force of the impact causes Obadiah to drop his ivory bow. Swinging his shield hard with his right hand, Halfdan smacks Titus across the head and shoulder, knocking him to the ground.

"You're next little girl" sneers Halfdan at Azra. Raising his shield to strike Azra in the head, Halfdan's attack is blocked by an invisible shield.

"Egill, Hyrue grab the scepter....it is free. I am pretty sure you can't protect yourself and put a shield around my scepter at the same time little girl" yells Halfdan.

"Tiwa help us! We need your help! Now!" screams Azra.

Hearing Azra call out her name, Tiwa snaps out of her daze. Turning around she sees the battles being fought and hears Halfdan telling his brothers to get the scepter. She pulls out three boomerangs and hurls them as hard as she can at the back of the heads of the unsuspecting Ice Lords.

Slicing through the air the boomerangs violently strike Egill, Hyrue, and Halfdan in the side of their heads knocking them out cold. Grabbing Halfdan's scepter, Tricar, and the snow leopard race to get outside.

"Secure the enemy. I will be back soon" shouts Tricar, as he turns the corner.

Tricar and the snow leopard exit the escape hatch at the top of the glacier, making their way down to the warring armies below.

Keembo, Titus, and Obadiah tie up the unconscious Ice Lords.

Azra rubs her hand over the crimson red and white fur of the fallen leopard and says, "I can't save her. She is already dead." Azra picks up the blue crystal knife next to the leopard's tail and retrieves Sakia's whip.

"Tiwa, how is Sakia?" asks Azra.

"Battered and bruised, but she'll live."

Keembo removes Halfdan's throne revealing a frozen shield underneath. Taking out his daggers, Keembo chips away at the ice until he frees the shield. The silver and gold oval-shaped shield has the symbols Alpha and Omega etched on it. "We have another piece to the Armor of God!" bellows Keembo.

~~~

The ambush by the Pulka clan and the animals quickly kill a hundred Ecclesian soldiers. The remaining soldiers regroup and mount a strong offensive attack using their superior weapons. Their blue crystal weapons easily penetrate the Pulka clan's shields rendering them useless.

As the war rages on more bears and leopards fall to the overpowering might of the Ecclesian Army. The battle gradually shifts in the Ecclesians favor. A third of the Pulka warriors along with half the bears and leopards fall in battle.

Belix calls for the animals and his warriors to retreat. The Ecclesians chase after them determined to crush the invading army. The retreat abruptly stops when Belix and his army find themselves boxed in by a tall wall of glacial ice.

Belix yells out, "Turn around and fight! If we are to die today, then we will take as many Ecclesian scum with us as we can!"

The Ecclesians raise their shields and lower their spears to impale their enemies. Victory is imminent.
~~~

Suddenly the sound of a loud piercing horn halts the marching Ecclesians. Standing on top of the glacial wall, Tricar raises Halfdan's scepter in the air with his right hand and shouts, "Ecclesians, your Ice Lords have been defeated. I now wield Halfdan's scepter of power!"

Shooting an ice beam at the Ecclesian Army, Tricar freezes fifteen soldiers. "You have the choice to surrender or die. Which do you choose?" demands Tricar.

Knowing their Lords have been defeated and looking at their frozen comrades, the Ecclesian Army reluctantly surrenders, putting down their shields and spears.

Belix shouts out, "Seize their weapons men and take them back to our new home!."

Having secured the prisoners of war, Belix joins Tricar and the snow leopard in the Ice Lords throne room.

"I see you have found what you seek. May I look at it?" asks Tricar, holding Halfdan's scepter in his hand. Keembo warily shows Tricar the Shield of Faith.

"This is an exquisite shield. You have kept your end of the bargain in helping my people overthrow the Ice Lords, so I will keep my end of the bargain. The shield is yours to keep. We have much to celebrate and mourn about. My people and I will reside in our new home tonight. Rest and make yourselves at home. Belix have some food and water brought up for our friends, take the Ice Lords to an isolated cell and carry out our fallen ally" instructs Tricar in a somber voice.

Tricar looks at the Chosen Ones and says, "Before I take my leave, is everyone alright?"

"We're fine, thank you. Just have someone hurry up with the food will ya" utters Sakia, rubbing her head.

They all laugh and Tricar and his men leave the throne room. Before leaving, the snow leopard hands Titus his blue crystal knife back with his tail, then slowly walks out.

"Sakia, I'd like to have a word with you alone outside," says Keembo.

"Alright, let's go" responds Sakia, receiving her whip back from Azra.

"I'll go with you guys" volunteers Azra.

"We don't need a babysitter, Azra. Besides, I said I want to speak with Sakia alone" states Keembo emphatically.

"Azra everything will be fine. Just be sure to save us some food for when we get back" jokes Sakia.

Keembo and Sakia exit the escape hatch and stand a few feet from each other on top of the icy glacier. Keembo's hands rest on his daggers and Sakia's right-hand rests on her whip. They stand silently staring at each other for two minutes, neither moving a muscle.

Then in a low voice, Keembo says, "I forgive you Sakia."

Sakia's hand slides off her whip.

"I forgive you, but my trust in you has been shattered" continues Keembo.

"I do plan to rebuild your trust in me through my actions. I hope over time, one day, we can be good friends again" responds Sakia sincerely.

"Fair enough" Keembo replies.

Tiwa pops her head out of the escape hatch and says, "Food is here, and no, I don't see any blood, Azra."

Sakia and Keembo chuckle as the tension subsides and they head inside to eat with the others.

Night arrives as does Tricar and Belix with the Chosen One's gear that was left in the mountains. Titus immediately looks through his gear to see if his toolkit is intact. Titus lets out a loud sigh of relief, as all eyes turn to gaze upon him.

"I was looking for my toolkit. I needed something in it" says Titus in a low mumble.

"So my friends, where does your journey lead you next?" inquires Tricar.

"There are two more regions we must venture to on our quest, the Sky Citadel, and the Defiled Marshlands. There lay the final two pieces of the armor we seek" shares Obadiah. An uneasiness comes over Tricar's face as Obadiah finishes his sentence.

"To go to the Marshlands is a fool's errand. There is a reason that place is called the Defiled Marshlands. Belix is my witness that I fear no man or beast, but that witch, causes even me to pause. Legend has it that the Defiled Marshlands are protected by powerful creatures and if you happen to make it past them, you still would have to face the witch and her endless army of undead souls."

"Well, we'll just go to the Sky Citadel first" interjects Sakia.

"Alas, the only way to reach the Sky Citadel is through the Defiled Marshlands. It is said the witch possesses powerful dark magic. From the determination, on your faces, I see I cannot dissuade you from traveling there. Therefore, I will aid you as much as I can. Titus, you are an alchemist, correct?" asks Tricar.

"Not really, I'm more of a scientist" explains Titus.

"Same thing.... Anyway! I found another white crystal in Halfdan's quarters. It is the exact same shape and size as the one in my new scepter. Here, it is yours" says Tricar, as he hands the crystal to Titus.

"Thank you, Tricar!" exclaims an awestruck Titus.

"Little girl - I mean Azra, come hither, I have something for you as well. You are an herbalist correct?" asks Tricar.

"Yes, I make potions from herbs" replies Azra.

"An herbalist, that's what I said…. Anyway! I give you the scroll of invisibility, to make invisibility potions. Here take all the lichen that I have and collect as much as you can, for lichen will not grow here again until next summer" says Tricar.

"Thank you very much!" shouts Azra, giving him a big hug.

"My people will begin settling into our new home immediately. You are welcome to stay as long as you like" offers Tricar.

"Thank you for the offer, but we will be leaving for the Defiled Marshlands tomorrow" states Obadiah.

"Then I bid you all good night."

The Chosen One's camp out in the throne room for the night, exhausted from the day's battle.

All rise to a cool, brisk sunny day. Packed and ready to leave, breakfast is the last meal shared with the Pulka clan. Tears are shed and hugs exchanged.

"How did you sleep Keembo?" asks Tricar.

"The last two days my sleep has been peaceful. Thank you for your encouraging words of wisdom, both my heart and mind are at peace" declares Keembo with a slight nod.

"You are welcome my son," says Tricar, placing his hand on Keembo's shoulder and addressing the others.

"Azra you can find lichen at the base of the mountains. Follow the water's current heading west, it will take you into the Defiled Marshlands. My people and I thank you for helping us reclaim our land. Good luck and farewell."

Waving goodbye, they make the long trek back to their original camp near the water. "Keembo, when we get back to camp can you help me cook the rest of the bear meat?" asks Obadiah.

"Sure, I'll give you a hand" replies Keembo.

"I need to collect as much lichen as I can. Who wants to come with me?" asks an overly-excited Azra.

"I really don't feel like cooking, so I'll come with you," says Sakia.

"Titus, are you going with Azra?" asks Tiwa.

"Oh, no. I'm going back to camp to work on creating my own Ice Scepter" states Titus.

"Yea, that sounds like fun. I think I'll hang out with the girls" says Tiwa.

"Okay suit yourself, but don't ask to shoot it when I'm done" jokes Titus.

"Make sure you're back before nightfall" instructs Obadiah.

"Alright, dad!" shouts Sakia sarcastically.

They part ways, the guys heading back to camp and the girls heading towards the mountains.

Keembo puts the last piece of bear meat on the fire as the sun hides behind the snow-capped mountains. The girls arrive back in camp listless and tired, except

Azra who skips into camp, smiling with a bag full of lichen.

"Welcome back, ladies" greets Obadiah.

"Yeah, yeah," says a visibly bothered Tiwa.

"My hands stink from those nasty plants. Where's the soap" murmurs Sakia, walking into the shelter.

"Well, I had a great time. I think we collected all the lichen in this region! Hey girls want to help me wash the herbs we collected?" asks Azra.

Tiwa and Sakia both respond with a resounding, "NO!"

"Uh, I would leave them alone if I were you, Azra. I'll help you wash them. We better hurry before it gets completely dark" says Obadiah, as he and Azra walk down to the water.

"Yes! That's it! It should work now!" shouts Titus, running out of the shelter.

Yelling at Obadiah, Titus screams, "Obadiah shoot one of your regular arrows my way, I want to test my new ice ray."

Obadiah shoots an arrow in Titus' direction from the water. Titus squeezes a device that fits in the palm of his hand. Instantly an ice beam shoots from the large white crystal embedded in the ice ray, hitting Obadiah's arrow in mid-air. Frozen solid the arrow falls to the ground and shatters.

"It works! It works!" shouts Titus.

"Wow, that thing fires just like Halfdan's scepter," says an astonished Keembo.

Filled with excitement, Titus blurts out, "Oh yeah! Now, who's afraid of the big bad witch? Not me, I'll freeze her eyebrows off. I'll freeze the wart off her nose. I'll, I'll-."

"Calm down Titus for all we know your ice ray may not even work against her dark magic" quips Sakia.

"No we don't, but we'll find out soon enough. I was thinking of adding a freezing element to your whip, but it might not work against the witch's dark magic" comments Titus, walking off to practice his aim with his new ice ray.

"Adding a freezing element to my whip would be a great idea, Titus! Hey Titus, wait up. Let's talk about this" yells Sakia, running after Titus.

Laughing and shaking her head Tiwa says, "Things seem to be getting back to normal, wouldn't you say Keembo?"

"Yes, things seem to be moving in that direction. Dinner's ready; let's round-up everyone while it's still hot" says Keembo.

Tiwa and Keembo get the others for dinner. They eat and talk awhile before going to sleep. The cold wind howls past their shelter as they sleep. Only Azra stays up, preparing invisibility potions. Azra uses all the lichen to make ten vials of new potions before going to bed.

Obadiah is the first to rise and the others quietly stretch and yawn as they get up and start to prepare for their journey to the Defiled Marshlands. "Wake up Azra, it's time to go. Everyone has packed their bags and Keembo has placed the boat near the water's edge. Hurry up and pack your stuff. Here eat this" says Obadiah, handing Azra some cooked fish for breakfast.

"Thank you, Obadiah, I'll be ready in fifteen minutes" replies Azra.

Thirty minutes later, Azra comes out of the ice shelter. All eyes rest upon her.

"What took you so long? What were you doing in there?" asks a bothered Titus.

"I was combing my hair and getting ready" responds Azra.

"Leave her alone Titus, she's ready now," says Tiwa, as the girls laugh out loud. The guys shake their heads as Titus quips, "I tell ya, girls will make you late to your own funeral."

As they walk to the boat Sakia says, "I think we should speak with the Spirit before we sail to the Defiled Marshlands."

They all agree and quickly build an ice altar. Azra places the red ruby on top of the altar, summoning the Spirit of Truth.

"Congratulations Chosen Ones on retrieving the Shield of Faith, which can quench all the fiery darts of the Wicked One. The Shield of Faith will strengthen your belief in what the Creator has established as true in your worlds. Keembo, you have chosen wisely in forgiving Sakia. I command the shackles of loneliness and bitterness be released from your heart."

Instantly, unseen spiritual chains break loose from around Keembo's heart. Keembo takes several deep breaths and touches his heart, as a huge heaviness lifts and a feeling of peace settles in.

"Keembo you have experienced firsthand how the supernatural power of forgiveness can free a soul from the bondage of bitterness and its companion, loneliness. My Chosen Ones in the upcoming battle you will face natural and supernatural enemies. You will only be able to defeat these supernatural enemies by using supernatural weapons. You must believe and have faith that despite what you see in the natural, these spiritual weapons will work. *Songs of Deliverance* will be the spiritual weapon you will need to defeat the demons you face. Sing this verse several times, *The Creator fights for me. He gives me the victory.*"

With a half-laugh Titus says, "Are you telling me we're supposed to defeat a bunch of demons with a song? That's kind of hard to believe."

"Titus, of all the Chosen Ones you are the most logical. You use science to explain natural phenomena, but science cannot always explain the supernatural. It will be harder for you to believe than anyone else because you rely too much on what you see. Therefore, you will wield the Shield of Faith. It will remind you that faith is the key that activates supernatural weapons, even when you cannot see it with your natural eye."

Titus remains quiet at the saying of the Spirit.

"Tiwa, you are a Chosen One from this world. You are just as vital and important as any of the other Chosen Ones. The Righteous One chose you and called you by name before you were even born" says the Spirit.

"I feel strengthened and more confident by your words," says Tiwa.

"You all have grown and matured much through your journeys and trials. There are only two pieces of armor left, the Boots of Peace and the Sword of the Spirit. Remember, only together, can you defeat the Wicked One and retrieve the rest of the Armor of God. Also, remember when your hearts are still and full of faith you will hear me speak to you. Farewell, my Chosen Ones and remember what I have spoken to you."

The Spirit of Truth disappears.

CHAPTER 12

DEFILED MARSHLANDS

zra puts the spirit stone back into her pouch and gives everybody a healing potion to hold on to. Keembo puts the blue crystal spears into the boat along with everyone's bags. Waving goodbye to the Arctic Plains, the Chosen Ones shove off heading west towards the Defiled Marshlands.

Sakia is the first one to break the silence, "Tiwa it's awesome, you're officially one of us. How do you feel?"

"I feel fantastic! For the first time in my life, I have real purpose and hope for my life. I am no longer a slave. I am a Chosen One of the Creator" declares Tiwa boldly and confidently.

"I must admit I didn't see this one coming, but you've been an integral part of the team since we've been here Tiwa," says Obadiah.

"Thank you. You all feel like family to me, even you Keembo" says Tiwa emotionally.

"Yea, yea. I feel the same way too. Don't go getting all mushy on me" says Keembo, wiping his eyes.

"Are you crying big guy?" asks Titus.

"No. I just got something in my eyes" explains Keembo.

"Yeah, a tear. Go ahead and let it all out Keembo, I hear crying is good for the soul" grins Titus.

Keembo raises an oar out of the water to hit Titus with.

"Keembo put that oar down" fusses Azra in a gentle voice, holding her hands up.

"Naw, that little twerp keeps pushing me" grunts Keembo.

"It's okay to show your emotions Keembo" jabs, Titus.

"Don't you say another word Titus" reprimands Azra.

"What? What makes you think I'd say something?" smiles Titus.

"Keembo, I'm proud of you. You forgave Sakia and as a result, the Spirit set your bound heart free. That's wonderful" comments Azra.

Putting the oar back into the water Keembo says, "I feel really good right now, my heart's at peace. I've never felt this peaceful and happy in my life. I'm feeling all these different kinds of emotions for all of you guys. It's kind of weird. Good, but weird. I feel like a new person.

Now, if only 'Doubting Titus' would change, the world would be a better place."

"Excuse me! Doughboy, are you talking about me? I don't doubt what I can see and I have faith in things I cannot see. So what are you talking about *'Doubting Titus'*?" says Titus angrily.

"Well, the Spirit of Truth said that you're more logical than all of us and that it would be harder for you to believe than the rest of us. So, *'Doubting Titus'* seems to fit. By the way, hold on to the Shield of Faith, will ya?" smirks Keembo, handing Titus the shield.

Titus says nothing as he examines the Shield of Faith.

Riding the river's current for several long hours, a noticeable change in the weather occurs. Touching the water and taking off his bearskin coat Obadiah says, "We're in warmer waters now. You can take off your coats and boots if you like."

"We can also prepare for a safe landing because I see land up ahead" points Titus.

"Hey, guys the water is starting to turn a dirty brown color. What's going on?" inquires Azra.

"I'm not sure but it seems to be getting darker and darker the closer we get to land" utters Titus.

~~~
~~~

Every world has a Defiled Marshlands, where evil takes root and grows. It is the place the Wicked One goes to when tempting new worlds and seeking new souls. He lures them with the promise of untold riches and ultimate power. Unwittingly, they become slaves to an unmerciful tyrant, who wishes to kill, steal, and destroy everything good in their lives. The Demon King knows the more souls who pledge their allegiance to him, the stronger his power becomes in that world.

The Defiled Marshlands is a vast, dense, murky swamp engulfed by dark waters. Dryland protrusions holding clusters of fat mossy trees litter the wasteland. Only animals of prey live here, alligators, pythons, large snapping turtles, and Baboon Spiders. Sitting atop the most dangerous creatures list is the witch. She is the sole ruler of the Defiled Marshlands and has pledged her allegiance to the Demon King.

~~~

Approaching land, the rowboat gets bumped from underneath and almost capsizes.

"What in the world was that?" screams Sakia.

"Something big I know that" exclaims Obadiah.

"I'm scared" frets Azra in a low voice.

"Hold on a second let me switch to infra-red vision. Oh my gosh!" yells Titus as he continues, "There's some
~~~

kind of gigantic snake swimming beneath us. It's coming right at us! Fast!"

Ramming into the rowboat a giant, green, fifty-foot long Anaconda, with black zigzag lines down its entire body, wraps its midsection around the boat. Azra raises a shield surrounding the boat, saving it from the crushing power of the Giant Anaconda.

As the Anaconda tightens its grip, Azra cries out, "The mental pressure is getting more intense as the snake tightens its grip. I won't be able to keep it from crushing us much longer."

As the snake's body twists, it lifts the boat out of the water and over dry land.

"Azra open a hole in your shield so we can jump out" instructs Titus.

Azra focuses and opens a hole in her shield. Tossing everything out of the boat they all jump four feet to the ground before Azra releases her shield. The boat is crushed into splinters by the Giant Anaconda.

"Sakia, Obadiah get to higher ground and draw the snake's attention away from us! Keembo what kind of weapon can we use to impale that giant snake?" bellows out Titus.

Looking around, Keembo uproots a tall Cedar tree.

"Tiwa, I need your help in turning this tree into a sharp pointy stick. I'll impale the snake with it" says Keembo.

"Perfect" nods Titus, as Tiwa goes to work sharpening the tree with her four boomerangs.

Just as it lifts its head out of the water Obadiah shoots the snake with four fiery arrows. Angered, the Giant Anaconda slithers towards Obadiah with its mouth wide open.

"Quickly, get on!" yells Sakia, securing her whip to a nearby tree branch. Obadiah jumps onto Sakia's back, swinging away they narrowly escape the Anaconda's deadly bite. Missing, the large snake slams to the ground.

Hurling her boomerangs, Tiwa hits the snake in the head drawing its ire. Whirling around with its mouth wide open, the snake lunges to swallow the four who are still on the ground.

With both hands, Keembo swings the sharp pointy tree up through the roof of the Anaconda's mouth and out the back of its head. The Giant Anaconda falls to the ground, curling and withering violently back and forth as blood streams from its head. The withering starts to slow and becomes less violent until it stops altogether. The Giant Anaconda is dead.

"Welcome to the Defiled Marshlands!" shouts Keembo.

The Chosen Ones regroup, gather their belongings and head deeper into the Marshlands in search of a place to make camp. A quarter-mile in, they find a dry mound suitable to make camp.

"I don't feel safe sleeping outside in a swamp full of killer animals. We have nothing to cover or hide us from them while we're sleeping" states Azra.

"I agree with Azra if we had some kind of tarp we could make a tent that would cover us at night," says Sakia.

"A tent! That's a great idea Sakia and I know where we can get a tarp. Better yet, how about a snakeskin tarp? I bet no animals will come near our camp tonight, fearing they might become snake food. Who wants to skin a snake?" asks Obadiah.

"I'll skin it since I killed it" volunteers Keembo.

"I'll give you a hand... or four," says Tiwa.

Titus gives Tiwa his two blue crystal knives to use. Obadiah gives his knife to Keembo. Keembo also grabs a crystal tipped spear, as he and Tiwa head back to where they killed the Giant Anaconda.

It takes three hours to skin the Giant Anaconda. Tiwa and Keembo return to camp with the snakeskin and large chunks of meat. To Keembo's surprise a fire and a long free-standing, wooden structure has already been made.

"Impressive. I thought when I got back here, I'd have to build our living structure as well" utters Keembo.

"We can't let you go around thinking you do everything now can we?" responds Sakia.

"Fair enough. Give me a hand securing the snakeskin tarp over this structure" barks Keembo.

"A control freak and a slave driver" mutters Sakia under her breath.

"Did you say something Sakia? I didn't hear you?" asks Keembo.

"I said I'd love to. You really need to get your ears checked out Keembo" replies Sakia.

"Dinner will be ready shortly. I found some edible mushrooms for us to eat" says Azra.

As the sun goes down a dense fog engulfs the marshland. An eerie evil presence can be felt spreading across the area.

"Does anyone besides me feel a creepy sensation around here?" inquires Azra.

"I feel it, Azra" states Tiwa.

"The witch or demons must be conjuring up some evil magic. Maybe we should check it out" suggests Obadiah.

"Check it out! Have you lost your mind, Obadiah? How many of those mushrooms did you eat? You do realize we can't see a thing out there in this thick fog. Well, you guys can't, I have my goggles. Nevertheless, you can count me out. I'm staying right here in this tent until I can see daylight" snaps Titus.

"I'm with Titus on this one, Obadiah. And how many mushrooms did you eat?" asks Keembo.

"I only ate six. Why?" retorts Obadiah.

"Because you're not thinking like your normal self. Azra, no more mushrooms for dinner. We should wait out the night here and find out what's going on in the morning" suggests Keembo.

Everyone agrees and tries to get some sleep.

The ominous noises of the night give way to a still and quiet morning. Dawn comes and the Chosen Ones awaken to find the thick dense fog completely gone. The eerie evil presence they felt last night has also disappeared.

Finishing breakfast, Obadiah says, "We should find the source of the evil presence we felt last night, while the sun is still out."

"I'll climb up a tree and take a look around" states Sakia.

Using her whip and agility, Sakia scampers up a nearby tree. Looking over the Defiled Marshlands, she notices a hill in the distance which appears to have three structures on it. Making her way back down, Sakia tells the others what she saw.

Collecting their weapons and gathering their gear, the Chosen Ones head out in the direction Sakia pointed out.

"I haven't noticed you wearing that necklace before Titus," says Tiwa.

"Oh, I just put a chain on my new handheld ice ray. It makes it easier to carry. Especially now that I have to carry the Shield of Faith."

Walking up the hill, they notice three structures that are broken down and in ruins. The middle structure is the ruins of a church or temple. The two structures beside it are broken down pillars, looming above two holes in the ground. The two holes have stairs leading down into underground catacombs. The tombs are home to many dead warriors.

As the Chosen Ones enter the dilapidated temple, the whole hill begins to shake from a violent earthquake, knocking them to the ground. Getting up, they hear noises coming from the holes in the ground.

"We better split up and check out those noises. Obadiah, Azra, and Sakia you three check out the hole on the left. Tiwa, Keembo and I will check out the other one. We meet back here when we're finished. Be careful everyone" instructs Titus, as the team splits up and enters their respective catacombs.

"It's dark down here. How are we supposed to see anything? Obadiah has the fiery arrows" states Keembo. Reaching into his bag Titus hands Keembo his yellow crystal.

"Here Keembo, take this light stone. Hit it once and it'll light up, as bright as a lantern. Keep it, I have night vision."

Turning on their light stones, Tiwa and Keembo walk in front of Titus down the catacomb stairs. The loud noises echoing through the catacombs are the sounds of stones splitting open and smashing to the ground.

"Who or what could be making all that noise?" inquires Tiwa, as they reach the bottom of the stairs.

Looking around Titus says, "I see movement in the room to our left. Wait, I also see movement in the room to our right. Turn off your light stones."

Keembo and Tiwa turn off their light stones. "Tiwa toss your light stone in the room to our left and Keembo toss yours in the room to our right. Once they hit the ground and light up, you'll be able to see what's coming."

When the two stones hit the ground, they illuminate their respective rooms revealing dozens of dead warriors coming out of their tombs and advancing towards them.

"Destroy them, destroy them all!" yells Titus.

~~~

Obadiah ignites a fiery arrow to light the way as he begins to walk down the catacomb stairs. Azra and Sakia pull out and turn on their light stones.

"We can make our own light now" states Azra.
~~~

"Good, the more light the better" responds Obadiah.

"This place reminds me of the catacombs in my clan's temple back home. I hope that noise isn't the sound of tombs breaking open" comments Sakia, grabbing her metal whip.

Waiting at the bottom of the stairs are four undead warriors.

"Ahhh!" shouts Azra at the sight of the walking dead.

Quickly, Obadiah shoots two of them in the chest with his fiery arrows. The undead warriors explode into clay and ash. Sakia swings her electric whip cutting the other two undead warriors in half. They fall to the ground and break into pieces.

Reaching the bottom of the stairs, Obadiah says, "There are dozens of them coming from both sides."

"Then I guess they'll have to die all over again and I have just the plan to do it. Azra, block the entryway to the room on the right with your shield; this will hold the creatures in that room at bay while Obadiah and I eliminate the walking corpses in this room. Once we're done here, we'll do the same thing to the other" smirks Sakia.

"Sounds like a good plan to me, Captain Sakia," says Azra, putting up an invisible shield blocking the entryway to the room on her right.

Obadiah repeatedly fires his arrows destroying dozens of undead warriors. Sakia slashes her whip back and forth destroying three warriors per swing. Several minutes of nonstop fighting results in well over a hundred dead corpses lying in ashes.

"How are you holding up?" asks Sakia.

"I'm fine but my arm is starting to get a little tired" responds Obadiah.

"Mine too. We only have one more room to go, I hope. You did great Azra, now release your shield. It's time for these warriors to go back where they came from" states a resolute Sakia.

Several more minutes of fighting yield the same results, lots of broken clay and ash on the floor. Reaching the back end of the room, they find a corridor leading into a much larger room.

~~~

Keembo dashes into the left room smashing dead warriors to pieces with his fists. Titus and Tiwa fight the undead corpses in the room to the right. Tiwa hurls four boomerangs into the crowd of dead warriors; each boomerang shatters five warriors before coming back to her hands. Titus uses his ice ray to freeze any close approaching corpses.

Picking up bodies and smashing them into the walls, the floor and each other, Keembo quickly clears out the left room of all its attackers. Tiwa continues to throw her boomerangs shattering frozen and unfrozen
~~~

enemies alike until there is nothing left but puddles of wet ash and clay laying on the floor.

"We defeated them all! That was fun" says Tiwa breathing heavily.

"Tiwa, do you see something over there?" asks Titus.

"I can't see anything, let me grab a light stone and take a closer look. Hey Keembo, grab the other light stone and come over here" directs Tiwa.

Keembo collects his light stone and jogs over to the others inquiring, "What is it? What did you find? What's that strange light?"

~~~

Walking through the corridor, Obadiah, Azra, and Sakia enter a wide room. In the corner, they see a large stone doorway covered with ancient symbols. A pulsating, green light swirls inside the door's archways.

Getting closer, Azra concludes, "That must be a portal. It's similar to the one we used to enter Demon's Realm. Except this one is green and gives off an eerie, evil vibe."

Suddenly, the ground starts to vibrate and shake. The green light in the portal starts to get bigger and brighter.

"The portal has been activated! Something or someone is about to come through. Quickly get against the wall" shouts Sakia.
~~~

The three brace themselves against the wall waiting for who or what passes through the portal.

~~~

A burst of bright light explodes into the room from the portal. As their eyes adjust from the blinding light, Tiwa, Keembo, and Titus see nine creatures hovering in the center of the room.

In a sinister, guttural voice one of the creatures growl, "These are the ones we were sent to exterminate."

"What are these creatures?" asks Tiwa.

"These must be the demons the Spirit said we would face. They're a lot uglier than I imagined" answers Keembo.

The crimson red and black demons are three feet tall with bat-like wings. They have long pointy ears and horns that extend from the top of their heads. The demons have sharp facial features and rigid jawlines. They have three long claws for hands and feet. Their fleshy, human-like skin is covered with a thin layer of scales. Moving behind them is a long, thick, ominous tail with a sharp arrow tip at the end.

The demons have come from the Infernal Pit with one objective in mind: kill the Chosen Ones and take back the Armor of God.

Having passed through the portal, the demons calmly approach their victims saying, "We will kill you
~~~

slowly and painfully. Then once you are dead, we will drag your souls to the pit and torment you for all eternity." They screech and laugh in a creepy tone as they continue to advance towards the Chosen Ones.

~~~

"Shoot them, Obadiah!" screams Azra.

Firing his bow, Obadiah releases several arrows that pass right through the demons, having no effect. Sakia swings her whip and it passes harmlessly through them.

"I'll block them with my shield!" hollers Azra. The demons pass through Azra's shield unhindered.

"Hey guys, I think we're in trouble here. I hope that others are faring better than we are" says Sakia.

~~~

Keembo pulls out his daggers and charges the demons, swinging wildly. A demon catches Keembo's right arm and immediately it begins to burn. Keembo lets out a loud scream as the demon hurls him across the room and into the wall.

"What the-? Did you see how they man-handled Keembo?" cries out Titus, as he fires an ice beam at the demons.

"It went right through them. Tiwa, try your boomerangs" Titus shouts.

Tiwa hurls her boomerangs at the demons to no avail.

"Your natural weapons are useless against us. Accept your fate and die" shrieks a demon, swinging its spear-tipped tail towards Titus' head.

Raising the Shield of Faith, Titus deflects the demons attack. The surprised demon says, "The Shield of Faith, but you do not have the Sword of the Spirit. Ha, ha, ha. Then you can not harm us and you can only block our attacks for so long human."

"Tiwa, run! Try to get out of here and find the others" yells Titus.

Tiwa runs out of the room and several demons follow her. Keembo rises to his feet holding his badly burned arm as three demons close in on him. Titus swings the Shield of Faith knocking a demon to the ground.

"I can still defeat you with this shield!" hollers Titus at the demons.

"You cannot defeat the three of us together mortal," says a demon as the three of them converge on him.

Keembo faintly hears singing coming from the other room. Who could be singing at a time like this, he thinks. Then, he remembers what the Spirit of Truth said about the *Songs of Deliverance.*

Instantly, Keembo remembers the words to the song and begins to sing, "The Creator fights for me. He gives me the victory."

Stopping in their tracks and putting their claws over their ears, the three demons yell, "Stop singing!"

Keembo keeps singing as the demons scream in agony and pain. "I can't stand this. Retreat!" screams a demon as the three flies back through the portal.

With the three demons gone, Keembo runs to go check on Tiwa, leaving Titus alone. The demons attack Titus simultaneously. He blocks two of their attacks with his shield, but the third demon stabs him in the leg with its tail, knocking him to the ground and leaving a large gaping hole in his leg. Blood oozes out of Titus' leg as the demons gloat over him.

"Foolish, prideful mortal, you thought you could defeat supernatural beings using natural means. Now you will die a fool's death" screeches a demon.

"The Creator fights for me. He gives me the victory" sings Titus.

"Hey, stop. What are you doing?" screeches the demons.

"I'm defeating supernatural beings by using supernatural means" stammers Titus, holding his bleeding leg and continuing to sing.

"Stop singing or we will kill you" scream the demons in agony.

"His praise is killing us, we must flee" the three demons cry out, as they fly back through the portal.

Titus continues to sing the *Songs of Deliverance* as Tiwa and Keembo run into the room and kneel by his side.

"Titus are you okay? You're losing a lot of blood. Did you drink your healing potion?" inquires Tiwa, looking into Titus' eyes.

Titus shakes his head, signifying no.

Tiwa holds Titus' head up as he drinks the healing potion.

Azra, Obadiah, and Sakia enter the room where Tiwa, Keembo, and Titus are. "Hey, guys, what happened here? Is Titus okay?" asks Sakia.

"He'll be fine. We just gave him a healing potion" responds Tiwa.

"Let me take a look at that wound. I'll need to treat the outside of the wound as well" states Azra putting medicinal herbs on the outside of Titus' leg.

"You haven't destroyed the portal yet!" shouts Obadiah.

"I'll destroy it," says Keembo calmly.

Keembo picks up a stone block from off the floor and starts bashing the portal until the green light flickers out and the stone portal collapses to the ground.

"How did you guys escape your battle without any injuries?" inquires Tiwa.

"Well you see, the three of us were surrounded by demons and Sakia started singing in this high pitched, screechy voice. I covered my ears and looking up I saw the demons covering their ears too" explains Obadiah.

"Wait a minute now Obadiah" interrupts Sakia.

"Let me finish. Azra and I quickly realized that Sakia was singing the *Songs of Deliverance* and we joined in, sending those grotesque demons back where they came from. We destroyed the portal and came looking for you guys" finishes Obadiah.

"I'm glad everyone's okay. Azra, it's been five minutes already. Why isn't Titus' wound healed yet?" inquires Tiwa.

"There appear to be sulfur granules in his wound still burning his leg. The healing potion and the ointment I applied will heal him, but it'll take longer before his wound is totally healed" informs Azra, turning her attention towards Keembo. "Keembo?"

"I know. I know. Here I come, doctor Azra" utters Keembo.

"Let me see your arm. The same thing is happening to you. The sulfur granules are continuing to burn through your skin. Drink a healing potion and I'll put some ointment on the burnt spots. You'll be good to go in no time" says Azra.

"Thanks, doc" Keembo replies.

Titus stands up and starts to walk around. "My legs totally healed. Thanks, Azra, now let's get out of this death pit. I've been down here long enough" states Titus, picking up his shield.

Reaching the top of the stairs, feeling the sunshine on their faces, Azra says, "Let there be light. I hate dark creepy places. Can we go back to camp now?"

"We still have four hours of daylight left. We should take this time to find the witch's hideout" suggests Obadiah.

"I agree with Obadiah. The sooner we find and defeat the witch, the sooner we can get out of this God-forsaken place" remarks Tiwa.

Everyone nods in agreement except Azra. "Alright. I guess I'm outvoted again. Fine, let's go find this wicked old witch" murmurs Azra.

Azra pulls Keembo aside to speak with him. "I thought you were on my side, Keembo."

"I am" Keembo replies.

"Then why did you vote against me?" says Azra with her hands on her hips.

"Azra I was looking at the bigger picture. You can't take this personally" responds Keembo.

"I'm not, Keembo. Do you know how many times I saved your life?" Azra ensues.

"Aw, not this again," says Keembo, throwing his hands up in the air.

Azra's lips continue to move as Keembo quickens his pace to catch up with the others.

After an hour of walking over land and trudging through muddy swamp water, they stop to rest and eat on top of a hill. Sakia scrambles up a tree and scans the area.

"I see smoke rising above the trees to the east of us. It could be the witch's hideout."

"Okay break time is over. We need to locate the source of that smoke" barks out, Obadiah.

"You're aware that if the source of the smoke is indeed the witch's hideout, she'll probably notice us approaching from a ways off. I have an idea, and for it to work we need to implement it starting right now" Titus says.

Wading through blackened waters, the Chosen Ones come upon a small open area surrounded by a circle of thick, interwoven trees. Inside the circle of trees is a raggedy, old cabin with a fireplace burning inside. On the right side of the house is a beautiful garden full of colorful flowers and growing vegetables.

Approaching the cabin Sakia questions, "What is that? This can't be the witch's hideout."

At that moment a young, beautiful woman emerges from the cabin and announces, "Oh, I see you are admiring my garden. All women love to look at beautiful things and a girl has got to eat, right. However, looks can be deceiving. For I am the witch you are looking for, and this is the place you will make your grave. I have been ordered by the Demon King to bring him your dead corpses. I think I will just deliver him your heads."

Waving her hands in a circular motion, the witch summons her fiercest creatures. "Abominations come forth and kill these intruders" commands the witch.

Emerging from the ground climbs two grotesque creatures.

The abominations are raging, weathered creatures, twice dead, to whom is reserved the blackest of darkness forever. These gifts from the Demon King have big red eyes, long-clawed human hands, black hair, pinkish skin, and black crooked chipped teeth. One is tall, long and lanky and the other is short and stocky. Both creatures foam and froth at the mouth as if they can smell and taste dinner.

"Hey guys, I don't like the way those creatures are looking at us and licking their lips. I feel like a piece of meat" says Titus.

"Now you know how us girls feel when you guys gawk at us" comments Sakia.

"This isn't the same thing and you know it. Besides I haven't gawked at any of you girls" Titus replies.

"So what are you saying, Titus? Are you calling us ugly?" insinuates Sakia.

"No! I just-" attempts Titus before being interrupted by Obadiah.

"Stop it you two, this isn't the time or place for this. Focus on the problem in front of us."

The abominations run toward the Chosen Ones. Titus shoots the small stocky abomination with his ice ray, freezing it in a block of ice. The other creature lunges to grab Sakia who ducks and slides under its legs. She wraps her whip around its right leg, shocking it with electricity.

Feeling the pain, the abomination turns and grabs Sakia's whip jerking it out of her hand. The snatching force of the abomination pulls Sakia to the ground. He grabs Sakia and lifts her up by the arm.

Tiwa turns two of her boomerangs in a vertical position and hurls them at the monster, stabbing it in the back. Making a loud growling noise the abomination drops Sakia and turns its attention towards Tiwa.

Shattering the block of ice to pieces, the small stocky abomination swings a powerful right hand towards a surprised Titus. Titus blocks the punch with his shield. The impact of the blow rolls Titus into the trees behind him. Obadiah shoots him in the head and back with exploding arrows, stealing its attention away from Titus.

Tiwa holds two boomerangs in her hands as the tall abomination rapidly approaches her. Keembo runs and tackles it, slamming it against the circle of trees.

Raining down left and right punches to the abomination's face, Keembo yells, "Leave my friends alone, monster!"

The tall abomination kicks Keembo off of him, sending him flying a few feet away.

Titus freezes the small abomination again as it attacks Obadiah. Then he freezes the ground beneath it.

"Sakia, Tiwa! Lure the tall abomination onto the sheet of ice" shouts Titus.

Sakia retrieves her whip as she and Tiwa yell at the monster. Tiwa hurls her remaining boomerangs at the abomination to draw it towards the frozen ice.

The block of ice explodes again as the small stocky abomination breaks free of its icy prison. Moving forward, it slips on the ice beneath. Running after Tiwa, the tall abomination slips on the ice and slams into its partner.

"Obadiah, melt the ice underneath the monsters" instructs Titus.

Obadiah shoots fiery arrow after fiery arrow into the sheet of ice beneath the abominations. The ice begins to melt and forms a large puddle underneath them. Struggling to their feet the abominations stand dripping wet in the puddle of water. "

Sakia, shock the water!" yells Titus.

Sakia flings her whip hitting the large puddle, sending a surge of electricity into the water. The water magnifies the electrical voltage tenfold, electrocuting the two abominations. Their smoking charred bodies stop convulsing and fall to the ground.

"I am impressed. You defeated my abominations. But they have served their purpose. I now know your abilities and powers. Sadly, they pale in comparison to mine" states the pretty, red-haired witch with an evil grin on her face.

The witch walks out into the garden looking at each of the Chosen Ones as they spread out. "So you are the Chosen Ones prophecy has foretold would come. Unfortunately, you will die by my hand today and the Creator will have to send another five in your place."

"Shut up witch. It's you who will die today" retorts Titus, shooting an ice beam at her.

Raising her left arm the witch shoots out a stream of fire colliding with Titus' ice beam, canceling each other out and forming a steamy cloud.

Obadiah and Tiwa attack her with their weapons. The witch raises her right hand, expelling wind that deflects Obadiah's arrows and Tiwa's boomerangs. Noticing Keembo charging, the witch stomps her foot. Keembo smacks right into a slab of earth, that rises up instantly from the ground.

"I don't see any holes in her defense. I can't get close to her" shouts Sakia.

"We must find a way to defeat her and recover the Armor of God!" yells Titus.

"Are you referring to the boots that I have in my possession? You are welcome to them if you can kill me."

"Witch, your big mouth has sealed your fate. Now that we know you have the boots here, we don't need you alive any longer" snickers Titus.

"Why you insolent human! I am the most powerful elemental witch in the universe. Die!" roars the witch.

Waving her hands above her head in a circular motion, the witch utters some unknown words summoning the strength of the Demon King. The sky turns black, with thunder and lightning. Lightning flies down from the sky striking several trees, splitting them in half.

The Chosen Ones quickly huddle together. The witch sends several lightning bolts directly at them. The lightning bolts strikes the Chosen Ones.

"Impossible! How could you survive?" screams the witch, summoning another round of lightning strikes. With each new wave of attack, the lightning bolts become more powerful.

After three more failed attacks the witch shouts, "What dark magic protects you from me? It is impossible for the Creator to intervene directly on your behalf. He decreed it so himself! But how?"

The dark black clouds begin to disperse. "Your power wanes as you grow tired witch. You are finished" declares Titus, as the Chosen Ones walk closely together towards the witch.

"Never!" screams the witch, shooting out a stream of fire from her hand.

"Why can't I kill you?" cries the witch.

"The truth of the matter is that your powers are pathetic" taunts, Titus.

Enraged by Titus' insults the witch summons her remaining strength to launch one more lightning strike. Falling to her knees, the skies clear and the Chosen Ones surround her. Slowly lifting her head up, her body exhausted and her powers spent, the witch looks at the Chosen Ones just as Azra's invisibility potion wears off.

"No! No! There can't be six of you. The prophecy said five. You deceived me!" yells the witch.

"What was it you said earlier? 'Looks can be deceiving.' Now it's time for you to die witch" says Keembo, stabbing her in the heart with his dagger.

Eyes wide open grabbing Keembo's arm, the witch gasps her last breath and dies. Her beautiful face starts to age quickly and her body starts to decay and turn into ash. A strong breeze suddenly blows taking the witch's ashes away over the circle of trees.

"Great teamwork everyone, we defeated the wicked old witch. Your plan worked out perfectly Titus, the witch never suspected there were six of us. Azra you did great staying hidden during the fight" says Obadiah.

"It was hard not getting involved, but I saw the witch intently watching you guys, so I bit my lip and stayed out of it. Protecting you guys with my shield was easy. Although, those last few lightning strikes gave me a headache. I'm glad she's dead" states Azra.

"Me too, now let's find those boots" responds Keembo.

Tiwa pulls her boomerangs out of the dead abomination's back as everyone else heads into the witch's cabin.

"It's too late to make it back to camp. We'll have to stay here for the night" states Obadiah.

"Well, at least we'll have some vegetables for dinner" laughs Sakia.

"I found them!" shouts Keembo, pulling a pair of armored boots from a secret compartment behind the fireplace.

The silver and gold boots have the symbol Alpha and Omega etched on the heel.

"This adds up to five pieces of the Armor of God, leaving the sixth piece somewhere up in the skies" declares Sakia.

"How are we supposed to fly up in the sky?" asks Tiwa.

"We'll cross that bridge when we get there. Right now we should eat and get some rest. We earned it today" says Titus.

Exhausted, they eat and prepare for a short night's sleep. They grab anything warm they can find and instantly fall asleep on the cold cabin floor.

At the break of day, the Chosen Ones rise in search of the Sky Citadel. Wading deeper into the Defiled Marshlands, Obadiah raises his hand and says, "Everybody stop. You hear that strange noise?"

"I don't hear anything other than these annoying swamp sounds" states Sakia.

"Just close your eyes and listen" exclaims Obadiah.

"Wait. I hear something. It sounds like it's coming from up ahead, through that clearing" points Keembo.

As they get closer to the clearing, Azra says, "I hear it now. It sounds like splashing water."

"I hear something too. But it sounds like steam to me" says Tiwa.

Reaching a clearing, everyone stands in awe as they watch a hot spring geyser erupt hundreds of feet into the air. High in the sky, far above the geyser, is a floating island camouflaged by thick clouds.

"That's one big, strange-looking cloud" comments Azra.

"I don't think that's a cloud, Azra. Let me take a closer look" says Titus, switching the lenses on his goggles.

"It's the Sky Citadel! We found it!" shouts an excited Titus.

Everyone cheers and laughs as they celebrate finding the final stop on their long journey to retrieve all of the pieces to the Armor of God.

Settling down from the excitement and looking up into the sky, Tiwa says, "Uh, guys. This brings me back to the question I asked yesterday. How are we supposed to fly up there?"

"If only we could ride the steam current of the geyser we could fly up there. But we don't have wings" Azra says.

"That's it! Azra you're a genius. Well really I'm the genius, you just came up with half of a good idea" utters Titus.

"Stop jabbering Titus and get to the point will you" barks Sakia.

"Azra's idea of riding the steam current is brilliant, except we won't use wings to fly. We'll ride the steam current up to Sky Citadel in an air balloon. All we have to do is build one" Titus exclaims.

"Where are we going to get the balloon from?" asks Obadiah.

Before Titus can answer the question Tiwa interjects, "We'll make the balloon out of the snakeskin we have back at camp."

"Precisely," says Titus. "Sakia and Obadiah I need you two to journey back to camp and collect the snakeskin. Tiwa, Keembo, Azra and I will begin working on the air balloon."

The journey back to camp takes several hours. Obadiah kills half a dozen poisonous snakes on the way.

"I'm getting tired of killing snakes, let alone eating them. Any other kind of meat would be a welcomed change" mutters Obadiah.

"How about a nice steak or chicken? Rabbit even sounds good" suggests Sakia.

"I tell you what. You find a rabbit around here and I'll catch it. I hear turtle meat is good. You want that instead?" asks Obadiah.

"Uh, no, that's okay. I'll stick with the snake meat" replies Sakia.

"Finally, we're here," says Obadiah, pointing to their snakeskin tent.

Sakia and Obadiah retrieve the snakeskin and start making their way back to the others.

"Azra, I need you to collect as much papyrus reeds as you can. We'll use the papyrus to make ropes for the balloon."

"I'm on it, Titus. I saw a lot of them by the witch's cabin."

"Good. Tiwa, can you help Azra? Bring back as much as you can carry" Titus instructs.

"No problem Titus, we'll be back soon" replies Tiwa, as she and Azra head off.

"Keembo, I need you to find some strong wood to make our basket. But make sure it's light in weight" explains Titus.

"Light but strong, okay I can do that. What are you going to do?" inquires Keembo.

"I'm going to work on designing a balloon that will safely get us up to Sky Citadel. All the calculations have to be precise for this to work" responds Titus.

"Okay, I was just asking," says Keembo, as he leaves to go about his task.

Bringing back the papyrus reeds, Tiwa and Azra start braiding it into strands of rope. Meanwhile, Keembo returns from his last trip of gathering wood.

"That should be enough wood Keembo. Now can you help me tie the pieces of wood together with the rope the girls made?" asks Titus.

After several hours of tedious work, the carry basket and balloon frame are complete.

"It's time for a break. My hands and fingers are killing me" says Tiwa.

Laughing, Azra says, "Tiwa, you did twice as much work as I did."

"Yes, I did" replies a smiling Tiwa, rubbing her four hands together.

Relaxing in the open clearing, Keembo, Titus, Tiwa, and Azra stare in amazement at the geyser as it erupts again. The geyser erupts every ninety minutes.

"That never gets old" states Keembo watching the steam rise.

"It's beautiful," says Azra.

"As soon as Sakia and Obadiah get back all we have to do is put the snakeskin over the balloon frame, tie it tightly together and, *voila,* off into space" declares Titus.

Tiwa leans over to Azra and whispers something in her ear. "Oh yes, that would be so great" shrieks Azra.

"What would be so great?" asks a curious Keembo.

"It's a surprise. Azra and I need to go back to the witch's cabin and get something" says Tiwa.

"Uh, okay. But hurry back, it'll be getting dark soon" Keembo says.

"Now what are they up to?" inquires Titus, as Azra and Tiwa disappear back into the swamp.

Returning an hour later, Tiwa and Azra arrive carrying two large iron kettle pots. Struggling, Tiwa yells, "Keembo can you give a girl a hand. We should have brought you along with us."

Keembo easily lifts the two extra-large pots and asks, "Where do you want these?"

"Please set them next to the geyser" Tiwa says.

"Next to the geyser? What for?" asks Keembo.

"We girls have been working hard in this dirty swamp and we feel we deserve a nice hot bath" states Azra.

"That's a great idea! I think I should test it first, to make sure you girls don't harm your nice delicate skin" says Keembo with a sly grin.

"No way buster, it was our idea and we're going first," says Tiwa emphatically.

"Exactly" blurts out Azra.

"Okay, okay, calm down. You two can go first. I don't care when I go as long as I get one" says Keembo, as he places the large cauldrons near the geyser.

The geyser erupts. The falling water quickly fills up the two large pots. Just then Obadiah and Sakia walk through the clearing carrying the giant snakeskin.

"We're back!" shouts Obadiah, as he and Sakia drop the snakeskin on the ground. Everyone greets them with excitement, happy to see them safe and sound.

"I'm filthy, tired and hungry" complains Sakia.

"Oh, do we have a surprise for you, Sakia. Guess what it is?" asks Azra excitedly.

"Hmm, let me think. You caught a rabbit" scoffs Sakia.

"No, silly. Everyone gets a hot bath tonight!" erupts Azra.

"That's not funny Azra. You shouldn't tease me like that. Do you know I would die for a hot bath right now?" says a simmering Sakia.

"She's not joking. The hot water is in those pots right now" says Tiwa, pointing towards the geyser.

Looking at the pots overflowing with water Sakia yells, "I go first!"

"Sorry girlfriend, Azra and I are going first" states Tiwa.

"And Keembo and I are going after them," says Titus.

"Titus can I have your place in the bath line?" asks Sakia nicely.

"No. You have to wait your turn. Tiwa! Azra! I believe the bathwater is ready. You two hurry up because I'm next" says an eager Titus.

After they all take a hot bath, they decide to finish working on the air balloon in the morning. Worn out from the day's activities, they fall sound asleep on the ground.

Waking up clean and refreshed, the Chosen Ones continue to work on the hot air balloon. They place the giant snakeskin on top of it.

Titus conducts a final inspection of the air balloon and says, "Guys it's finished and ready for takeoff! We leave in forty-five minutes. That's when the geyser will erupt again."

"Hey with all the excitement last night over the hot water baths, we forgot to decide on who'll wear the Boots of Peace. Tiwa, Keembo do either of you have a preference or want to wear them?" asks Sakia.

"With all the recent changes in my life, I really could use some extra peace right now. If that's okay with you, Keembo?" asks Tiwa.

"The boots are all yours Tiwa. You'll probably look better in them than I would anyway" smiles Keembo.

"We should talk to the Spirit before we go" suggests Azra.

"We don't have enough time Azra. As soon as we land on Sky Citadel that'll be the first thing we do" says Titus.

"Okay, I'm going to hold you to that" glares Azra.

"I'm sure you will. Everyone gather your belongings and put them in the balloon" instructs Titus.

Keembo puts the snakeskin cover right on top of the geyser.

With a concerned look on his face, Obadiah asks Titus, "How is this supposed to work? What about the scalding hot water? Will we walk away from this?"

"Excellent questions, Obadiah. I need everyone to listen up, especially you Azra. When the geyser erupts hot steam will shoot out first, then hot water quickly thereafter. The hot steam will fill up the snakeskin cover lifting us up in the air and onward to Sky Citadel. Before the water gushes out, Azra will place a shield around the bottom of the basket protecting us from the scalding hot water. My calculations of the balloon's size and the steam temperature indicate that we should travel two times higher than Sky Citadel. But we can land anywhere on the floating island we want too. Did I address your concerns Obadiah?" smiles Titus.

"Yes you did, but I'll feel better once we land on Sky Citadel" exclaims Obadiah.

"It's time. Everyone in the basket quickly" bellows Titus.

As they enter the basket the ground begins to rumble. Hot steam shoots out of the geyser and fills the snakeskin cover lifting the balloon up in the air.

"Azra shield us!" yells Titus.

Azra raises her shield moments before hot liquid shoots out of the ground. Slamming into Azra's shield, the hot water jolts the rising balloon as it ascends skyward.

"We're flying! Ha! Ha! We're really flying! Woo! Titus, you did it. I'm not going to lie, I didn't think this air balloon trick was going to work" comments Keembo excitedly.

"Keembo, I'm deeply offended. Have I ever missed on my calculations?" inquires Titus.

"No. But there's always a first time and I thought this was it. Anyway, I was wrong. You're still the man, pipsqueak!" hollers Keembo.

"Don't worry about him Titus, that was a great idea," says Sakia.

The air balloon floats right above the island called Sky Citadel.

"Something's flying towards us. It appears to be closing in really fast. Wait! It's headed straight for us and it's huge. Ahhhhh!" screams Tiwa.

CHAPTER 13

SKY CITADEL

A magnificent view from above camouflages the inherent dangers waiting below. The picturesque landscape making up Sky Citadel consists of lush green terrain that butts up against cavernous mountains to the north. Acres of fertile soil separate the mountains from the large sparkling lake to the south. To the west, is a forest of thick green trees nestled with various colorful birds. To the east lies The Citadel, a fortress designed to protect the town and the Royal Palace. The beautiful white palace is covered by sapphire roofs and outlined in gold.

The Citadel is surrounded by a deep moat filled with water. All nobility lives inside the walls of The Citadel. The peasants live on the other side of the moat where they farm, mine and tend to the livestock.

A massive wooden drawbridge is the only way in and out that connects the Queen to her subjects. The drawbridge is always down allowing the Queen's army of knights and archers to travel back and forth.

Five guard towers are strategically placed throughout the peasant's homes, to protect them and the Queen's resources. The stone guard towers are big enough to provide the knights and archers a place to eat and sleep, while also providing a front-line defense against intruders.

Tiwa screams from inside the air balloon, pointing at a gigantic vulture with an enormous wingspan, heading straight towards them. The gigantic vulture rams its razor-sharp beak right into the top of the air balloon, while its dagger-like talons rip the snakeskin hide to shreds. Pulling and jerking on its prey, the enormous vulture overturns the balloon's basket.

The Chosen Ones scream as they fall headlong out of the balloon towards the ground. The fall feels like an eternity before they splash into the lake. All their weapons and gear are scattered across the terrain as the huge vulture flies off with their air balloon.

Swimming up to the top of the water, Obadiah looks around and cries out, "Is everyone alright?"

"No! I'm not alright. I just got knocked out of the air by Sky Citadel's welcoming committee and I'm soaking wet" shouts Sakia.

"My tool bag! Where's my tool bag?" cries out a frantic Titus.

"Oh no! The spirit stone is gone. What are we going to do? We have to find it or we'll be lost here forever" whines a desperate Azra.

"Calm down everyone. We're alive and unharmed. Let's be thankful for that. We'll search for our missing items as we explore this new land" states Keembo.

"That flying creature was heading in a northwestern direction. That's where we should start our search. At least we didn't lose any pieces to the Armor of God" Tiwa says.

"You guys are right. We need to look at the positive side of our situation. No one was hurt, we still have the pieces to the Armor of God and we made it to Sky Citadel. Hopefully, what was lost can be found. So let's go find this welcoming committee" says Obadiah.

Wet and uncomfortable, the Chosen Ones follow the direction the gigantic vulture headed in, to find their lost items and the spirit gem. Walking underneath the large vulture's flight path Keembo, Tiwa, Sakia, and Obadiah recover their bags. Further down, three spears are recovered.

"Aw, look at that beautiful red and blue bird up ahead. What's that in its beak?" asks Azra.

"My toolkit! That bird has my toolkit!" hollers Titus, running towards the bird as it starts to fly away. "Shoot it down! Someone shoot it down! Get it before it reaches the forest."

Obadiah takes aim with his ivory bow and shoots a fiery arrow killing the beautiful red and blue bird before it reaches the trees in the forest.

Titus, running to retrieve his tool bag from the dead bird screams loudly, "You did it! You got my toolkit!"

Titus' loud scream frightens the hundreds of birds resting in the nearby trees. They all screech and caw as they fly out of the trees and up into the air. This awesome site does not go unnoticed by the Queen's tower guards.

Sounding an alarm, the tower guard blows his trumpet summoning an infantry of knights and archers. Soldiers run across the drawbridge to assemble near the town hall.

"What is the reason for sounding the alarm?" Commander Wentar inquires.

The tower guard responds, "Commander I observed several strange occurrences that I believe should be investigated. A strange object appeared over the horizon and was attacked by Vermilion. A little while later, all the birds at Tree Hill scattered and took to the skies. Something strange is happening west of us, Commander" replies the guard.

"Good job. We will investigate these disturbances. Knights! Archers! Let's move out" shouts Commander Wentar.

"Titus hurry and retrieve your bag. We need to leave here now. All this commotion has given away our location. Someone is sure to have noticed" says Obadiah.

"Okay, I got it. Let's go" Titus replies.

The Chosen Ones head north still in search of Azra's bag with the spirit gem in it.

Heading north the Chosen Ones reach the Cavernous Mountains. These rocky mountains are home to a bunch of cave bandits called Nomads.

Nomads are grey gargoyle-like creatures that scavenge, pillage and steal whatever they can to survive. They constantly mount raids on the town, stealing their food and livestock. Several cave bandits watch as the Chosen Ones get closer, waiting for them to get in attack range. Arrows whiz by and stick in the ground.

 Keembo shouts, "We're under attack!"

"We walked right into an ambush!" shouts Titus.

Azra and Titus raise their shields to deflect the barrage of arrows and spears flying at them. Letting out a high-pitched scream, the bandits alert their comrades in the nearby caves. Their banshee cry can be heard over a long distance.

"Commander Wentar, the cave bandits' cries are coming from the north. Should we investigate?" asks an archer.

"Yes" replies Commander Wentar, ordering his army to change direction and head north.

"We have to retreat away from these mountains before we get pinned down by their reinforcements. Obadiah, Tiwa, fan out and find higher ground. Once you get there start attacking the enemy and provide cover for the rest of us to retreat. Sakia find a good place for us to mount a counterattack from. Hurry, more of these creatures are pouring out of The caves" dictates Titus.

Several minutes pass as Titus, Azra, and Keembo slowly move backward away from the mountain behind Azra's protective shield.

"What's taking Obadiah and Tiwa so long?" cries out Keembo.

From a short distance behind them, a loud voice shouts, "Archers! Fire when ready!"

A blanket of arrows shot from crossbows traverses the skies, killing several bandits and scaring off the rest.

Turning around Azra says, "Thank you for saving us."

"Knights, bind these prisoners up with the others if they try to escape kill them" commands Commander Wentar.

Their weapons confiscated, bound in chains, the captive Chosen Ones are taken into The Citadel.

The large, hexagonal-shaped castle is home to the royal family and two hundred and fifty knights and people of noble birth. The Sky People, both nobles and peasants, have orange skin, purple eyes, blonde hair, and pointy ears and chins. Their facial features have an elfish look to them.

The royal family, Queen Vita and her two daughters, Princess Sunda and Princess Retta differ from their people in that their eyes are yellow and their hair is purple. Only the royal family possesses the ability to manipulate wind. Queen Vita rules Sky Citadel with an iron fist and rarely leaves the castle. Her two daughters frequently travel outside of the castle and are their mother's eyes and ears.

Princess Sunda greets Commander Wentar at the drawbridge. "Commander, did you find out what the disturbance to the west was?"

"Yes, we did Princess Sunda. These six intruders were found fighting with the cave bandits. We are taking them to the Queen now to be interrogated" he replies.

Intently looking at the Chosen Ones, Princess Sunda responds, "Yes, take them to my mother."

Commander Wentar enters the castle throne room and kneels before Queen Vita and Princess Retta, sitting on their thrones. Princess Sunda passes by Commander Wentar on her way to sit down on her throne, to the left of her mother.

Speaking with a regal voice Queen Vita says, "Speak Commander. What do you have to report to your Queen?"

"My Queen we have captured six intruders to your realm. Bring forth the prisoners" orders Commander Wentar.

Dragged in chains, the Chosen Ones are lined up in front of the Queen. Looking at the prisoners before her, the Queen is unimpressed.

Glancing at Obadiah's breastplate the Queen's eyes widen as she jumps up. "Bring that breastplate to me" commands the Queen, visibly bothered.

"What is it, mother? What disturbs you?" inquires Princess Retta.

"Silence!" yells the Queen, as one of the knights hands her Obadiah's breastplate. The Queen passes her hand over the symbols Alpha and Omega on the breastplate.

Looking at the prisoners again the Queen gasps, "It can't be."

Sitting back down, the Queen commands, "Bring me all of their armor."

The knights lay the boots, helmet, belt, shield and Azra's bracelet before the Queen. Examining the armor the Queen angrily inquires, "Who are you? Why have you come here?"

Boldly, Sakia says, "We're the Chosen Ones of the Creator. We've come here to retrieve the last piece to the Armor of God. You can hand it over to us or we will forcibly take it from you like we did all the others."

"Why you insolent little wretch!" screams the Queen, as she sends a blast of wind from her right-hand smashing into Sakia and slamming her against the wall.

"Stay calm, Keembo" whispers Titus.

Knowing exactly what Titus means, Keembo breathes and relaxes his muscles.

"Bring me their bags and take them to the dungeon. I will speak with them later" commands the Queen.

Chained and thrown into separate cells, two guards stand watch outside the captives prison doors.

"Mother, what is wrong? Please tell us what is going on" cries the two princesses.

"My daughters before you were born, the Demon King granted me rulership over this realm, a royal lineage, and special powers in exchange for protecting the Sword of the Spirit. The prophecy states that five beings chosen by the Creator would defeat the Demon King using the Armor of God. These intruders have come to retrieve the last piece to the Armor of God. We can not let that happen!"

"Then let's kill them mother and be done with it" states Princess Retta.

"I want to question them before I kill them. I am interested in the Armor of God's power. How I can make it mine" utters the Queen.

The Queen has all the armor and items of the Chosen Ones placed under a sword mounted on the throne room wall.

"I need to think, my daughters. Leave me. I will interrogate the prisoners further in the morning" Queen Vita says.

"Yes, mother" replies the two princesses.

As night descends on Sky Citadel, Tiwa calls out to one of the guards, "Can we get something to eat?"

"Food should be the least of your concerns, deary. The Queen will probably have you all killed tomorrow" laughs the guard.

"It's time, Keembo!" shouts Titus from his cell.

"You shut your mouth before I come in there and bust you in the chops, shorty" yells the other guard.

"I'd like to see you try, ugly" taunts Titus.

"That does it, I'm going to smash your face in runt," says the guard, as he unlocks Titus' cell.

The other guard laughs as he keeps an eye on the other cell doors. Quietly breaking his chains, Keembo calls the second guard to his cell.

"What do you want?" asks the guard, as he stands in front of Keembo's cell.

Suddenly, Keembo kicks open the cell door slamming it into the guard, knocking him to the ground. Taking his sword, Keembo forces the guard to open everyone's cell. Upon reaching Titus' cell the guard gasps in horror as he sees his fellow guard frozen in a block of ice.

"Nice job Titus, I thought you were going to get your face rearranged" jokes Keembo.

"I told you I can take care of myself" states Titus.

"Unlock his chains" commands Keembo.

As the guard unlocks Titus' chains, Titus asks him, "Tell me how to get to the Queen's throne room from here? If your directions are wrong, I'll come back and shatter you and your friend here into little pieces of ice. Understand?"

The guard nods and gives Titus the directions to the throne room before being frozen in a block of ice.

Leaving the dungeon, the Chosen Ones move stealthily through the castle to the Queen's throne room. Simultaneously, the curious Princess Sunda decides to pay the Chosen Ones a visit in the dungeon.

"There are two guards in front of the throne room. I don't see anyone entering or leaving. All appears to be quiet. Okay, let's take those guards out" says Obadiah.

Titus freezes both guards with his ice ray.

"I'm glad they didn't take your necklace, Titus. They must have mistaken my bracelet for armor. I can't wait to get it back" exclaims Azra.

Entering the throne room, Keembo and Tiwa slide the frozen guards inside and lock the large double doors.

"Our weapons. The Armor of God. There they are" points out Sakia, as she runs towards the stone wall.

Everyone runs behind her, gathering their weapons, armor, and bags. Keembo reaches up and grabs the mounted sword off the wall. Inspecting the silver and gold sword, Keembo notices the symbols Alpha and Omega etched on the blade.

He cries out, "It's the Sword of the Spirit! We've found the last piece to the Armor of God!"

Princess Sunda reaches the dungeon and says out loud, "Where are the guards? If they have left their posts I will kill them myself."

Princess Sunda looks into the empty cells and finds the two frozen guards.

"The prisoners have escaped! Sound the alarm!" shouts the princess repeatedly, as she runs out of the dungeon.

Hearing the princess' screams, the castle tower guard blows his trumpet loudly three times, signaling intruders in the castle. The knights and archers rally in front of the castle drawbridge. Queen Vita orders the drawbridge to be raised and the prisoners found. The cave bandits hear the trumpet sounds and see the castle drawbridge being raised.

"That trumpet sound means they know we've escaped. Hurry back to the dungeon. That's the last place they'll look for us" says Titus.

"Commander! How did the prisoners escape? Never mind that now. Go secure my throne room. They must not retrieve the Armor of God" commands the Queen.

Half the army searches the castle and half stays by the drawbridge.

Reaching the throne room Queen Vita screams, "NO! Find them! Kill them and bring me back my armor."

Hiding in the dungeon Tiwa says, "Titus I need to hear your plan for getting us out of this castle alive. The six of us cannot defeat the Queen and her army of knights and archers. What shall we do? They'll find us here soon enough."

A somber Titus responds, "Tiwa I have no foolproof plan to get us out of the castle and across the moat. I noticed on the way down here that they raised the drawbridge. So even if we're invisible, they'll see us splashing in the water and shoot us. We're going to need some divine intervention...luck. Call it what you will. We're going to need help to get out of here alive. Azra, give everybody an invisibility potion. Once we drink the potion we won't be able to see each other. We'll have thirty minutes to make it across the moat before the potion wears off. If the drawbridge isn't lowered by then, we take our chances in the water. Be careful, don't make any noises. See you all on the other side."

They all drink the invisibility potion and start to leave just as ten soldiers burst into the dungeon.

"No ones in here. Keep looking" shouts a knight.

~~~

"Commander we have searched the entire castle and there is no sign of the prisoners," says a reluctant knight.

"Impossible! Search the castle again" orders the commander.

"Commander Wentar, I will hold you personally responsible for the prisoners' escape, if they are not found. Do I make myself clear?" yells the Queen angrily.

"Yes, my Queen. We will find them" replies the commander.

The north tower guard blows his trumpet four times, signaling an attack from the cave bandits.

"My Queen the cave bandits are attacking the town and half of our army is inside the castle. What are your orders?" asks the commander.

"Lower the drawbridge and repel the cave bandits. We can't let them take our food and supplies" commands the Queen.
~~~

The cave bandits descend upon the livestock and ravage the fields, killing peasants and the handful of knights and archers left in the guard towers.

As the drawbridge slowly descends, cries and screams can be heard from the injured and dying. The bridge finally lowers and a battalion of two hundred men run across the bridge to fight the cave bandits and recover the livestock and food that were taken. The eighty-plus bandits retreat back to the mountains with lots of stolen goods in their hands.

"Commander, the cave bandits have taken most of the livestock and stolen half of our winter food supply" reports an archer.

"We must recoup everything that was taken" declares Commander Wentar.

Queen Vita and her two daughters stand in the middle of the drawbridge waiting for the prisoners to try and pass over. Commander Wentar reports the losses to Queen Vita.

"They dare take our livestock and winter food supply! They would try to kill us through starvation. Commander, the time for tolerating these pesky cave bandits has come to an end. Today we go to war with the Nomads. I do not want one single soul to survive, destroy them all. Gather the explosives and take the entire army with you. Princess Sunda will go with you to battle. Retta and I will deal with the escaped prisoners" yells an irate Queen.

"Yes, my Queen. It shall be as you command" replies Commander Wentar.

~~~

Titus slowly walks across the drawbridge, avoiding knights and archers running back and forth across the bridge. Reaching the other side of the moat, he says to himself, "We have a few minutes before the invisibility potion wears off. I hope the others have made it across safely."

A knight walking on the drawbridge utters to a fellow knight in a loud voice, "Hey, shove me again and I'm going to push you off the bridge! This is the second time you slammed into me."

"What are you talking about? I didn't touch you. The fear of war must be getting to you" retorts his fellow knight.

Pulling out his sword the soldier responds, "Are you calling me a coward? I'll-."

Princess Retta interrupts, "Knights stop fighting with each other and fight the enemy unless you prefer to fight against me."

Dropping to their knees both knights plead, "Yes princess. We're sorry. It won't happen again."
~~~

"Whew, that was close," thinks Azra as she steps off the drawbridge across the moat.

~~~

Commander Wentar reaches the Cavernous Mountains and positions his army for battle. The bandits hunker down in their caves, waiting for the advancing army to attack.

Crik, the leader of the Nomads, instructs his people, "Take two lives for each life lost. If we are to die this day, then we will take these self-righteous dogs down with us. Fight to the death."

"Commander, how do you plan on defeating the bandits?" asks Princess Sunda.

"We will use our explosive bombs to force them out of their caves and then we'll strike them down with arrows and swords. Only problem is, we need to get closer to throw our bombs. And they have the high ground. We have to figure out another way to deliver our bombs or we will be stuck in a stalemate" explains Commander Wentar.

"Commander, light two bombs and throw them in the air" instructs Princess Sunda.

As the bombs rise in the air Princess Sunda raises both her arms and shoots out a blast of wind from her hands, taking the bombs all the way to a cave opening. The bombs explode on impact, killing several bandits.
~~~

"Take out the wind witch" commands Crik.

Arrows whisk through the air under the cover of a darkening sky. Night has arrived and war has begun.

~~~

The invisibility potion wears off and slowly the Chosen Ones become visible again. Obadiah reappears atop a guard tower, Tiwa and Sakia appear behind the town hall, Keembo reappears under the drawbridge, Titus appears along the edge of the moat and Azra reappears at the end of the drawbridge across the moat.

Princess Retta does a double-take and cries out, "Mother, I have found one of the prisoners at the end of the drawbridge."

Lifting her right hand Princess Retta shoots a blast of wind at Azra, slamming her head into the ground. Azra passes out. Creating a gust of air under her feet, Retta floats over to Azra. Queen Vita floats over to Retta's side.

"Shall I finish her off mother?" gloats Princess Retta.

"Yes. Kill her" commands the Queen.

Upon hearing that, Titus jumps out and shoots an ice beam at Princess Retta. Queen Vita blocks Titus' attack with a whirlwind blast and engages him. Retta uses her wind power to lift a large boulder to crush Azra with.
~~~

Obadiah shoots several fiery arrows at Retta, forcing her to drop the rock and block his attack with a wind blast. Putting both her hands together, Princess Retta shoots a whirlwind blast at Obadiah on top of the guard tower.

Just as she fires, Keembo leaps out from under the edge of the bridge and grabs both of her arms. Squeezing tightly, Keembo shatters both of Retta's arms. Screaming loudly from the pain, Princess Retta passes out and crumbles to the ground.

Queen Vita, startled by her daughter's scream, turns and shoots a vortex of air that blasts into Keembo, lifting him off the ground and slamming him into the roof of the town hall. Picking up her unconscious daughter, Queen Vita encircles Retta and herself in a defensive ball of wind.

The attacks of Obadiah, Tiwa, and Titus are unable to penetrate Queen Vita's defensive wind sphere. Causing the ball of wind to float, Queen Vita takes her daughter back to the castle.

While departing she yells out, "You all will pay for what you have done to my daughter. I will make each of you suffer horribly before you die."

Sakia runs over to help Keembo out of the rubble and Titus pours water on Azra's face, awakening her.

Gathering in the damaged town hall, the Chosen Ones try to figure out a way to defeat Queen Vita.

"How can we penetrate her wind defense?" Keembo asks.

Azra interrupts the train of thought and says, "Wait, everyone listen. While I was unconscious the Spirit of Truth appeared to me and told me where the spirit gem is. She said my bag is tied around one of the vulture's talons."

"Did she by any chance tell you how we're supposed to summon that monstrous beast?" Sakia asks.

"No" replies Azra.

"Did she tell you how to defeat the Wind Queen?" inquires Keembo.

"No, she didn't" replies Azra.

"Are you sure you weren't just dreaming Azra?" asks Obadiah.

Frustrated, Azra says in a loud voice, "You guys are acting like I'm making this up! The Spirit said, *'When your hearts are still and full of faith you will hear me speak to you'*. I know the Spirit spoke to me."

"I believe you, Azra. We need to figure out a way to call that monstrous bird back here" says Tiwa.

"I have an idea on how we can summon the bird, but we can't do it until daybreak. We should go to the forest and camp out there till morning. We don't want to be here when the wind witch returns" states Titus.

The Chosen Ones depart walking into the dark night.

~~~
~~~

"Princess Sunda it is too dark to continue fighting. We must wait till dawn's first light. A garrison of men will stay here and the rest of the army will camp out in town" says the commander.

"Very well" agrees Princess Sunda.

Commander Wentar places his garrison and takes the rest of the army into town. "Take your rest now men, we fight in the morning. I'm heading back to the castle" he says.

Upon seeing Commander Wentar, Queen Vita yells at the top of her lungs, "Where are they, commander? Where are the escaped prisoners?"

"We have not seen them your Majesty" the commander humbly replies.

Grabbing him by the throat the Queen says, "They have seriously injured Princess Retta. I want them dead, now!"

Gasping for breath the Commander responds, "Ugh! My Queen your army is set to fight the cave bandits at first light and recapture our livestock and stolen food supplies. Do you wish to redirect our efforts to find the prisoners?"

"No, Commander. Stay your course. I will find and defeat them myself."

"Mother, I will fight with you," says Princess Sunda.

"No daughter, you assist the commander. After tomorrow, everything will be back to normal" declares the Queen.

As morning breaks, Princess Sunda and Commander Wentar's army gather at the battle line. Several black bombs are tossed up in the air. Princess Sunda catches them with her wind tunnel and sends them into the bandits' cave. The battle reignites once again. Queen Vita heads south towards the lake in search of her escaped prisoners.

Waking up to bombs exploding Titus says, "Get up everyone there's no time to waste, we must find the bird that attacked us when we first arrived. I believe that giant bird attacked our air balloon because it thought we were food. So, if we provide morning breakfast, it should come to us. On the count of three everyone shout."

Standing in front of Tree Hill Forest, Titus counts, "One, two, three."

All six shout at the top of their lungs. Breakfast flies out of the trees in droves, catching the attention of two deadly predators, Vermilion and Queen Vita. Vermilion leaves his lair and Queen Vita changes course, they both head west towards Tree Hill.

Vermilion arrives first, catching birds with its long talons and beak.

"It's here!" shouts Azra.

Obadiah shoots multiple arrows hitting the tough underbelly of the gigantic vulture.

"My arrows have no effect on this bird. How are we going to bring this thing down? We need something that packs a harder punch to get its attention" says Obadiah.

"Then try this" shouts the Queen shooting a strong wind blast that slams into Keembo knocking him twenty feet away.

Putting both hands together, the Queen shoots a vortex wind blast at the rest of the Chosen Ones. Azra raises an invisible force shield that blocks the wind. Strong winds blow over the top and around the sides of Azra's shield.

Suddenly Azra's eyes get big and she shouts, "Everyone get in a straight line behind me!"

"Azra, what are you trying to do?" inquires the others.

Ignoring their questions, Azra reshapes her shield and tilts it to a sixty-degree angle. The Queen's violent wind attack ricochets off Azra's shield and smashes directly into Vermilion, causing him to flip end over end in the air. Angered by the wind blast, Vermilion turns its attention towards Queen Vita. Flapping its large wings, it flies straight at the Queen.

Seeing the bird flying towards her Queen Vita yells, "Blast you! You little meddlers."

The Queen shoots her violent wind attack directly at the large bird heading her way, slowing its descent to a crawl.

Keembo gets up and finds the fourth blue crystal spear lying next to him. Joining the others Keembo says, "Look at what I found, it might come in handy."

Titus smiles and says, "Excellent, Keembo! Give the spear to Sakia. Sakia, take the spear, climb up the trees and get as close to the vulture as you can. When the time is right, jump onto its back and drive the spear into the base of its neck. The skin should be softest there."

"Wait a second. You want *me* to jump on the back of that monstrous bird and stab it in the neck with this little spear. Are you crazy? Why me?" asks Sakia, in bewilderment.

"Sakia, I'm not crazy. You're the only one who is fast and agile enough to climb the trees and make the jump onto the birds back. The wind witch has brought the bird to almost a dead stop, but she can't hold it off much longer. You have to go now or we'll lose our chance at getting the spirit gem back" explains Titus.

"Alright, I'll go. Wish me luck" replies Sakia.

Sakia gives Titus a big hug and leaps up into the trees.

"Be careful" whispers Titus.

"I can't hold it off much longer. I'm going to have to switch from attack mode to defensive mode, in order to conserve my energy" mutters Vita.

The Queen ceases her wind attack on Vermilion and encloses herself in a ball of wind. Vermilion hovers over the grayish sphere of wind.

Leaping from the trees, Sakia jumps onto the huge birds back, unnoticed. The large vulture grabs the ball of wind with both its talons and squeezes down on it as hard as it can. Its talons slowly start to pierce the Queen's wind defense.

Sakia carefully makes her way up to the base of the bird's neck. Raising the sharp blue crystal spear above her head, Sakia plunges it into the base of the bird's neck.

Vermilion tenses its muscles from the pain, forcing its talons to penetrate deeper into the Queen's defensive wind sphere. Vermilion starts to flap its large wings and move skyward.

Sakia holds on and pulls out her whip, wrapping it around the spear. As the massive bird rises above the trees, Sakia zaps the spear sending electricity through the puncture hole directly into the bird's body.

Vermilion lets out a long, loud screech as its insides are electrocuted. The bird's muscles tense and spasm as the electric shock pulses through its body.

The gigantic vulture's talons pop the Queen's defensive wind sphere. A loud scream of agony can be heard as the Queen is skewered to death.

Vermilion's wings stop flapping and it falls headlong towards the ground. Sakia leaps into the nearby trees before the bird crashes, dead to the ground.

"She did it!" cheers everyone as they run towards the monstrous bird.

"Anyone see her?" asks Titus.

"Not yet" replies Tiwa.

"There it is! The bag with the spirit gem in it. It's still wrapped around the bird's talon, just as the Spirit of Truth showed me. Keembo can you help me cut it free?" asks Azra anxiously.

"Step aside, Azra. I got this" says Keembo pulling out his dagger.

Sakia jumps down from the trees startling Titus and Tiwa saying, "A job well done if I do say so myself."

"Thank God you're okay," says a visibly concerned Titus.

"Yea, you did a great job up there" states Tiwa.

"Why, thanks, guys. What happened to the wind witch?" Sakia asks.

"The wind witch is dead. The vulture killed her with its talons. I guess you can say we killed two birds with one stone. Let's all get some rest before we move on" chuckles Obadiah.

Exploding bombs can be heard in the distance.

"We can't stay here any longer. We need to build an altar and summon the Spirit" declares Azra.

"I remember seeing a lot of stones down by the lake. We should go there" suggests Tiwa.

"Good idea. The lake is southeast of here" says Obadiah, as he leads the way.

~~~

Commander Wentar and Princess Sunda are still engaged in battle with the cave bandits. Both sides have suffered many casualties.

"Princess, we cannot win this war without losing eighty-five percent of our army. If the peasants decide to revolt, we will not have enough men left to bring them back to order. Please find the Queen and apprise her of the situation. It is imperative that we get instructions on our next move. I noticed birds flying in the sky earlier this morning. You should probably check over by Tree Hill first, princess" informs the commander.

"Very well, I will venture to Tree Hill and see if my mother is there. I will return soon" Princess Sunda replies as she creates a large gust of wind under her feet and whisks away.

~~~

Reaching the lake, the Chosen Ones build an altar and summon the Spirit of Truth. She looks at them and says, "Greetings, Chosen Ones! I see you have found and acquired all the pieces to the Armor of God. That was no small feat. Congratulations! Your teamwork and trust in each other have forged into a strong bond of unity. It is this bond of unity that has caused you all to maximize your abilities and overcome all the trials you have faced thus far.

"Azra, I am greatly pleased that your faith allowed me to speak to you through visions and dreams without the use of the spirit gem. Your heart was full of faith and your spirit was quiet before me, allowing me to make known to you the way you should go. I wish to communicate with all of you in this manner, individually. Titus, I hope you have learned that not all things can be solved and understood through logic and science."

"Yes, Spirit. I'm starting to understand how to separate earthly things from spiritual things. Thank you for teaching me this lesson" responds Titus.

"Titus, since you have humbled yourself to walk by faith and not by your logic and intellect, I grant unto you even more worldly wisdom and knowledge. However, when it comes to spiritual matters you will have to seek me out and not lean on your own understanding.

"My Chosen Ones, you must learn how to hear my voice. I will lead and guide you in all truth and show you the right way to go. You will travel to Demon's Lair, the home and unholy sanctum of the Demon King. In his lair, the Demon King will be at the height of his power. His minions have reported to him each of your victories. Because the inhabitants of your worlds foolishly gave their authority and dominion to the Evil One, he has the legal right to do what he wants without interference from the Creator. The Demon King is a powerful spiritual being. No natural being can defeat him or withstand his might. Only by blood and through the power of the Armor of God, will you be able to withstand and defeat the Wicked One. The Gateway to Demon's Lair is through the Great Temple" explains the Spirit.

Pointing to her left, the Spirit continues, "Go to the bottom of the ore mine, there you will find a stone door. Place the spirit gem into its slot and a portal to the Great Temple will appear. I will speak with you further at the temple. Farewell."

The Spirit disappears. The Chosen Ones remain quiet for several minutes reflecting on the words spoken by the Spirit of Truth.

~~~
~~~

Princess Sunda reaches Tree Hill and finds her mother's dead body in Vermilion's talons. She falls to her knees, wailing and crying loudly.

Holding her mother's cold dead hand, Princess Sunda shouts, "Mother, this is the Demon King's fault. He forced you to stay here and protect that accursed Sword of the Spirit. He filled your mind with empty promises of endless power. I will avenge you mother. I will kill the Demon King."

Returning to Commander Wentar, the princess informs him of the Queen's death.

"Commander, I am in charge now since Princess Retta is incapacitated. I command an end to this war. Make peace with the cave bandits commander and bring our food supply and livestock back home" commands Princess Sunda.

"Yes, your Majesty" replies Commander Wentar.

"Commander, when you get back to the castle, inform Princess Retta of our mother's death and that she is now Queen. I am leaving Sky Citadel to avenge my mother's death. Carry out my last orders Commander and serve my sister well. Farewell commander" says the princess.

"I will, your Majesty and farewell" responds the perplexed commander.

Princess Sunda manipulates the air and flies southward towards the lake.

"I must find those escaped prisoners. They must know where to find this Demon King" she mutters.

Several minutes pass before the princess says to herself, "There they are, headed towards the ore mine."

Princess Sunda lands between the Chosen Ones and the ore mine. Instinctively, Obadiah shoots off four arrows at the princess. She deflects them with a blast of wind.

"Stop! Hold on! I'm not here to fight you" she exclaims.

"Sorry, witch, but excuse us if we don't believe you!" shouts Sakia, pulling out her whip.

"Hold on everyone! But stand ready" yells Titus.

Looking at Princess Sunda, Titus says, "If you haven't come to fight us, then why have you come?"

"I want to avenge my mother's death. I want to kill the Demon King" declares Sunda.

Stunned by the princess's words, the Chosen Ones look at each other.

"Look, lady, the Demon King didn't kill your mother, a giant bird did" states Keembo.

"My name is Princess Sunda and I saw the bird that killed my mother. However, it was the Demon King who forced my mother to stay here and protect that stupid sword. I will not serve him any longer. I will destroy him. Now please, tell me where I can find him" asks the princess.

"Princess Sunda is it? We are going to defeat the Demon King, so take solace in knowing that his demise is coming soon" states Obadiah.

"I cannot and will not stand by and let others fight my battles. I will go with you and help you defeat him" demands Princess Sunda.

"Then you're gonna have to fight and kill us, lady, because you're not coming with us!" belts out Sakia.

"Wait! She should come with us" says Azra.

"I don't know where your head is at Azra, but I think you've lost your mind" retorts Sakia.

"Azra's right. The Spirit said Princess Sunda should come with us" exclaims Tiwa.

"Then how come I didn't hear anything?" asks Sakia.

"Probably because your spirit isn't quiet; it's racing with the excitement of battle. You can't hear anything else" explains Tiwa.

"Maybe my mind is racing right now, and I can't hear the spirit. But if you both heard the same thing, then I'll trust what you say" says Sakia reluctantly.

"Princess Sunda, we'll take you with us. However, we'll need to bind your hands so you can't use your wind powers against us. Also, if it turns out our two friends here were wrong, we will kill you. These are our conditions. Do you still want to come along with us?" asks Titus.

"If I die in search of the Demon King, then I die. I agree to your conditions" replies Princess Sunda.

"Alright then. Keembo, tie her up tightly with her hands behind her back" instructs Titus.

"I hope you know what you're doing, smart guy. But I'll keep an eye on her just in case" states Keembo.

"Oh and just for the record, I'm not calling you princess. Sunda will have to do" exclaims Sakia.

"Sunda will do just fine" retorts the princess.

The Chosen Ones and Princess Sunda head towards the ore mine. At the entrance, Obadiah spots a crossbow with fifty arrows sitting on top of a box containing twenty hand bombs left by the guards. Obadiah gets rid of his regular bow and replaces it with the more powerful crossbow. Titus excitedly places the twenty bombs into his bag as they enter the mine.

Walking down two levels, they reach the end of the mine. The back stone wall has an outline of a door on it. The yellow light stones illuminate the area. Azra walks over to the wall and places the spirit gem in a slot near the stone door.

"This portal will take us to the Great Temple. Once we're there we can summon the Spirit" Azra says.

"Yeah, then your fate will be decided, Sunda. Whether you live or die" states Sakia.

A yellow light starts to glow behind the stone wall. Immediately the wall disappears and a solid yellow light appears in its place. The portal to the Great Temple has been opened.

"Wait, I'm not going through there" states a nervous Sunda. "Untie my hands at least. I don't know what's on the other side of that portal" she continues.

"Don't worry, I'll protect you, princess," says Keembo sarcastically.

"Hold on! I have changed my mind. I will find the Demon King myself!" shouts out Princess Sunda.

"It's too late princess, you're coming with us now" declares Keembo as he picks up the screaming princess and walks through the portal.

Azra retrieves the spirit gem as she walks through the portal.

The Chosen Ones and Princess Sunda are teleported inside the Great Temple. The Great Temple is a large, luminous, sun-filled room with tall, ivory pillars. The spacious temple is empty except for a long golden basin resting between two giant golden statues of a lion and a lamb. The statues and basin sit in the center of the temple. Off to the right is a stone altar. The Chosen Ones stand in awe at the celestial lights glistening off the ivory pillars, the golden basin, and the golden lion and lamb.

"Let me down!" shouts Princess Sunda.

Keembo gently sets Sunda down.

Turning around Sunda gasps, "Wow! I have never seen anything as splendid as this sight in all my life. Who lives here?"

No answer is given and the deafening silence cues Princess Sunda to be quiet as well.

Gazing around, they walk closer to the center of the temple. Azra spots the stone altar and immediately walks over and places the spirit gem on top of it. Celestial light rains down on the Spirit of Truth, revealing her glorious beauty. The radiant light is blinding.

The Spirit utters, "Greetings, Chosen Ones and Princess Sunda of Sky Citadel. Welcome to the Great Temple. This is your last stop before you face the Demon King. Untie Princess Sunda's hands."

Keembo quickly unties the princess.

"Why have you come here, Princess Sunda?" the Spirit asks.

"I have come to find and destroy the Demon King" she sheepishly replies.

"Have you heard of the Creator?" inquires the Spirit.

"My mother told me that he is the sworn enemy of the Demon King and that he was our enemy as well. However, any enemy of the Demon King, I gladly call friend" responds Sunda.

"Well said, young princess. However, the only way to side with the Demon King's sworn enemy is to choose to serve him and you will only serve him faithfully, once you know him. The Creator is good and righteous, he has given every living being in every realm and world the free choice to choose good or evil. When you choose good you choose life and servanthood to the Righteous One. When you choose evil you choose death and slavery to the Demon King. Princess, if you want to side with the Creator, then you must choose him and learn to do things his way. If you choose not to be one of his servants, then I will safely teleport you back to Sky Citadel" explains the Spirit.

"But I have never seen this Creator. How can I decide without knowing him?" inquires the princess.

"Princess, you have gladly served the Demon King for years without seeing him. Know this, the Creator and I, the Spirit of Truth, are one. I speak to you the things he speaks to me. Since you have seen me, you have seen him. Now choose whom you will serve" states the Spirit.

"Spirit of Truth, I choose to serve and follow the Creator" answers Princess Sunda, surprising her own self.

"Wise choice, my dear, for today you seven will be baptized by blood and become the new rulers, the new Kings and Queens of your worlds. Today, you will fight the Demon King as true Kings and Queens. Walk over to the golden basin and place both your hands in it" instructs the Spirit.

Reaching the basin Sakia says, "Is that blood in there? I'm not sure if I want to stick my hands in that."

Sticking both his hands into the golden basin full of blood Keembo says, "You can do as you like, but I'll become a King and destroy the Demon King. I'll free my family and my people from his evil domination."

Princess Sunda, Titus, Azra and Tiwa immediately place their hands into the blood-filled basin.

"Count me in," says Obadiah, placing his hands in the blood.

"You know you guys can't defeat the Demon King without me. You need me" states Sakia, slapping her hands into the basin.

"Hey, watch it. You're splashing blood all over us" says Azra.

Everyone laughs and turns their gaze upon the Spirit.

"You have received the blood seal. Now you may enter into Demon's Lair. I cannot physically aid you in this battle, but if you quiet yourselves you will hear my voice telling you what you should do. One of you will need to wear all of the pieces to the Armor of God in your battle with the Demon King. You must decide who that person will be. Be on your guard, for the Demon King and his horde of demons will be waiting for you. Take the spirit gem and open the portal door on the far back wall. I bid you farewell and good luck, Chosen Ones."

The Spirit disappears.

"Uh, wait a second. I need a moment to process all that just happened" says Princess Sunda.

"Don't worry, take all the time you need. We still have to decide who will wear the Armor of God" says Obadiah.

"Well, that's an easy decision. I should wear it" states Sakia.

"No, I should wear it. I'm the strongest" declares Keembo.

"I want to wear it" utters Tiwa.

"Me too," Titus says.

"I think I should be the one to wear the armor," says Obadiah.

"I don't care who wears the armor" states Azra.

"You guys hurry up and figure this out. I have a Demon King to kill" quips Sunda.

"I have an idea that'll settle this once and for all. Azra, pick a number between one and a hundred, tell Sunda the number and the closest one will wear the Armor of God. Does everyone agree?" asks Titus.

Everyone agrees.

Azra whispers twenty-eight in Princess Sunda's ear.

"Okay, pick a number," says Azra.

Sakia chooses fifty-two, Titus picks forty-five, Obadiah selects sixty-four, Tiwa chooses twenty-five and Keembo picks thirty.

"Congratulations! Keembo, you get to wear the full Armor of God. Do us proud" smiles Azra.

"Aw, that's not fair. You better not lose, Keembo" says a disappointed Sakia.

"I never lose" states Keembo as he puts on the Armor of God.

"Keembo, test out the armor as much as you can before facing the Demon King, there has to be some special powers with all the pieces of the armor together" mentions Titus.

"Remember everything the Spirit told us and know we have your back Keembo" declares Obadiah.

"Alright Azra, open the portal. It's time to take down the Demon King!" shouts Tiwa.

Azra places the spirit gem into the wall and the stone door is replaced by a red portal. The Chosen Ones leave the Great Temple and enter Demon's Lair.

CHAPTER 14

DEMON'S LAIR

Demon's Lair is a large asteroid that travels across worlds. It is the Demon King's seat of power and the place he calls home. Inside the hollowed-out asteroid, a dreary orange light flickers off the rock walls. The foul stench of fire and brimstone fills the air. Large and small ominous cliffs, ledges and pathways are scattered throughout the massive multi-leveled asteroid. A hot, fiery pit covers three-quarters of the bottom floor.

The Demon King's army, his horde of demons, reside here in Demon's Lair. Sitting on his throne, annoyed and visibly angry, the Demon King awaits the arrival of the Chosen Ones.

"They are here! Attack them!" screeches a demon.

Hundreds of fiery darts are shot at the intruders.

Keembo, wearing the full Armor of God takes point. Raising the Shield of Faith, he deflects some of the oncoming darts. Azra standing to the left of Keembo raises her impenetrable shield and blocks the incoming darts from their left side. Princess Sunda, standing to the right of Keembo, shoots out a vortex of air that scatters all incoming darts to the right of them. Obadiah shoots off four arrows.

The four demons hit instantly vaporize from the impact. Several Demon Lords, the stronger, more powerful demons, say in a loud eerie voice, "They have the blood seal which allows them to fight supernatural beings. It matters little that their natural weapons can harm us, for we will defeat them with sheer overwhelming numbers."

"Our weapons can kill the demons!" shouts Obadiah as he unleashes more arrows.

Keembo swings the Sword of the Spirit, a wave of white energy shoots out, obliterating several legions of demons in front of him.

"We must press forward! I think I see the Demon King's throne room up ahead" yells out Keembo.

They continue to move forward in tight formation, Keembo destroys a multitude of demons with several swings of his sword. Tiwa hurls her four boomerangs, each one killing ten demons.

"Woo! Now that's how you kick some demon butt around here!" shouts Tiwa.

Sunda's wind vortex slams twelve demons into the rock walls, vaporizing them. "These demons are easy to kill, but for every one we take out, it seems like two more take their place. They just keep coming" states Princess Sunda.

"Keep moving forward! The throne room is right up those stairs. I see the Demon King" shouts Keembo.

~~~

The Demon King arrogantly sits on his throne wearing dark ashy-gray armor, consisting of his helmet, breastplate, boots, and belt. His shield lies against his chair. He wears a crown that encircles the two long, milky, white horns protruding from the top of his head. His deep orange skin is scaly and rough. His white teeth are pointy and sharp.

"So you have finally come and I see you wear the complete Armor of God" utters the Demon King in a deep, echoing voice.

Grabbing his shield, the Demon King rises, standing nine feet tall.

"Shall we take this fight outside?" inquires the Demon King.

Titus speaks up and says, "Keembo, you can't defeat the Demon King and his horde of demons. Battle the Demon King outside and we'll hold off his army of demons, even if it means our lives. Destroy the Demon King and free our people."
~~~

Keembo nods his head in response to Titus and then answers the Demon King. "Let's take the fight outside then."

The Demon King walks up a flight of stairs to the surface of the asteroid. Keembo follows a short distance behind him.

~~~

"This is where we make our stand people! No demon is to make it up those stairs to the surface. If we go down, we go down swinging" says a resolute Titus.

"Good. Now I can stop running and start fighting. The big ones are mine" states Sakia, as she evades several darts and cuts three demons in half with the crack of her whip.

Sakia bounds onto a ledge and zaps two Demon Lords who explode into vapor. Tiwa hurls her boomerangs killing another forty demons.

"Take out the one with four arms" cries a Demon Lord.

Azra's shield protects Tiwa from dozens of fiery darts. Hundreds of demons converge on the throne room floor. Titus freezes ten demons at a time with his ice ray, the demons freeze and explode. Princess Sunda shoots wind blast after wind blast into a sea of demons; they smash into each other and explode into a puff of vapor. Obadiah continues to kill demons with his fiery arrows.
~~~

"Watch your backs!" yells Obadiah.

Protecting Tiwa, Obadiah, and Titus, Azra does not notice the demons sneaking up behind her.

"Argh!" screams Azra, as six darts pierce her back. She is the first to fall, her body hits the ground, motionless.

"Get away from her!" shouts Tiwa, as she flings her boomerangs at Azra's assailants. Forty more demons fall.

Six Demon Lords continue to bark out orders.

"Take out as many of the big demons as you can, they seem to be giving out orders. Sunda, protect our flank with your wind vortex!" shouts Obadiah as he shoots and takes down two Demon Lords.

Dozens of darts fly straight towards Tiwa. Sunda fires a wind blast knocking away the incoming darts. Tiwa falls to the ground as two darts get through, piercing her neck.

"No!" screams Sakia as she goes after the remaining Demon Lords.

A fiery dart hits Obadiah's ivory bow snapping it in half. Pulling the crossbow from off his shoulder Obadiah continues to fight, knowing he only has fifty shots left. Titus continues to freeze demons with his ice ray.

"The demons are surging in on us. Stand your ground!" shouts Titus.

Swinging over to a cliff, Sakia takes out a couple more Demon Lords. The two remaining call back some of the surging demons to their side for protection.

Shouting at the top of her lungs, Sakia says, "What was it you said, Titus? If we go down, we go down swinging? Well, I'm taking out the last two lead demons before I go."

"Noooo!" shouts Obadiah as he unloads his remaining arrows in Sakia's direction, creating an opening for her to kill the last two Demon Lords.

Sakia lands on her feet and wraps her whip around the neck of both Demon Lords. Fear can be seen in the demons' eyes before their heads and bodies explode into vapor.

Sakia is quickly swarmed by dozens of demons. She fights them off the best she can before being pierced in the side by several fiery darts. Sakia falls to her knees and slowly falls face-first into the ground.

Obadiah, out of arrows, is quickly swarmed by demons. Several darts puncture his skin causing him to fall backward hitting the jagged, rocky floor beneath him. The demons, sensing victory, head towards Princess Sunda and Titus, who are blocking the stairway to the surface of the asteroid.

"Sunda I need you to buy me some time so I can seal up the stairway entrance to the surface" instructs Titus.

"Okay, I'll try" replies Princess Sunda.

Putting both hands together Sunda creates a mighty whirlwind that decimates fifty demons, causing the others to hesitate for a moment.

"Now go upstairs and aid Keembo, I'll be right behind you" yells Titus.

Princess Sunda runs up the stairs. Slowly walking and looking around Sunda gazes upon Keembo and the Demon King facing off with each other. Titus glances over his shoulder and sees the horde of demons making their way to the only opening to the top of the asteroid.

With strong resolve, Titus says within himself, "My last stand will be to keep these evil creatures from reaching the top. Sorry, Sunda."

Titus places his handheld ice ray in the middle of the stairway and places several bombs next to it. Activating the bombs, Titus runs behind a large rock bracing for the explosion. The bombs explode shattering the white crystal ice ray causing a giant glacier of solid ice to form engulfing the entire stairway, creating a formidable blockade. The icy barrier separates Princess Sunda, Keembo and the Demon King on top of the asteroid, leaving Titus and the demon horde locked down below.

Startled by the large explosion Princess Sunda turns around expecting to see Titus, who isn't there. She lets out a loud scream, "No, Titus!"

Standing up, Titus hurls bomb after bomb into the sea of demons killing hundreds of them. With no bombs left, Titus pulls out his steel baton and continues to fight until he gets overrun. Stabbed several times in the stomach and back, he doubles over and hits the ground. The demons are unable to penetrate Titus' icy blockade. With no more Demon Lords to tell them what to do, the demons move around aimlessly.

~~~

Standing on the dusty, rock surface of the asteroid the Demon King and Keembo face off. The Demon King glares at Keembo, sizing him up, looking for any traces of fear, doubt, or uncertainty. "Let me introduce you to my three hellspawn."

The Demon King channels his energy summoning his three hellspawn. He places half of his power into their bodies which he controls telepathically. The hellspawn Volstag is a creature made of electricity. Bluish white sparks ripple in and out and all around its malleable body. Volstag's round form hovers off the ground waiting for a command from its master. Krustis is a monstrous rock creature. This hellspawn is living granite. It can change its density to rival that of titanium steel. Krustis stands at the ready clinching its boulder-like fists awaiting orders. Burnem is the third hellspawn summoned by the Demon King. Scorching the area beneath its oval bottom, this living flame stares at Keembo content to only look, for now.
~~~

Princess Sunda flies over to Keembo's side and shouts, "So you are the dreaded Demon King. I've come a long way to destroy you."

With disdain and disgust in his voice, the Demon King bellows out, "Traitor! I gave your family the powers you possess and you would dare turn them on me. I will make a gruesome example out of you to remind the rest of my slaves to fear and obey me. Shall we begin?"

The Demon King instructs Burnem to attack Princess Sunda knowing her wind powers are weakest against fire. Volstag and Krustis advance towards Keembo. Burnem shoots a steady stream of fire at Princess Sunda. A wind blast from Sunda collides with the stream of fire making the fire explode with greater intensity and heat.

"Oh my traitorous one, didn't you know wind is the fuel of fire" laughs the Demon King.

"Sunda!" shouts Keembo, his hands full with Volstag and Krustis.

"Now now Keembo you have your own playmates. You might want to pay closer attention to them" taunts the Demon King.

Volstag shoots an electricity bolt at Keembo while Krustis hurls boulders from his hands. Keembo blocks both attacks with his shield. Their synchronized attack keeps Keembo on the defensive. Like a puppet master, the Demon King telepathically pulls the strings of his three hellspawn.

Princess Sunda takes to the air putting distance between herself and Burnem who continues to shoot fire at her. With a thought, Krustis breaks from Keembo and shoots several boulders at an unsuspecting Sunda. One grazes her left shoulder forcing her back to the ground. Burnem moves in for the kill.

With just Volstag attacking him, Keembo has time to unsheathe the Sword of The Spirit. His shield raised with his left hand, blocking electricity bolts, Keembo swings the sword in his right hand sending a white energy blast directly at Burnem. As quick as a thought, Burnem splits in half letting the energy blast pass harmlessly through him. Merging back together the fire hellspawn steps closer into attack range of Princess Sunda. Unable to flee from her attacker, Sunda seals herself in a defensive wind sphere. Burnem repeatedly blasts the sphere-like he is using a huge blow torch. Each fire blast lasts ten seconds, followed by a three-second delay.

Sweat drops from Princess Sunda's body as she is being cooked alive by the hot flames exploding against her wind sphere. A thought enters her mind, "Is this how my life will end?"

Krustis and Volstag's combined attack knock Keembo off his feet. Krustis creates a large boulder to smash Keembo with, while Volstag continues to electrocute him.

"I can't reach Sunda in time. I'm at my wit's end. Spirit, help me!" yells Keembo. Instantly, the Helmet of Salvation activates, calming Keembo's panicking mind and releases the Spirit's thoughts directly to him.

"Access the armor's power."

Krustis smashes the large boulder into Keembo's body again and again and again. Standing safely at a distance, the Demon King commands Krustis to deliver the final crushing blow.

"What is that bright light emanating from Keembo's armor? No, this can't be. Where is this unbelievable power coming from? I can sense the presence of the Creator" gasps the Demon King.

Imbued with the power of the Righteous One, Keembo opens his eyes and shoots out a beam of yellow light, obliterating the large rock held in Krustis' hands. Taking two steps back the Wicked One feels an emotion he's never felt before: Fear.

As long as the Demon King has existed he has always conquered and destroyed worlds. He manipulated Kreel and humanity and ultimately conquered the Earth. By deceit and betrayal, he conquered the kingdoms of Demon's Realm. In every world he rules over, there has always been a remnant of souls who have resisted his authority, but none of them had enough power or strength to overthrow him.

Fear, the Demon King's favorite weapon, is now turning on him. Fear is like an infection that enters the body through the eyes, ears, and even the words spoken out of one's own mouth. It grows and gets bigger like an unborn child growing inside its mother's womb. Fear weakens one's resolve and saps their strength. For the first time in his life, the Demon King was experiencing fear and it was quickly spreading and sapping his strength.

Keembo clearly hears the Spirit say, "Switch opponents with Princess Sunda and make the hellspawn fight for you. Relay this to Princess Sunda."

Understanding only half of what the Spirit has said, Keembo shouts to Princess Sunda, "Sunda the Spirit spoke to me and said we need to switch opponents and have them fight for us."

Hearing those words gives Princess Sunda hope and a desire to live.

"I need to escape this fiery prison."

Noticing she has a three-second window between Burnem's fire blasts, Sunda releases her defensive wind sphere at the exact moment the fire blast ceases. She hurls a gust of wind directly at Burnem causing his body to burn brighter and hotter. The sudden burst of heat causes Volstag and Krustis to turn and look at their fellow hellspawn.

At that moment, clarity hits Keembo and he knows exactly what to do.

"Princess! Fly over to me and shoot a vortex of wind that forces the electricity hellspawn into the rock hellspawn."

Sunda does exactly what he says. Keembo protects Sunda from Burnem's fire blasts with his shield as she sends a vortex of wind at Volstag, slamming the vile creature into Krustis. Getting up off the ground, Krustis shoves Volstag.

"Did you see that?" asks Sunda.

"Yes. Now do you understand?" replies Keembo.

"Divide and conquer. Now let us see how the Demon King likes chaos in his midst" comments Princess Sunda.

Telepathically, the Demon King commands his hellspawn to refocus on their true enemies, finding it harder to control their ferocious nature. The three hellspawn attack simultaneously. Princess Sunda moves behind Keembo as he blocks fire blasts with his shield and electricity with his sword and body armor. Krustis' stone boulders are caught in a wind vortex and shot back at Burnem and Volstag. Enraged by Krustis' perceived attack Burnem shoots a stream of fire at

Krustis, hitting both him and Volstag. In fighting begins and chaos abounds.

"No! No! No!" screams the Demon King.

Volstag and Burnem unleash a vicious assault of electricity and fire on Krustis. His molecules expand and contract under the intense onslaught. Reaching its critical point Krustis' body explodes outward in a blast of dirt and rocks. The debris thoroughly covers Burnem and Volstag. The dirt and rocks smother Burnem's flaming body morphing it into a massive, solid red-hot charcoal. Volstag covered in rocks and dirt releases a massive electrical shock wave from his entire body, extricating himself from his dirt tomb. The electric shock wave shatters Burnem's hot, solid, charcoal body to ashes. Only a weakened Volstag remains. Throwing his shield into the air, Keembo directs Princess Sunda to drive the shield through Volstag's body and into the ground. Sunda manipulates the wind and slings Keembo's shield through Volstag's body, grounding it into the asteroid. Volstag screeches as the remaining electricity in its body flows through Keembo's shield and is dispersed throughout the asteroid.

Standing alone and at half strength, the Demon King leers at Keembo and Princess Sunda and defiantly says, "You can't defeat me."

Looking back at the Demon King, Princess Sunda remembers her dead mother and Keembo recalls his fallen comrades. A wave of emotion surges through their bodies. Sunda summons one of her largest wind blasts yet and Keembo simultaneously charges up his armor to attack. The Armor of God begins to glow in a gentle yet fierce manner and a ball of blinding, white energy forms in front of Keembo's chest. A heartbeat later, both attacks are ready and are shot, in sync, at the Demon King. Their attacks slam into the Demon King's chest, sending him flying and crashing to the ground. Keembo picks up his shield as he and Princess Sunda walk over to the Demon King. Smoke rising from his armor.

"Keep him pinned down Sunda as I rip off his armor" instructs Keembo.

"No... this... can't.. be... happening" utters the Demon King faintly.

Driving the Sword of The Spirit into the joints of the Demon King's armor, Keembo pries the armor off his arms, legs, and chest. As each piece of armor is broken away from the Wicked One's body, invisible chains are simultaneously broken over the kingdoms he once ruled. Earthquakes and volcanic eruptions occur on all the worlds he has conquered signifying the end of the Demon King's rule.

Princess Sunda pounds her fists on the charred, unmoving body of the Demon King screaming, "Die! Die! Die! You took my mother from me! And for that, you will DIE!!!"

Keembo gently places his hand on Princess Sunda's shoulder, beckoning her it is time to go. Keembo and Princess Sunda drag the Wicked One's limp body to the frozen stairwell leading off the surface of the asteroid. Keembo swings his sword shattering Titus' icy blockade into tiny chips of ice. Throwing the Demon King's bloodied and battered body down the stairs, the remaining demons see their lord defeated and back up slowly.

"The Demon King has been defeated! Run! Retreat!" screech several demons.

The demons scatter and flee back to their caves. Princess Sunda flies around and gathers the bodies of her new comrades, bringing them next to Keembo.

A small, still voice speaks to Keembo and tells him, "Before you aid your friends, cast the Demon King into the fiery pit."

Obeying the voice of the Spirit, Keembo lifts the Demon King over his head and hurls him off the cliff into the fiery pit below. His body slowly sinks and then disappears into the sulfur pit. The Demon King is dead.

Turning his attention to his fallen comrades, Keembo searches through Azra's pouch looking for healing potions. Finding them, he lifts everyone's head up and administers the potion.

As they all regain consciousness, somberly Titus asks, "Did we do it? Did we defeat the Demon King?"

Keembo replies, "Yes, he has been defeated."

"Good, I can't wait to go home and see my mother and father again" states Azra looking into the fiery pit.

"Do you think we'll miss the adventures?" asks Obadiah.

"After a few months, I'm sure we will" replies Sakia.

"I'll return to Sky Citadel and convince my sister to serve the Creator," says Princess Sunda.

"I don't know where I should go" states Tiwa.

"We need to summon the Spirit of Truth," says Keembo.

Building an altar, from the rubble and debris, Azra places the spirit gem on the makeshift altar and the Spirit appears.

"Well done, Chosen Ones. The Prophecy of Old has been fulfilled and the Demon King has been defeated. The inhabitants of your worlds have been freed from bondage and slavery to the Demon King. They, like you, can now choose their own fate. As Kings and Queens, you have dominion over your realms, rule well as servants of The Righteous One. Each of you continue to fight evil wherever it raises its head and listen for my voice, for I will always be with you. I have one last request before I send you home. Help free Tiwa's people, the Serconians, from slavery under their current king and establish her as their new ruler."

"Sure. Okay," they all respond looking at each other happily.

"Keembo, give the others back their piece of the Armor of God" instructs the Spirit.

Waving her hand, the Spirit opens a portal to the Sand Province. The young warriors depart Demon's Lair.

~~~

The seven Kings and Queens liberate the enslaved Serconians and help Tiwa become the new ruler of the Sand Province. Tiwa uses the wise advice of the Spirit to lead and rule her kingdom through its new transition. After several months, Tiwa establishes her power base and starts to win over the hearts of her people.

"Well Tiwa, it looks like your kingdom is well on its way to greatness. It's time for us to go back to our homes. I'll miss you" says Sakia, starting to tear up.

"I'll never forget you, Sakia. Thank you for all that you've done for me. Thank you all" says Tiwa, tears dropping from her eyes.

"Aw, man. I hate mushy goodbyes. My eyes always seem to hurt afterward" says Keembo, giving Tiwa a big hug.

Everyone takes time to say goodbye to each other, for they know when they leave the Sand Province, they will return to their own homelands.
~~~

The Spirit opens a portal in Tiwa's royal chamber. King Obadiah is the first to walk through the portal and return home to the frozen Siberian Wasteland. He is greeted by Cephas, his clan's high priest. They converse well into the night.

Queen Azra is the next to leave and reappears in China. Recognizing her surroundings, Azra runs home and finds her mother and father working in the rice fields. She calls out to them. Seeing their little girl, they stop what they are doing and run over to give her a big hug. No words are spoken; only sobs of joy can be heard.

Queen Sunda teleports to Sky Citadel and is greeted by Commander Wentar. He updates her on the current state of affairs and takes her to see Queen Retta, her older sister.

King Keembo waves goodbye and steps through the portal back to the scorching hot sands of Saudi Arabia. His little brother and sister are the first to greet him. Keembo starts to cry, glad to be home and see his family again.

Sakia and Titus embrace one another as they say goodbye.

"I'll miss you. Promise me you'll find a way to see me again" says Sakia.

"I'll miss you too. And I *will* figure out a way to see you again" declares Titus.

"I know you will" smirks Sakia, stepping through the portal.

Queen Sakia returns to the Amazon Jungle in South America. Entering her clan's temple, Sakia finds her father and mother praying.

"Thank goodness you made it home safely!" cries her mother loudly, as she runs to hug her.

Titus studies the portal before he leaves saying, "I'll create one of these when I get back home."

Returning to the Silicon Valley in North America, King Titus is greeted by his family and all the members of his clan. A few days later, Titus begins working on a new project.

Far away, a mysterious, sinister presence observes all that has transpired between the Chosen Ones and the Demon King through a crystal ball.

~~~

Two years later, Titus closes his toolkit and says with a deep sigh, "I've done it. It is finally complete."
~~~

www.ingramcontent.com/pod-product-compliance
Lightning Source LLC
Chambersburg PA
CBHW071152100726
47908CB00002B/342